A Brush

with

Murder

A Brush with Murder

Murder

A PAINT BY MURDER MYSTERY

Bailee Abbott

CROOKED
LANE

NEW YORK

Copyright © 2021 by Kathryn Long

Published in the United States by Crooked Lane Books, an imprint of The Quick Brown Fox & Company LLC.

Crooked Lane Books and its logo are trademarks of The Quick Brown Fox & Company LLC.

Library of Congress Catalog-in-Publication data available upon request.

ISBN (hardcover): 978-1-64385-774-9
ISBN (ebook): 978-1-64385-775-6

Cover illustration by Rob Fiore

Printed in the United States.

www.crookedlanebooks.com

Crooked Lane Books
34 West 27th St., 10th Floor
New York, NY 10001

First Edition: October 2021

10 9 8 7 6 5 4 3 2 1

To my family—Gary, Kristin, Sean, Jenn, and my furry pal, Max.
You all are so awesome, and that inspires me to work harder and do better.
Love you to pieces!

Chapter One

I rounded the next bend in the road and at once gripped the wheel. Flashing lights bordering a huge sign grabbed my attention.

"Road closed. Detour ahead. How ironic is that, Max?"

My life was a sign, too. A regrettable, take-ten-steps-back detour sign. Now, if I figured out which road to choose next, one that hopefully wouldn't lead me to another dead end, my story might have a happy ending. I slammed my hand on the wheel and the horn blared.

A sharp bark made me bounce in my seat and swerve the car. Tires bumped and vibrated over the graveled surface of the highway berm until I jerked the wheel and steered back onto the road.

"Good grief." I gulped. "I appreciate your feedback, Max, but maybe tone it down a bark while I'm driving. You don't want me to wreck the car, do you?" I dared a quick glance in the rearview mirror and laughed at the pint-sized ball of fur.

He lifted one paw in the air to scratch at the bars of his crate and whined.

1

"I know it's hot and uncomfortable, and this cute little piece of junk is overdue for the scrapyard." I worked my lips into a smile. "Don't worry. Someday we'll have lots of money. I'll buy you all the kibble and doggie biscuits your little heart desires. Promise." I tapped fingers on the wheel then turned up the dial on the AC. The motor chugged and clinked until a large puff of air whooshed out of the vents. Warm air. "Yeah, someday." I powered down all four windows. "Fresh air is nice too. Right, Max?"

Flipping on my turn signal, I slowed to form a place in line behind a trail of cars as it snaked around trucks and guys wearing yellow hard hats and orange vests. Sharp odors of tar and diesel fuel permeated the air and filled the car. I coughed and waved one hand in front of my face. Thankfully, the billboard advertising the Blue Whale and fresh haddock came into view. Whisper Cove was only two miles away. My heartbeat quickened. "Now, stop your worrying and count your blessings, Chloe Abbington. Not everyone gets a chance at a do-over."

Swerving around the last hard hat and work truck, I picked up speed along the road that bordered Chautauqua Lake. Rays of evening sunlight sparkled like tiny jewels on the cobalt blue water. I glanced at the tranquil scene of boats and bathers lazing on their docks along the shore. Lifting my chin, I sniffed the fresh piney air. For a brief moment, I wondered why I ever left, but then remembered my dream had been to conquer New York.

The sudden shrill ring of my phone blasted from the car speakers and made me gasp. Seeing the name on the screen, I grinned and pressed the button on my steering wheel. "Hi, Izzie."

"Hi, yourself. What's taking you so long? You should be on our doorstep right this minute so we can be talking face to face."

I laughed. "Calm down. I'm only five minutes away."

She hiccupped. "Thank goodness. I worried you'd changed your mind."

"Sweetie, I swear New York City and all its baggage are only unpleasant memories, and I'm sure as heck glad I left all of it behind." At least, I kept telling myself as much.

Around the next bend, a welcome sign announced my arrival to Whisper Cove, New York, population four hundred thirty-nine. I smiled. The number hadn't changed in two years, which was fine with me. Staying here for a while, surrounded by familiar sights, folks I'd grown up with, and a cozy atmosphere, would be a huge relief.

"You're a life saver, Chloe. I've mentioned that, right? Of course I have." Izzie hiccupped once more. "Sorry. My nerves are frazzled, and my brain's turned into goo. Did you know four out of five businesses fail in the first year? I do. I researched it. Yet here I am, taking the leap, and that's huge for me. Lord, I hope this isn't a huge mistake."

I swerved to miss a fallen branch. "Take it from me, the queen of huge mistakes, your plan is practical and well thought out. You were stuck in a rut at the bakery, working part-time and only snagging a commission here and there to paint somebody's portrait. Besides, you've got Mom and Dad backing you, and don't forget about me. I'll be your dutiful servant for however long you need." I chewed on my bottom lip. I projected as much enthusiasm as possible. "Your shop will be the biggest hit since Gwen Finch opened Go Fly a Kite twenty years ago."

"Ha. I wish. You can stop with the dutiful servant line. We're sisters, and you're older than me. I can't boss you around."

"Please. You've been dishing out orders since I was six and you were five." I made a left onto Seneca Drive and passed the town hall before reaching Main Street. Claire's bakery, For Sweet's Sake, carried a banner announcing today's special—fresh-baked bagels, four dollars a dozen. Catty-corner from Claire's was La Chic, with its trendy but pricey selection of clothing. Artisan Alley and the shoreline were only a block away. I was anxious to take a peek at Izzie's shop, but the desperate tone in my sister's voice on the other end of the phone warned me to go home. "I'm about to turn onto Sail Shore Drive. See you soon." I tapped the end call button and slowed the car to a crawl. In a few hundred yards, I steered the car to the right. "We're home, Max."

On one side of the road, trees formed a natural border, and on the other was Chautauqua Lake. The Abbington house was a huge, white clapboard, two-story structure that stood out from the others on our block. Pale green shutters framed the windows, and a widow's walk topped the roof. Izzie and I often joked about our granddad's choice to build something intended for houses overlooking the ocean. Of course, Granddad Abbington once lived on New York's Atlantic coast. He owned a fleet of fishing trawlers and spent most of his life on the sea. Moving inland and clear across the other side of the state made him homesick. Sound enough reason to build the widow's walk, he claimed, and he spent most every evening up there until the day he passed away.

Pulling into the drive, I let the engine idle for a minute. I studied the details of the yard and house. Nothing about this scene had changed. Not a tree or shrub, not even the porch swing painted tangerine orange. Then again, why should it? Our parents' belief was to embrace new experiences, but they never changed what they loved. That included adding a fresh coat of bright, tangerine orange paint to the swing every summer.

"Okay, Max. Let's go see your auntie." I turned off the ignition and stepped out of my car. Opening the crate, I let Max free so he could run around the yard.

Izzie stood on the front porch. She waved both arms with an energy that moved her whole body. Thick, brown curls hung loose almost to her waist.

I reached up to smooth my poker-straight short bob of black hair and heaved a sigh. Two sisters couldn't be more opposite. Izzie was tall and thin, with the graceful moves of a ballet dancer, while I was petite and curvy, the older sister who tended to stumble over things. She was the perfect runway model, and I was the classic geek. On the other hand, where Izzie often lacked the confidence to tackle new ventures, I braved those moments, excited to begin something different. Together, we checked all the boxes on a personality test. Maybe that was why we were so close and depended on one another.

"Hey, you. Looking as beautiful as ever, hiccups and all." I greeted her with a smile and a hug.

"You, too." Izzie hung onto me for several seconds while Max jumped up and down. "Sorry about what's his name."

A flush of heat spread throughout me as my heartbeat flip-flopped. With my face planted against her chest, my words were muffled. "Let's leave him out of the conversation. Where are Mom and Dad?"

"They went on a retreat at a winery up north to drink and paint." She lifted Max in her arms and snuggled him, while he licked her face. "The spontaneous, carefree behavior of our parents never changes. They'll be back late this evening." She put Max on the porch floor and shook her head. "I can't believe you're really here."

I laughed. "Neither can I." I glanced over my shoulder at the lake and the empty dock. "Did they go by boat?"

"Of course." Izzie wrapped her arm around mine. "How about we give Max a chance to snoop around inside and get acquainted with his new digs? I have his water and food dishes out on the kitchen floor, filled and ready. You and I can take a walk to Artisan Alley. I'm super excited for you to see the shop." She opened the door to let Max in the house, while we remained on the porch.

"Before unloading my luggage?" I moved alongside her down the sidewalk.

She wagged her head as we descended the porch steps. "Your things can wait. We have less than twenty-four hours to get ready for the pre-opening event I've arranged. I call it Paint Your Shop." Izzie let go of my arm and hurried on to the next block, heading toward Artisan Alley.

I picked up my pace. "Izzie, please. I'm sure you've got everything in order."

She was the think-and-plan type. That careful procedure kept her sane but drove me and my impulsiveness crazy. We stopped to wait at the corner while a few cars drove through the intersection.

"Tell me about the event. What's the theme?"

"Oh—well, all the guests are local shop owners. Nine are coming. Small and intimate gives it a cozy feel, don't you think? Anyway, they'll paint a scene of businesses in Whisper Cove, with the lake in the background, and then label one of them with their shop's name." She picked at the hem of her blouse sleeve. "I hope getting the merchants together will stop all the arguing and bad karma."

I raised my brows. "Bad karma?"

The traffic cleared, and Izzie grabbed my hand. We ran across Whisper Cove Boulevard and down Whisper Lane, leading to Artisan Alley. Lake water lapped against the rocky shore in an even rhythm while the cries of gulls echoed in the distance. The breeze off the lake carried the musky scent of algae and pondweed. I took a breath and filled my lungs. I'd missed those sounds and smells.

"I'll explain later." Izzie smiled and pointed at the corner building, the last in a string of craft shops that trailed along a road facing the lakefront. "Right now, take a look. Theo owns the building, but she gave me a sweet deal on rent. I imagine our parents' generous donations to the *Gazette* every year influenced her decision."

I stepped onto the pathway to get a closer view of the cottage structure with its huge picture window. Painted canary yellow, the building fit perfectly in this cheery setting along the lake. Above the front door, a sign with bright blue letters spelled out Paint with a View, and a tin box decorated with colorful butterflies hung from the wall.

Izzie reached around me and plucked a flyer out of the box. "See? I had these printed in case people were curious enough to take one. It tells you plenty about the shop and what we offer."

Clearing my throat, I skimmed the flyer and nodded. "'Paint with a View. Experience a fun time painting with friends and relatives. Sign up and join the party.'" Underneath the message was a schedule of upcoming events and themes.

"I even created a website, which I included along with my phone number."

I shook my head at Izzie. Her eyes brightened while a grin lifted her cheeks.

"I'm having a landline put in soon, and I've filled all the slots for the grand opening. I can't believe that's only two days away. In fact, we'll need to schedule a second Paint Your Pet event next month because dozens more people want portraits of their fur babies. Isn't that great?"

I folded my arms and chuckled. "I don't think I've seen you this excited about something since the fifth grade when you won first prize in the Chautauqua Art Festival."

She patted my shoulder. "Just you wait. More excitement is around the corner. Would you like to take a look inside?"

Before I could respond, she unlocked the door. A bell tinkled to greet us. I followed her into the spacious room. Three rows of tables were set up with easel stands and cupholders. There were enough stations to seat twenty-five to thirty customers. A small platform stage was situated at the far end, and a huge projector screen hung above it. Painted canvases decorated the walls with images of various subjects, like cute, furry animals, peaceful lake views, and panoramic mountain scenes. I walked the length of the room and paused near the stage. I lifted one of several hair dryers dangling from hooks. "You've thought of everything."

"I researched businesses and chose the best setup. Some of the designs need to be dried in stages. Got to keep the events moving along if folks are getting out of here by the scheduled nine o'clock." Izzie straightened one of the canvases.

"It's certainly impressive." I sat on one of the stools.

Our family possessed loads of artistic talent. However, I hadn't been satisfied with local success. I wanted more. I went to New York, determined to fulfill my dreams of a gallery showing and taking my place in the artists' world. Of course, that career move fell way short of expectations. After a couple of years, spending my days as a clerk in an art supply store and evenings attending every art event I could manage to talk about my work, I was exhausted and discouraged. Then the situation with *what's his name*, aka Ross Thompson, added to my frustration and misery. No doubt, for me, the Big Apple had a few worms. Thankfully, Izzie's call to help open her shop had come at the perfect time.

I twirled the stool around so I faced her. "You did good, sweetie."

Izzie chewed on a fingernail. "If only Mom and Dad agreed."

"You're doing what makes you happy, right? Doesn't matter whether they're totally onboard."

Izzie wagged her finger. "Ha. This coming from the daughter who spent two years in the French Quarter in Paris to study the masters and paint while living on bread and cheese, all because our parents, in their unconventional way, encouraged you."

"You mean their bohemian way, don't you?" I laughed. "That period lasted until I wanted to expand my diet to include lobster and prime rib." I spun off the stool and landed squarely on my heels. "I'm still craving that lobster."

Our parents could afford to live a carefree, spontaneous lifestyle, painting only when inspiration hit them. The Abbington family trust gave them that choice. Thankfully, Kate and Joe didn't put on airs or snub their noses at anyone. They were good people.

At once, a burning in my gut spread and left a sour taste in my mouth. "I dread hearing them say I told you so and giving me advice on what to do next."

Izzie nodded. "They will, though. Mom and Dad can't help themselves."

I opened my mouth to respond with a witty comment when loud voices outside interrupted.

"What the . . ." Izzie ran to the door, with me close on her heels.

In front of the shop, two women were caught up in a heated exchange as their arms flailed and fingers pointed. I recognized the younger one with her blonde curls and stocky figure. Megan Hunt, Izzie's closest friend, stood almost nose to nose with a much older woman. She was painfully thin and had a short bob of white hair. A crowd of gawkers surrounded them, but the sparring pair didn't seem to notice.

"Your column stinks, Fiona Gimble. It's full of hate and lies." Megan sniffed and jutted out her chin. "My candles get rave reviews and win prizes. They sell by the dozens."

"Do they really, Megan?" With a slight tilt of her head, Fiona pursed her lips. "My column is an editorial. I state my opinions, and I'm entitled to say what I feel. Freedom of speech is still part of the Constitution, isn't it?" The pursed lips spread into a thin smile.

Megan balled her fists and smacked them against her thighs. "You're a wicked person. Nobody in this town likes you, so why do you insist on staying here? Leave, Fiona. Leave before you and your precious column push somebody over the edge and—oh, what the heck." She threw up her arms and turned. "Get out of my way."

The gawkers parted, leaving Megan a path to escape.

Izzie stepped forward and grabbed her friend's arm. "Megs."

Megan turned to glare, her green eyes flashing. "You know what I'm talking about, Izzie." Her lips trembled as she spoke. "You've been her target too, and you haven't even opened your shop yet." She blinked away tears before pulling her arm free and disappearing into the crowd.

I ran my tongue across my upper lip as I cocked my head toward Megan. I took a wild leap. "Bad karma?"

Izzie bit down on another nail. "Yep. Super bad karma."

That sour taste curdled my stomach again, only this time for another reason. Before making my decision to return home, I'd listed the pros and cons of what to expect, like confronting my parents, whom I loved with all my heart, and suffering through their questions about New York. Even adjusting to the small-town life I missed so much, where everybody knew everybody and everything, would be a huge challenge. Quite a different picture from city life. Yet I had never pictured a disgruntled journalist angering the merchants and stirring up trouble. I sighed. The saying to expect the unexpected echoed in my head.

"Izzie, dear. Do you think I could trouble you for a glass of water?" Fiona sneaked up, suddenly appearing at my side, and I hop-skipped sideways.

The gawkers had gone about their business, leaving the three of us. I didn't care for sharing alone time with the supposedly toxic journalist.

Izzie wrinkled her nose and stiffened her shoulders. She marched back inside the shop and returned within seconds. She thrust a bottle of water into the journalist's hand. "We were just leaving, Fiona."

Fiona cleared her throat, and the prim smile surfaced as she turned to stare at me. "I'm sure Izzie doesn't mean to be rude. You must be her sister, Chloe. So very glad to meet you."

I blinked at Fiona without speaking, then glimpsed Izzie, whose face had turned tomato red. Awkward didn't begin to cover this moment.

Fiona barreled on. "I imagine our little display wasn't exactly a warm welcome, was it?" Fiona chuckled. "Megan tends to be overdramatic. No harm done, though. She'll forgive and forget by morning. Have a wonderful evening, ladies."

She took several swigs from the bottle, then turned on her heel and strode down the shoreline.

"She is . . . certainly interesting," I said.

Izzie scoffed. "Interesting isn't the word I'd choose. Fiona Gimble stirs up more trouble than a springtime tornado." She tapped her foot. "More than this town can handle."

I rubbed the back of my neck. "Is she really that bad? She seems totally unaware."

"More like she refuses to admit her nasty comments hurt people." Izzie shrugged. "Could be she's a lonely spinster who's

12

desperate for attention, whether good or bad. She never talks about the life she had before coming to Whisper Cove, so who knows for sure? It's like she put up this wall to keep folks from getting too close." She folded her arms, hugging her chest. "None of that excuses her vicious column. I'm with Megan. Fiona Gimble needs to disappear."

I hitched my breath. "That's kind of harsh, don't you think?"

Izzie screwed her face into a scowl. "If her agenda is to ruin people's reputations and businesses rather than to get along with folks, I'll be first in line to help pack her bags and point the way out of town. That's all I'm saying."

My concern surged along with my heartbeat. What happened to her treat-people-with-kindness motto? "Izzie—"

She shook her head and let out a nervous titter. "Don't mind me. I'm worried about Megan is all. I'll give her a ring to make sure she's okay."

She pressed her phone to one ear. After a few seconds, her brow creased. "Straight to voice mail. Okay, let me lock up, and then we can head for home. I'm sure you're tired after that long drive."

Without argument, I walked alongside her toward Whisper Cove Boulevard. Sure, I had questions. They pummeled my brain. I especially wanted to know more about Fiona. Who was she, really, and why was she causing such a stir when, as a newcomer in town, making friends should be a priority? I couldn't remember hearing about her or running into her when I had visited last Christmas. Obviously, she had riled Izzie and Megan, who insisted many others, especially shop owners, voiced the same concern. How could anyone cause such a reaction with a newspaper column?

Reaching our drive, Izzie helped carry my luggage inside the house. She set the cases next to the coat rack before leaning over to give me a quick hug. "Let's make some hot cocoa and sit out on the deck." At once, she turned and took long strides down the hallway.

I opened my mouth but then snapped it shut. Izzie had already disappeared into the kitchen. I stared at my suitcases piled in the foyer for a second. Cocoa did sound nice. "Do you have anything to munch on? I'm starving." I followed her path to the rear of the house.

When I reached the doorway, I spotted Max curled up in his favorite spot, sound asleep, but found no sign of Izzie. "Seriously?" I shook my head. Too much caffeine or too many sugary desserts had turned her into a jumping jackrabbit. "Izzie? Where'd you go?" I stepped across the room to the back door. The porchlight glowed, revealing Izzie's silhouette. I frowned. She was talking on her phone in a hushed tone. I leaned my ear against the screen.

"Stop. Of course I'll help you. See you tomorrow evening at seven." Izzie pivoted on her heel and gasped. "Good grief! You scared the heck out of me."

I opened the door and moved aside to let her through. "You mentioned a hot beverage?"

She lifted her shoulders and managed a weak smile. Sliding past me, she reached the kitchen counter. "Sorry. I had to take that call."

I grabbed the can of cocoa and scooped the powdery mix into mugs while she filled the kettle with water. I sorted through the choice of comments that filled my head to find the right one. I desperately wanted to avoid behaving like the pushy, older sister who couldn't resist being nosy and patronizing. I cleared my throat. "I couldn't help overhearing your phone conversation. Everything okay?"

She turned and laughed. "Why shouldn't it be?"

I walked closer and reached around her to set the mugs next to the stove. "How about we start with tomorrow evening when you plan to meet someone. What about the Paint Your Shop event?"

Izzie's eyes popped wider, and she gasped. "Oh, wow. The event with the shop owners. I totally forgot." She gripped my arm. "Chloe, I'm so sorry."

I frowned. Izzie wasn't the kind to forget her own agenda. No doubt, opening a business caused stress, but this behavior measured several heaps of anxiety into the mix. I pointed at the steaming kettle. "Do you want to get that, or should I?"

She grabbed the potholder and wrapped it around the kettle handle. "Look. This really stinks, but I can't be at the event tomorrow evening."

While she poured water into both mugs, I let her comment sink in. I narrowed my gaze and pointed. "What exactly are you saying?"

Izzie motioned me to the table. "Sit. Drink your cocoa. You'll feel better." She opened a tin can that sat on the lazy Susan. "Try one of these. I made them especially for you. Chocolate coconut bars. Your favorite, right?" She hiccupped.

I slid onto the bench. While studying her face, I chewed on a bar, savoring the generous amount of coconut. Izzie's behavior advertised like a neon road sign flashing *watch out for trouble ahead.*

I dabbed my lips with a napkin, then set it next to the mug. "Now, you want to tell me what you're thinking?"

She pressed a hand against her lips to stifle the next hiccup. "I need you to run tomorrow's event without me." The words rushed out.

I gripped the handle of my mug. "Izzie."

"I know. I promised we'd iron out the wrinkles of my crazy plan together, working side by side." She squirmed in her seat. "Hey, at least my assistant will be with you. Willow knows what to do. We've practiced the drill. I know that to look at her most people would think she's too young, but wow, is she super talented." She leaned back. "Besides, you love a challenge."

I sniffed. "I do when they're *my* challenges to screw up, but this is your business. Don't you want to be there to make sure the event runs perfectly? If something goes wrong, you'll never forgive me or yourself." I picked up the napkin and twisted the ends into pointy nubs. Truth was, I'd had it with screwed-up moments in my life. I needed a win to boost my confidence.

"Nonsense. I totally believe you'll do fine." She squeezed my hand. "Please, Chloe. Do this for me."

Before I could answer, her phone rang.

"Oh!" Izzie jumped out of her seat. "It's the art supplier I've been waiting to hear from. Be right back." She hurried out of the kitchen and down the hallway.

"Don't hurry!" I called out. "I'm turning in for the night."

"Sleep well," she hollered as her footsteps faded.

I drummed my fingers on the mug, then picked up my half-eaten chocolate bar. If Izzie wasn't worried about me handling the event, then why should I be? I slumped in my seat and groaned. Still, she must have an important reason for missing the pre-opening event. She was a type A personality, and micromanaging was her specialty. It would take quite a bit to keep her away from this opening. I chewed on my lip as I recalled her earlier comment. Izzie hoped this event would bring the merchants together and stop all their bickering, or, as she phrased it, bad karma. I popped the rest of the bar into my mouth. Acting so sneaky and secretive about wherever she planned to go tomorrow evening wasn't like her, either.

I picked up my empty mug, then stared at Izzie's. She hadn't taken one sip, and hot cocoa was her favorite beverage.

"Hopping like a jackrabbit is right."

Walking to the sink, I peered through the window. Pine branches swayed in the wind, and the sweet fragrance of lilac carried through the screen. I hoped the phone call and her behavior were nothing to worry about. Still, why all the secrecy? What sort of craziness had taken hold of people in Whisper Cove? Could Izzie and Megan be right? Was Fiona the real cause of the trouble, or was something else at the center?

I walked to the foyer and picked up two of my suitcases. Carrying them upstairs, I entered my bedroom and paused to study the familiar walls and fixtures. A sigh escaped. After a nine-hour drive, every bone in my body ached with exhaustion. I listened to the faint click of paws on the hall floor and smiled as Max pranced into my room. Lifting him in my arms, I gave him a smooch, then set him on the bed. Tomorrow, I'd be the big sister and push harder to get answers. After her strange secretive behavior, Izzie owed me.

Chapter Two

The burble and pop of the coffee maker finishing its second brew filled the moments of awkward silence in our conversation. This was like playing a game of dodgeball, where my job was to avoid the topic my parents were desperate to discuss while Izzie, the spectator, stood off to the side, totally entertained.

"More coffee?" Mom leaned over my shoulder to pour.

"We're so very glad you're home, Shortcake." Dad raised his glass of buttermilk in the air. "This is where you belong."

Rather than respond, I took a generous swig from my cup, willing the caffeine to do its job. No point in interrupting when I lacked a line of defense. My bullet points fell into the negative column. Plus, my heart wasn't into arguing.

Without skipping a beat, Mom set a plate of flapjacks in front of me, smothered in butter and syrup. "He's right. You can't live among those big city art snobs fighting their way to the top for long without turning into one." She pointed. "Eat. You're skin and bones." Turning, she picked up Max and carried him away from the table. "And *you* stop your begging. You have your own food."

A thick braid of auburn hair lay over one shoulder. The fringes of her suede leather vest swayed as she moved. We both possessed green eyes and fair skin, but that was where the resemblance stopped. She was tall and willowy, like Izzie. Only the red hair color was uniquely Kate's.

Dad, on the other hand, was my perfect match. We both had black hair, though age now peppered his with gray. He stood at least four inches shorter than his wife. From appearances, most people would probably think them mismatched as a couple. However, Izzie and I knew they complemented each other perfectly. Their opinions, lifestyle, likes, and dislikes all blended together like paint colors on a canvas.

I forked a bite of pancake. "Don't worry. I've learned those art snobs and I have nothing in common." I shoveled more syrupy deliciousness into my mouth to avoid spilling any details of my New York City experience. With any luck, they'd move on to other topics.

Mom snuggled next to me on the bench and stroked my arm. "It's okay, honey. We all make mistakes and hopefully learn from them. As long as you remember who you are and what we taught both you and Izzie, you'll be fine."

I drowned my groan with a few swallows of milk and shot Izzie a lethal stare as she winked without comment. What happened to the loyalty of sisters to throw out a lifeline when needed?

I lifted my chin and returned the wink. "You know, Izzie gave me a tour of her shop. She's really brave to open a business, don't you think?"

Mom stabbed the table with her finger. "Art should never be treated as a commodity."

"Also, never sold for money," Dad added.

"Art is pure, an expression of oneself, not some cookie-cutter effort or a paint-by-numbers project." Mom wagged her head. "But that's all we'll say on the subject. We've also taught you girls to be independent and make your own way."

I heaved a sigh and pushed back from the table. Game, set, match. Kate and Joe Abbington for the win.

Izzie stared at her watch. "We should go, Chloe. I want to walk you through the program and have you meet Willow."

"You haven't finished your breakfast, ladies." Mom walked to the fridge and pulled out two containers. She placed one in my hand and passed the other across the table to Izzie. "At least take the blueberry and almond quinoa I fixed. Trust me. This power food will be the perfect pick-me-up come mid-morning." She gave me a peck on the cheek, then whispered in my ear, "I hope you stay a good, long while. Izzie needs you. We all do."

I pulled away and, tilting my head, studied her for a moment. "I'm not leaving any time soon. Promise." I turned to glance at Izzie.

She was busy chitchatting with Dad, which most likely meant she hadn't heard our conversation.

"Good. Now, go do your paint-by-numbers thing with your sister before she has a meltdown." Mom laughed, then, exchanging places with Dad, she skirted the table to hug her other daughter.

"Forgive your mom. She acts as if every time you leave it will be forever." Dad kissed my forehead, then tousled my hair.

I swung my hip sideways to nudge his. "I love her drama. It's what makes Mom so special."

Dad sighed. "One of her many qualities I fell in love with. Okay, enough mush. Katy dear, let's leave these two beautiful ladies to get on with their day. Besides, we have a boat to scrub down and give a fresh coat of paint."

Before they offered another round of hugs, I hurried out of the house and down the drive, pulling Izzie close behind me. Opening the car door, I scooted into the driver's seat.

"That wasn't so painful." Izzie buckled her seat belt.

I steered north on Sail Shore Drive and my breathing slowed into a normal rhythm. "Let me say I'm glad the homecoming trauma is over." No mention of my ex-boyfriend or sob stories about why I hated my job left me with at least some dignity.

Izzie stared at a makeup mirror and brushed her cheeks with bronzer. "Nice try distracting Mom with the paint shop comment, but we've argued the subject to death. One more go-around couldn't make a difference."

I shrugged as I drove through the intersection and onto Whisper Lane. "Sorry. I panicked. If she'd decided to dig for details about New York, well, I'm not ready for that."

"Hey! Perfect timing." Izzie clasped her hands. "We can get started right away."

I parked the car and turned to face the shop.

A pixie-faced girl with spiked hair in shades of blue and purple stood in the shop's doorway. She unplugged a pair of earbuds and waved. Her smile showed perfectly straight teeth and was punctuated with a set of dimples. "Morning! I opened the shipment that arrived yesterday evening and stocked the shelves. I'd say we have enough paints and brushes to last for months."

Izzie reached the stoop first. "You're the best. Thank you, Willow. I'd like you to meet my sister. Chloe, this is my assistant, and she's a genius at painting."

"Hi." Willow pumped my arm with a firm handshake. "Izzie has told me great things about you. I've gotta say, you coming here to help get the business started is so nice."

I cleared my throat. "Thanks. Izzie swears you have what it takes to do the job, and I'm counting on that, especially this evening."

Willow wrinkled her forehead as she stared at Izzie. "Oh? Why this evening?"

"Something's come up, and I can't be at tonight's event." Izzie fussed with her shirt button. "But you'll be fine, and, of course, Chloe's here. She's a whiz at this stuff." Her voice raised another octave.

"I am?" I grinned, then placed a gentle hand on Izzie's shoulder. "How about we go inside and you give me the crash course on painting events? Okay?"

Willow curled her arm around Izzie's and guided her inside. "Don't sweat it. We've got this, boss."

I followed them into the shop. Smells of paint, linseed oil, and turpentine combined in the air and triggered memories of Paris and my days spent creating art. I sighed. Mom and Dad might be right. This was where I belonged . . . at least for now.

* * *

"She did what?" My voice squeaked as I struggled to keep a grip on a fistful of paint brushes. I couldn't have heard her correctly. A huge box fan blasted noise and air into the room, which did nothing to alleviate the heat that lingered, thick and heavy, well into the evening. However, central air-conditioning wasn't a luxury Izzie could afford yet.

Willow stood with hands on her hips. "It's strategy. What's that saying? Keep your friends close but keep your enemies closer? For now, Fiona is our enemy."

My jaw dropped. I didn't know how to respond. If Izzie and Megan were right about Fiona's troublemaking, inviting her here this evening would be like throwing meat to the wolves since I suspected the shop owners were starving for revenge. "I don't know . . ." I shook my head.

"Really?" Willow blinked. "I would've thought Izzie told you. She invited her. First, she spoke with Theo to see what she thought. She agreed with Izzie that having Fiona attend this evening to observe, maybe talk with a couple of the guests, and then write about the experience in her column was a great idea." She moved down the middle row to place cups and napkins at nine of the stations, then tuned the stereo to a smooth jazz station. "Anyway, Izzie is desperate to squash all the anger and tension that's built up. I know she doesn't care for Fiona—hardly anybody in town does—but she wants this to work."

I scratched behind one ear with my free hand. Last night, Izzie's comments and attitude hadn't exactly screamed forgiveness. However, the shouting match between Megan and Fiona might have caused her to forget mentioning the invitation. "I understand trying to play peacemaker. What I'm finding hard to believe is how Fiona will help achieve that."

"Go ahead and place those brushes next to the napkins, then grab the flat and liner brushes. We need all three kinds this evening. I'll be glad to run the event, if you keep an eye on Fiona."

Willow's brow arched as if she were asking me rather than ordering. In any case, keeping an eye on Fiona might not be a bad idea. I sure didn't know if she was the sort to keep her promise. What if she came this evening to stir up more trouble?

Willow twirled around to face the stage, then rushed to one side and switched on the projector. "Look. I'll admit I've got doubts, too. But we both should have faith in the plan. Besides, any publicity put in the *Whisper Cove Gazette* will help business, right?"

Before I could answer, the bell chimed.

As the door flew open, a rush of damp, muggy air filled the room. "Hello, ladies! It took me awhile to get through town. A huge sale on summer wear at Casually Done is attracting a swarm of shoppers. Lord knows Aggie Rezno's business needs a major boost. She's not the best salesperson."

"Speak of the devil." I mumbled before raising my chin to smile. "Glad you could make it, Miss Gimble."

She waved her arm. "Please. Miss Gimble is too formal. I think it would be nice if we became friends. Don't you agree, Chloe?" She creased her mouth into a thin smile.

I bit down on my lip. "Fiona, would you like something to quench your thirst? We have bottled water, tea, and, of course, wine." I moved to the mini-fridge behind the front counter.

"Don't bother." Fiona dug through her carryall and pulled out a thermos. "I always carry my own drink. It's a special brew of sassafras tea with just the right amounts of cinnamon and ginger." She tapped the container. "Family recipe."

I blinked. "That's nice. Willow? You want something?" I jiggled a bottle of iced tea.

"Nope. Maybe later." Without looking at either me or our guest, she busied her hands with last-minute prep.

The bell jingled again. Two women entered, chatting and laughing. I recognized Megan and the owner of Quaint Décor, Sammy Peale. She had graduated a few years before me and starred in track and field. Her tall build remained athletic. A thick mane of chestnut brown hair swung across her shoulders as she waved at me.

"Chloe Abbington, how great is this?" Sammy squeezed me in a hug that threatened to cut off oxygen.

After a second, I pulled myself free. "Good to see you, Sammy."

I tried my best to keep up with Sammy's account of Whisper Cove news and kept my responses to an occasional nod. Several more guests popped inside to join the group of merchants. However, Megan remained near the door, clutching her bag close to her chest. I winked and smiled with a wave, attempting to chase away what I figured was her discomfort or embarrassment about yesterday's drama.

"Oh! There's Penny." Sammy squeezed my arm. "I don't think you've met. She owns a shop next to mine. Penny is pure genius when it comes to aromatherapy. I've got to ask her about my itchy skin problem." She hurried toward a slightly older, large-chested woman with platinum blonde hair pulled back in a bun.

I turned to search for Megan, but she'd moved on to take a seat. Her apprehensive mood must have vanished because she was carrying on a conversation with another shop owner. I mingled to chat with the guests, both old friends and new acquaintances, until Willow gave me the nod. She'd start the show any minute now. I pivoted on my heel and crossed the room.

Fiona raised her camera and snapped candid shots of the guests and shop. "Seems you have a nice gig going. With any luck, your sister won't tank the business before Christmas." She snickered and pointed to the stage. "The wine will help."

"Welcome, everybody. My name is Willow North, and I'm your instructor this evening. I'm new to Whisper Cove. So, if you want to know anything about me, just ask." She circulated the room to pass out tiny plastic goblets and quickly filled each one before returning to her place next to the easel. "Compliments of the shop for this special occasion. Enjoy, everybody! Oh, and if you'd prefer coffee or water, let us know." She set the empty bottle on the counter and wiped her hands on a towel. "Now, when you're ready, I want you to take the flat brush—that's the big, fat one—and dip it in the white paint. Add some blue. If you'll look at the projector screen, you can see from my painting, this gives the sky a softer appearance."

I crossed my arms and glared at the reporter. "You sure say whatever comes to mind, don't you?"

Fiona peered at me and sighed. "Too much lying and deceit going on in this world. About time people tell the truth to each other."

I stiffened and kept my voice low, though I wanted to shout. "Even if the truth hurts? I mean, going out of your way to tell somebody you hate their shop or how they do business seems cruel and uncalled for."

Fiona stuffed the camera back inside her carryall, then took a swig of tea. She capped the thermos and kept quiet.

"No comment?" I sniffed and recalled Megan's claim about Fiona.

Glancing across the room, I cringed at all the vicious stares cast in our direction, including a couple of ladies who held their brushes in a white-knuckled grip. My heart sank as Izzie's bubble of hope to mend fences popped and fizzled into nothing right before my eyes. Deep in thought, I almost missed the empty seat next to Penny. I scrambled to think and take a mental inventory of guests, but Fiona's rambling interrupted.

"Last year, my husband died and left me with a ton of debt. Meanwhile, at his funeral, my sister had the poor taste to confess how she and my dearly departed had been having an affair for several years and claimed I didn't care enough about him to notice. I wanted nothing to do with that man, including his name." Fiona's chin trembled. "Perhaps this heart of mine is too broken to mend. Maybe my misery tends to spill out in the column I write. My intention isn't to hurt anyone, Chloe. I figure truth is better than living in blissful ignorance."

I swallowed. Had anyone heard this story? Izzie claimed Fiona kept quiet about the details of the life she had before moving here. "You came to Whisper Cove hoping for a fresh start?"

Fiona nodded. "Landing my job at the *Whisper Cove Gazette* was like a touch of fate from an angel. You understand?"

I did. Izzie's suggestion to help her launch Paint with a View was my stroke of fate, wasn't it? How could I not sympathize, at least with that part of Fiona's story? I opened then shut my mouth, not sure what to say. If she told the others her tragic tale, they might offer to help her get through what was obviously a hard time. "Fiona—" I turned at the sound of Willow's voice.

"Take your painting knife and mix your white and green colors together. You'll apply this in thin lines to create waves in the water. That will give dimension and texture to your painting." Willow made some quick strokes on her canvas, then circulated to help the others.

Fiona poked my shoulder. "Would you look at our Olympic star? Talk about needing a dose of truth and a reality check, Samantha fits that sad tale. She'll never make it in the business world." Fiona snorted. "Her talent is mooching off of others and taking shortcuts to get what she wants. Lazy and dishonest are qualities to scar anyone's résumé."

My mouth flapped. What happened? A few seconds ago, I felt sorry for the woman, and then she cannonballed me with another round of lethal comments aimed at the Quaint Décor owner. To make matters worse, Sammy turned at that same moment to shoot Fiona a hateful glare, as if she knew the unkind journalist was talking about her.

"Wow. Would you look at the time? Flies by when having fun, right?" Fiona laughed as if none of what she'd said about Sammy was hurtful or wrong.

"Okay, people." Willow tapped the mic until everyone quieted down. "Before leaving, you'll want to use one of the hair dryers to finish your masterpieces. Trust me. Wet paint and car seats don't go together." Willow hopped off the stage and motioned to me with a wave of her arm.

This was my cue to circulate and thank our guests, which, after my talk with Fiona, would be the easiest part of the evening. I turned to say goodbye to her. However, she had her phone in hand, tapping keys at a frenzied pace while an ugly scowl creased her brow.

When she finished, the smile was back in place. "Sorry to rush off." She pumped my arm in a firm handshake. "I'll take a couple more quotes from the shop owners before I leave."

"Thanks for agreeing to write about our event. I'm looking forward to reading the article when it comes out."

Fiona lifted her chin. "That may not be for a while. I have other topics scheduled for my column. Don't worry, though. I'm sure I can fit you in by October or November. Good evening, Chloe."

My jaw dropped as heat spread through me. We'd been tricked. Or I should say, Izzie had been. Though Fiona had promised to write a nice article, I bet nothing had been discussed about when she'd have it published. I couldn't wait to let Izzie know. Possibly, she had some influence with the *Gazette*'s owner, Theo Lawrence.

I made a quick tour of the room to say thank you and goodbye to everyone, though the gesture was mechanical. I hoped no one noticed. Fiona's comments troubled me and dampened my mood.

"You okay, Chloe?" Willow stood close as the last two guests gathered their paintings and walked to the door.

I shook my head. "Nothing surprising, I guess."

"Fiona?"

"Yep." Having no desire to share the details, I gathered napkins off the table and tossed them in the trash.

"I warned you she's the enemy. It's a shame, though. Izzie is such an optimist and wanted this evening to work out."

Willow picked up all of the paint tools and plopped them in the plastic washtub she cradled under one arm.

"Fiona's the enemy, all right. She should never have been invited." I quickly heaved a sigh. "Sorry. That was uncalled for. Izzie meant well."

"No problem. Fiona tends to bring out the worst in people." Willow shrugged, then set the washtub on the table near the back. "I really hate to ask, but I have a date this evening, and I'm supposed to meet him in like fifteen minutes. Would you mind finishing the cleanup? I like this guy a lot and want to make a good impression." She twisted the hem of her shirt and blushed.

I chuckled. Youth and the innocence of love. Granted, Willow was probably only a few years younger than my twenty-six, but personal experience had left me somewhat jaded. "Sure. I've got this. Plus, you did most of the work already. Go have fun." I shooed her away.

"You're the best. Thank you! I owe you big time." Willow grabbed her bag and rushed out, letting the door slam behind her.

I locked the door then, with hands on hips, swiveled side to side to view the shop, and estimated the cleanup wouldn't take more than a half hour or so. After I washed and put away the brushes and knives, wiped the tables, swept, and dumped the trash, I'd be finished and on my way home. I sighed. "Easy-peasy."

I flipped the radio station to rock. The powerful beat of The Black Keys resonated through the speakers. Keeping time to the rhythm, I swept the broom back and forth across the plank flooring. A sense of accomplishment filled me. Except for the minor hiccup with Fiona and her contrary behavior, the evening had been a success. Izzie would be pleased. At once, I pulled my phone from my back pocket and tapped the call button.

"You've reached the number of Izzie Abbington. Sorry I missed your call. You know the drill."

I frowned but didn't bother to leave a message. We'd see each other soon enough. I could share all the details of the evening, including Fiona's announcement, over a cup of hot cocoa. Izzie wouldn't be happy about a long delay in printing the story. I shuddered. We were only halfway through summer. October might be too late. By then, the feud between the town and the columnist could spiral into a barroom brawl.

"I can't believe I felt sorry for the woman." I grabbed the bottled cleaner, aimed, and gave the table several squirts. "What's with her? Just because somebody treated her crappy doesn't mean she should do the same to others." I ripped paper towels from the roll and applied some serious muscle to wipe the surface dry. "All her honesty-is-the-best-policy garbage. What a crock of bull." I stuck out my tongue. After tossing the used towels into the trash, I hoisted the washtub and moved to the storage room.

Brushes and knives clanked together as I dumped them in the utility sink. Once I added soap to a sink full of hot water, I sat in the chair to relax. I could agree with Izzie and Megan. Running the woman out of town would be easiest, but she'd only take out her venomous attitude on somebody somewhere else. Dumping our problem on others wasn't kind. Besides, this wasn't a wild west show where the sheriff fired his gun and chased unwanted folks out of town.

I stood and turned to tidy up and reorganize the paint supplies on the shelf by size and color. All the while, my head kept spinning with ideas. We could invite Fiona to dinner, get to know each other, and send a message she was a welcome addition to our community. I snapped my fingers. "Or maybe we throw her a party on her next birthday! If we show her kindness, maybe she'll change for the better. Like flies and honey." I smiled and hummed along to the Stones belting out "Honky Tonk Woman."

My back pocket buzzed, along with a familiar ringtone. I plastered the phone to one ear while lining up bottles and tubes of paint with the other. "Hi, Mom."

"Oh, good. I thought your phone would go straight to voice mail like Izzie's. Listen, your dad and I are going to the Bixbys' for a late-night game of gin rummy. When will you be home?"

I glanced at the clock. "I'd say by ten."

"Well, if you're hungry, there's leftover pizza in the fridge. We should return by twelve or one. How'd everything go this evening?"

My hand jerked, and bottles of paint tipped over like a line of dominoes. "Dang it all," I muttered under my breath. "Except for Fiona's behavior, the event ran like a charm. I'll share the details later. Thanks for the pizza. You and Dad have a nice visit, and say hello to the Bixbys for me."

A nanosecond later, before she could ask more about Fiona, I stabbed the end call button and moved on to scrub and dry the brushes and knives. "Shoot. I forgot to mention my idea about the dinner invitation." I figured the sooner we got started on my strategy, the better.

With the paint tools cleaned, dried, and put away, the only task remaining was to take the trash to the dumpster in the alley. I collected the wastebaskets from the front, the bathroom, and storage room, and emptied everything into one bag. Taking a deep breath, I lifted the heavy load and staggered to the back exit. "Should have used two trash bags." I dropped my cargo and, with a swipe of my foot, shoved it to one side.

Closing my fingers around the handle, I pulled the door open and shuddered. Dark alleys shouldn't scare me. After all, I'd been a New Yorker for two years. But that label also meant I kept my guard up to prepare for anything. I flipped the switch to turn on the floodlight. I grumbled, then toggled the switch again and again, but the alley remained pitch black. "Well, that's just fantastic." I blew out air and dragged the trash bag across the floor. Lifting the load with both arms, I stepped into the alley. My foot caught on something lumpy. I frowned. Another bag? Izzie wouldn't leave trash in the doorway. Of course, I didn't know Willow or if she was lazy or careless enough to do so.

Frustrated, I pulled out my phone and switched on the flashlight app. "Somebody is going to hear about this." I scowled, waving the light across the alley pavement until it rested directly in front of me. My eyes widened, and the phone slipped from my hand as the floodlight flickered. A scream built in my throat, and I couldn't stop the sound. A body lay at my feet with arms and legs spread out in a disturbing, awkward pose.

I back shuffled but couldn't pull my gaze from the horrible sight. A knife protruded from the neck while blood tinged the mop of white hair with red. The curved handle of the weapon looked familiar. So did the body. I cringed and clamped one hand over my mouth to keep from screaming again.

Fiona was dead, and she'd been stabbed with what looked to me like a painting knife.

Chapter Three

"What time would you say you discovered the body?"

I pressed my lips together and fixed my gaze on the notepad Detective Barrett held. Members of CIT, his crime investigative team, filled the shop, busy collecting and filling bags with evidence. I struggled to block out the loud buzz of conversation, the crinkle and snap of the bags, and the laughs that seemed so out of place. I squeezed against one wall of the supply room to move away from the gurney being carried in by two men. "I told you. I believe it was close to nine thirty, maybe a few minutes after." My defenses rankled, and I flashed angry eyes at him. "I was too busy freaking out over a dead body to pay much attention to the time, Detective." My breath hitched. "Sorry."

He nodded and tapped his pen on the paper. "Understandable. I'll try and be quick." The slight upturn of his lips softened the effect of his rigid jawline.

I rubbed my arms. "Thanks. Do you mind if I grab a bottle of water out of the mini-fridge?"

"Hey, Lorenzo! Pull a water out of that fridge and bring it here," Barrett called out.

His eyes were a warm brown that matched the color of his hair. The summer sun had deepened the shade of his skin to bronze, and his tall frame was fit and muscular. A tiny scar traced a faint white line around the corner of one eye. The shape reminded me of a crescent moon. As if he knew I had noticed, he raised a finger to scratch the spot.

"Thank you." I took the bottle from Lorenzo and swigged nearly half the water, desperate to drown out the fear and panic. "I only met her yesterday."

Barrett arched his brow.

"Fiona Gimble. We talked at this evening's painting event."

"You've mentioned that." He flipped the notebook to a blank page. "Did anything unusual happen this evening? Arguments or something that struck you as odd? How about your conversation with the victim?"

I shivered at hearing the word victim. "Right now, I can't recall anything unusual." My comment was sort of true. All the glares from the merchants weren't anything new. Fiona's snide remarks were hardly a secret since, according to Izzie and Megan, she peppered her column with them.

"Hmm." He rested the pen on the notepad and raised his chin. "What do you do in New York?"

I blinked, totally caught off guard by the direction his questioning took. "I work in art supplies." I refused to go into detail about my job and career mishaps.

"You mentioned you came to Whisper Cove to help your sister start her business. I don't know many employers who let their people up and leave for, how long did you say? Several weeks?"

I shifted my weight and leaned back. My face heated. "Business is slow."

"I see. Any other reason why you wanted to get away?" He tilted his head.

A prickly sense of irritation rose to the surface. I anchored my hands on my hips. "What does any of this have to do with that poor woman's murder? My life in New York isn't important."

He shrugged. "I disagree. Every detail is crucial. For all I know, you came here because you're running from the law. Or could be you knew Fiona from another time and held a grudge against her." He crossed his arms and rolled back on his heels. "Lots of scenarios to explore."

My anger spiked and simmered under the surface. "Well, I never—"

"Oh, my poor baby!" Mom rushed into the storage room and cradled me in her arms.

Dad was on her heels, giving the detective an evil-eye glare.

I gently freed myself from the tight hold and stepped back. "Mom, Dad, this is Detective Barrett."

"We know who he is." Mom puffed her cheeks. "Weren't you the one who framed that unfortunate lady who lives up north on Haymaker Run? Not a smart way to start your job, if you ask me."

"Now, Katy." Dad patted her on the shoulder. "We're here to support Chloe and not spread rumors about Detective Barrett, who I'm sure will do his best to find the killer. Right?" He puffed out his chest and continued glaring.

I clenched my jaw. The call for their help had been a mistake. I'd tried Izzie, but again, her phone had gone straight to voice mail. "Say, why don't you both go out front and grab something to drink from the fridge while I finish answering the detective's questions?" I squeezed each of their hands, then gave them a tiny push toward the doorway.

"But—" Mom frowned.

"I'll be fine." I spread my lips into what I hoped was a positive smile.

"Don't worry. I only have a couple more questions, and then she's all yours." Barrett looked and sounded almost relieved to say he'd be done with me soon.

I scowled. Once we were alone, I pulled back my shoulders and lifted my head. "Okay, then. Let's get this over with, Detective Barrett."

He pulled a stick of gum from his pocket and popped it in his mouth. "Would you like some?"

"No, thank you. What I'd like is to get this interrogation over with, if you don't mind." I fanned my face with both hands. By now, emotional exhaustion was taking over. I could barely keep on my feet, but I doubted he cared.

Barrett chewed slowly for a few seconds. "What makes you think this is an interrogation?"

"Well, isn't it? You, the detective, are asking me, the suspect, questions." I sputtered my words.

He chuckled. "Who said you're a suspect, Miss Abbington? Unless you think you should be."

"I—can we get on with it?" I waved an arm. "We have a business to run and lots to prepare before our grand opening event, which is less than twenty-four hours from now." Why did I let him get to me? After all, he was a detective doing his job.

He shook his head. "Sorry, I can't let that happen. This place is a crime scene. Until I say we're finished, your shop remains closed."

I blinked, and my heart pounded. At once, the reality of what happened this evening hit me hard. "Okay. I—um—yes, I understand." I patted my pockets, searching for my phone, then remembered the crime team had taken it. "Do you think I can have my phone back for a minute? I need to call my sister, Izzie."

He pointed his pen at me. "About your sister. Shouldn't she be here this evening?"

A queasiness rolled through me. I clutched a hand to my stomach. From the corner of one eye, I saw Mom flailing her arms in all directions while talking to one of the crime team members.

Dad attempted to pull her away, but with no success.

His voice grew louder, asking her to calm down. However, nothing worked when she grew anxious.

"If you'll excuse me for a minute?" I rubbed the back of my neck and struggled to keep my nerves in check. Without waiting for his response, I hurried to the front.

"Mom, I think you should go on home and wait for Izzie." I turned to Dad. "Don't you agree that would be best?"

As if I'd handed him a lifeline, the officer slipped away and back to work. I waited until he reached the other side of the room, then snapped my head around to glower at my parents. "What the heck was that all about? Mom, you were moving your arms like you were winding up to take a swing at him. Not smart."

"I overheard the man spouting off about Izzie." Mom sniffed.

"About Izzie? What did he say?" I didn't like the sound of that. If the police knew Izzie had made snide remarks about

Fiona, not to mention her wish to run the woman out of town, those nasty details wouldn't look good to them. Then add her vanishing act this evening to the story with no explanation as to where she'd gone? Barrett would be locking her up and tossing the key in Chautauqua Lake.

"He claimed she and Megan were causing a stir and bad-mouthing Fiona. He—boy, does this make me hopping mad—he said he wouldn't be surprised if one of them killed the woman." Mom gritted her teeth and balled her hands into tight fists.

"That shouldn't happen, ma'am. If you point out the officer, I'll be sure to reprimand him for his conduct."

I gasped as Detective Barrett spoke over my shoulder. How much had he heard? Somehow, we had to get out of here and warn Izzie. The situation was looking worse by the second.

Mom pointed. "That tall man with short red hair. I believe his name tag said Collins."

Barrett made a note then looked at all three of us. "Where is Izzie, by the way? I'd like to speak with her."

"She's out of town on business." Mom blurted out the words.

I sighed. "She had another appointment. It was urgent." I hoped he'd buy the excuse. The blank expression on his face gave me no clue.

"Oh, my." Mom sobbed and covered her mouth.

Two crime team members pushed the gurney through the shop. Thank goodness a body bag covered Fiona and the gory details of her murder. I blew out air to ease the tight feeling in my chest.

A rather short and balding man followed close behind the gurney. Once he reached Barrett, he stopped. "Can I have a word?"

Barrett stood off to the side and leaned close to the man's ear. After a curt nod, he returned. "The coroner needs me, so I won't keep you. Please let Izzie know I'll be in touch."

Mom and Dad headed for the door, but I hung back. I wanted answers. Why was Fiona behind the shop in the first place? What or who had brought her there? I suddenly remembered what happened before she left the event. I paced over to where Barrett stood, engaged in conversation once more with the coroner.

"Her body temperature dropped only a couple of degrees." The coroner swiped his phone with the tip of one finger. "Sharp object hit the jugular vein." He cleared his throat, then paused and nodded at me. He pocketed his phone. "I'll give you the rest back at the precinct, Hunter."

"Thanks, Ed." Barrett took a moment to spit his gum into a cup. "Hate when it loses the sugary taste, don't you?"

I shrugged. "I hardly ever chew gum."

He set the cup on the counter and pulled one of the evidence bags from a box.

I flinched. The sight of the object inside, with its bloody tip, made me regret my decision to stick around. I wiped clammy hands on my thighs.

"Does this look familiar?"

I swallowed then pinched my bottom lip with my finger and thumb. "Um . . . I think that's a painting knife."

Barrett nodded. "The weapon used to stab the victim." Looking down, he ran his fingers along the zipper closure of the bag. "I have to admit, I don't know a painting knife from a kitchen knife." He lifted his chin and nodded. "Thank you for clearing up that mystery."

My heartbeat flip-flopped. I fell hook, line, and the proverbial sinker for the bait he'd cast. I stabbed the air with my finger. "Doesn't mean it came from our shop."

He dropped the bag into the box then turned. "You seem defensive, but it's natural after what you've been through. I'm not saying the murder weapon, that being a painting knife, is from this shop. However, I wouldn't be doing my job if I didn't consider the possibility. Don't you agree?"

I blinked. A painful lump of defeat lodged in my throat and left me unable to speak.

"Was there something else?" He bent down to lock the lid on the box. "Otherwise, I think we should call it a night. My team is finished for now, and you look beat."

I pressed two fingers to my neck. My pulse was racing. I took a breath. "I remembered a detail that happened right before Fiona left the event."

"Oh?" He pulled out his pen and flipped open his notepad.

"She got a phone message and was texting, really fast, like it was urgent. She had this scowl on her face, as if she was angry about something." I shook my head. "I'm not sure. Then she said a quick goodbye and left a little before nine." I grew quiet while Barrett scribbled notes.

"You have any idea who she was texting with?" He stopped writing and looked up.

"How would I—no, I don't." I sighed. "Why not check her phone?" I didn't mean to sound sarcastic, but his raised brows hinted I failed to hide the surly tone.

He rubbed the line of his jaw with one hand. "No phone on her. The killer most likely took it."

"Meaning, the killer might be the one she was texting?" I grew tense as my chest tightened and cut off my breath.

The crime team hadn't found a phone on her or in the shop. However, if I was the texter, I had plenty of opportunity to ditch the device and to delete any messages on my phone. Barrett's gloomy stare and his dead silence told me he was thinking the same thing. Fine, but where was my motive? I bit down on my lip. Izzie and her shop. People would do just about anything to help protect family. Even murder? I shuddered to think someone could be that desperate.

Barrett raked fingers through his hair. "Look, Miss Abbington. Chloe. Is it all right if I call you Chloe? I'm not jumping to any conclusions. That's not the way I do things."

"I heard the coroner." Panicking, I picked up speed. "He said the victim's temperature dropped only a couple of degrees. I watch lots of cop shows, and what he said means Fiona died within the last hour, and that means she was murdered while I was here alone. I—"

His hand gripped my shoulder. "Chloe, I have an investigation to run and several leads to follow. What you told me about Fiona's texting helps. Every detail helps. I'm not accusing you of anything. Please, go home and get some rest." He pulled a bag off the shelf and plucked out a device. "You can have your phone back. The team's all done with it."

I cleared my throat and steadied my wobbly legs. "Sorry. It's been a terrifying evening."

"Of course it has. Now, we'll talk tomorrow. Here's my card, in case you remember anything else. Meantime, don't forget to let your sister know I'll need to speak with her. Oh, and perhaps you should put a sign on the door?"

"Hmm?"

"Closed for business until further notice."

"Right." I rummaged through my bag until I found the spare shop key. "Here you go. Please lock up when you all leave. We don't need to add vandalism to the list of crimes committed this evening." I nodded. "Thanks, Detective Barrett."

"Hunter. Call me Hunter. I have a feeling we'll be seeing a lot of each other." He smiled and pulled out another stick of gum.

I waved. Yeah, I knew that trick. Pretend to make friends, get me to relax, and, all at once, I would let my guard down and spill all sorts of details that made me look guilty. "Nope. Detective Barrett works best for me, thank you." I walked out of the shop.

As I reached my car and slipped into the driver's seat, my phone rang. Staring at the screen, I slumped down and opened the call. My voice trembled. "Izzie. Where have you been?"

"Sorry. The evening's been crazy busy. How'd the event go? I'm anxious to hear all about it."

"Oh, you'll be anxious, all right. Izzie—" I gripped the phone. "Izzie, something horrible has happened. Fiona is dead." I winced as she gasped.

"What? How?" Her words ended with a hiccup.

I explained in as few words as possible about the murder. "The sight of her was so awful. Then that Detective Barrett with all his questions had my hair on end. Even worse, Mom and Dad came. They didn't handle matters well. I never should have called them, but you weren't answering your phone. Where were you?"

"This is terrible." Izzie whispered her words.

"I know. How awful for her." My head pounded. The sight of waves lapping against the lakeshore nauseated me.

"And for my shop. How will the business survive after a murder happened there?"

My throat tightened. "Izzie. A woman is dead. Don't you think—"

"Of course. I don't know what I'm saying." A nervous titter released. "Poor Fiona. She may not have been friendly or kind, but no one deserves that."

Was it my overly suspicious mind at work, or did her words sound emotionless and without a hint of sincerity? "Okay. I'm wiped and need some sleep. I'll see you at home." I stabbed the end call button before she could say another word and pulled onto the road.

Sure, the business could suffer, but we had more important concerns. Fiona was dead, and, as far as I knew, Izzie and I might end up Detective Barrett's prime suspects. Without a doubt, my alibi sucked. I had been alone in the shop doing cleanup. I had access to sharp objects, like painting knives. I clenched the steering wheel, picturing the look on Barrett's face when he showed me the evidence bag with the bloody knife. Thank goodness I hadn't touched anything from the crime scene. Barrett and his team wouldn't find a single print to match mine.

I turned onto Sail Shore Drive. Reaching within a few yards of the house, I spotted Izzie's jeep. What about her alibi? If she had been with someone this evening, he or she could prove

Izzie was nowhere close to commit the crime. I groaned. Lots of pieces needed to fall into place before I'd stop worrying.

I parked behind Izzie's vehicle and sat for a while. Through the front window, I could see into the living room. Izzie pulled the curtain shut and turned off the light. Coming to Whisper Cove was supposed to be my turning point and the chance to do something worthwhile by helping Izzie with her shop. I rested my chin on the steering wheel and closed my eyes. Only, right now, instead of sharing the opening of Paint with a View, we were sharing a murder.

Chapter Four

"I can't tell you. I promised." Sitting next to me on the edge of the boat dock, Izzie dipped her toes into the water.

A gull cried as it dove to catch a fish, then flapped its wings until it soared into the air once more. I tugged at the clamshell brim of my sun hat to shade my face from the morning sunlight. "Who did you promise?"

"I can't tell you that, either." She kicked her foot and splashed water on both of us. "Maybe we should talk about when to reschedule my grand opening, since the date I planned is ruined, all because the shop is a crime scene and off limits. The murder happened *outside*. Detective Barrett is being difficult." Her lips curled into a pouty expression.

"He's being thorough and doesn't want to overlook any evidence, inside the shop or out. In case somebody at the event last night turns out to be a killer, you know?" I scratched the top of Max's head.

"Seriously?" Izzie threw up her arms. "Whose side are you on?"

"Yours, of course. I'm thinking like a detective, and *you* are sidetracking the conversation. Even if you won't tell me your whereabouts, the detective will want to know." I pulled my feet out of the water and turned to face her, tucking one leg under the other. "In fact, he might suspect you're trying to hide something, which doesn't usually go over well in a murder investigation." At the very least, she shouldn't keep secrets from me. We'd always had that sister bond and supported each other. It was like she didn't trust me. I reached for her hand. "Look. You have an alibi, so tell him. Then he can scratch your name off his list of suspects. Isn't that how it works?"

"When the time is right, I'll tell him, and you, and everybody." She squeezed my hand. "Right now, I can't."

"There you are." Mom tiptoed with bare feet across the lawn, holding up the sides of her flowered silk kaftan to keep the hem from dragging in the wet grass. Her red tresses were piled on top of her head in a poofy bun. "I filled a huge bowl of strawberries, melon, and kiwi to go with breakfast. Come join your dad and me. We have lots to discuss." She waved her arm toward the door.

I grinned at Izzie then sprinted to the house. "Dibs on the strawberries!"

"That's cheating, Chloe."

Her footsteps grew louder as she hurried to catch up to me, which really wasn't fair since her legs were twice as long as mine. As she flew by, I stopped in the doorway and bent over to grab my knees and catch my breath. Even Max, with his short, tiny legs, scurried ahead of me and down the hall.

Mom patted my back. "Don't worry, sweetie. I have more strawberries and melon in the fridge."

I straightened and gave her a hug. "You're the best, Mom. Thank you."

"Always trying. Now, I'm hoping you got somewhere with Izzie?" Frown lines creased her brow.

Last night we'd stayed up way past midnight, too disturbed to sleep over the shock of Fiona's murder only a few hours before. Mom and Dad had urged Izzie to talk about where she had gone for the evening but had gotten the same answer I did this morning.

"Not even close." I linked my arm through hers, and we walked down the hall and into the kitchen.

The sizzle of tofu bacon frying, the garlicky scent of bagels toasting, and Dad manning the kitchen made me smile. He wore his denim Chautauqua Lake Yacht Club floppy hat, complete with the signature flag logo, and Mom's paisley print apron over his faded blue shirt and cargo shorts. Never one for stereotypes, he loved cooking, much to Mom's delight. She'd rather spend time in her she-shed, painting one of her sunset-over-water scenes. She and Claude Monet would've been a perfect match.

The toaster popped out a bagel. I grabbed for the cream cheese and spread on a thick layer, then took a generous bite. "Yum." Plucking two slices of bacon off the serving plate, I made my way to the fruit bowl.

Izzie winked as she held up her plate filled mostly with melon and grapes. "You didn't think I'd take all the strawberries, did you?"

I ignored the teasing jab. "I think we should discuss the topic we'd all rather avoid before Detective Barrett shows up."

"I agree." Mom sat at the table with her fingers curled around a mug of her Earl Grey tea. "No point in denying the obvious. He will look at both you girls as suspects. Especially when Izzie refuses to explain where she was last night." The disapproving stare darkened her eyes.

"Now, Kate." Dad placed the bacon and bagels in the center of the table, alongside the fruit bowl, then took off his hat before sitting next to me. "How about we try and stay positive? I'm sure Barrett and his team will find plenty of evidence to prove Chloe and Izzie had nothing to do with Miss Gimble's murder."

Mom slanted her head. "I say it's always better to be cautious."

"Look at us. The Abbington Detective Agency. Too bad we haven't a clue how to solve a murder." I took a bite of bagel and chewed, contemplating the odds.

"Hey. At least we have plenty of suspects." Izzie nudged Mom's arm. "That's one checkmark for the pro column."

"You mean if distaste or loathing Fiona is a motive?" I shook my head. "Hardly enough to point fingers."

Izzie scooted forward. Her eyes gleamed with excitement. "Loathing her is only a part of the equation. Think about it. Each scathing column Fiona wrote attacked one of the shop owners. Some even took a hit to their sales. I heard from Megan, who spoke to Sammy, that Gwen's Go Fly a Kite's profits dropped nearly twenty percent in the quarter after Fiona's first column about her was published."

"I warned Gwen not to write that letter to the editor." Dad shook his head.

I frowned. "What letter?" Like starting a book in the middle of the story, I was playing catch-up.

"Gwen wrote to complain about all the negativity affecting our town," Mom said.

Izzie cleared her throat. "Word for word, she wrote that the residents of Whisper Cove had become victims of a poisonous voice. Everyone knew who she was referring to, including Fiona, aka the poisonous voice herself."

Dad raised his brows. "Speaking ill of the dead? Maybe we shouldn't go there."

Mom waved an arm to dismiss his comment. "Fiona fired back with a vengeance. She claimed a six-year-old could design better kites than Gwen."

"Ouch." I cringed.

"Even worse, she wrote that maybe it was time for her to retire and let a young person with fresh ideas and more talent take over." Izzie shoved away her plate.

"Then what happened? Did Gwen fight back?" I couldn't imagine letting such brutal criticism go unchallenged. I'd hire a lawyer to say libel had cost my business money.

"Sorry to say, Gwen went into a depressing spiral. She closed up her shop, and no one we've spoken to has seen her since. Her neighbors say she hardly ever leaves the house, only pops out the front door to grab her mail." Dad carried the leftovers to the fridge.

"What about the other shop owners? Did none of them come to her defense? I'd have boycotted the newspaper or staged a protest to demand Fiona be fired." I pounded the table with my fist. "How could she get away with her slice-'em-and-dice-'em column for so long?"

"Are you kidding?" Izzie's eyes widened. "According to Theo, subscriptions and sales have never been better. Money talks."

I carried my empty plate to the sink, then placed it in the dishwasher. "I feel sorry for Gwen. Seems a shame to consider her a murder suspect." The sweet lady who always gave Izzie and me treats when we visited her shop didn't fit the profile of a killer.

Max danced on his hind legs and twirled in circles. Taking the hint, I filled his bowl with kibble and topped the meal with a few bits of tofu bacon. He devoured his breakfast.

Mom sighed. "The authorities will have to start somewhere. If Gwen turns out to be one of the suspects, I'll be as devastated as anyone. Shame on me, but I'm praying Detective Barrett will keep busy with plenty of other suspects to investigate. Otherwise . . ." She pointed at me and then at Izzie. "Time and place will bring the authorities around to look at you two."

"What about motive?" I avoided the obvious—Izzie now owned a business too, and she disliked Fiona as much as everyone else in town, including Gwen. But I knew my sister well enough to believe she couldn't commit such a horrible act. What seriously worried me, though, was Megan's comment. She'd said Izzie had already been targeted by Fiona. Something had happened to fuel that fire. Would Detective Barrett add the damaging information to reasons why Izzie should be a prime suspect? Yeah, I was worried and scared for her.

As for me? That time and place thing put me on the detective's radar for sure.

"Well, no point in worrying about it. I have better things to do with my time." Izzie stood and plucked her phone out of her pocket. "Like making a phone call to Theo to cancel that huge and way over-the-top expensive ad for the grand opening."

I stared at her, amazed at how she could be so dismissive. "Anyone else you can think of that'd have a strong motive and opportunity to get rid of Fiona?"

Izzie shrugged. "Who knows? This town is full of secrets. I imagine some are pretty dark and embarrassing."

"How many times have I told you to stop listening to all the gossip your friends tell?" Mom scolded with one of her long, dragged-out sighs. "We have good people in Whisper Cove."

"Of course we do, dear." Dad squeezed her shoulders and then winked at me. "What if we shelve this discussion for another time and get out of here? We have a date with a beautiful vessel named *No Regrets*." He pulled Mom to her feet.

"Guess that's my cue to leave." She gave us each a peck on the cheek. "We'll be back around noon. You can reach us on the satellite radio, in case you need us."

Dad pulled her toward the hall. "They'll be fine. No one's going to jail today." He nodded at me. "We'll return closer to dinnertime. If we're late, there's leftover chicken Parmesan in the fridge."

"Why do you always disagree with me? I swear, Joe, you can be so overbearing at times." Mom linked her arm through his and chuckled. "Good thing I love you so much."

I smiled and then turned my head, but Izzie had disappeared. I could see her through the window in the back door, phone slapped to her ear, looking none too happy.

The dinging of the doorbell grabbed my attention. I sprinted up the hallway and yanked open the front door. "What's the matter? Did you forget your nautical telescope? How are you going to find land if you—" I pulled back. "Willow! Sorry, I thought you were my parents, which you obviously aren't." I wrinkled my nose in embarrassment. "Come in."

Willow slipped by me. She clutched a manila envelope in one hand and her bag in the other. A denim jacket splashed with jagged circles in bold colors covered her top half. A short miniskirt and fishnet leggings finished the ensemble. "Sorry to bother you." She shoved the envelope at my chest. "Someone stuck this in the shop mailbox. I thought it might be important, and why is there yellow tape covering the front door?" She heaved her chest and blinked.

Despite Whisper Cove being a small town where everybody knew everybody, word about the murder obviously hadn't gotten around to Willow.

"Let's go into the kitchen. Have you eaten breakfast? We have plenty of leftovers. When he's on one of his healthy food kicks, our dad makes the best tofu bacon." I led the way while gathering my thoughts on how to break the tragic news without getting hysterical.

Izzie might be able to remain calm, cool, and collected, but I would be having nightmares for years. Then again, I was the one who had found Fiona with a knife sticking out of her neck. Not Izzie. Those kinds of images couldn't be erased.

"Would you like some fresh-squeezed juice?" I held up the pitcher.

Willow leaned back against the table with her arms crossed. "What I'd like is to know what's going on. Did something happen at the shop? An explosion? Fire? A break-in?"

I chewed on my lip then motioned her to sit down. "None of the above. You see, last night after you left, I found—"

"Oh! Hi, Willow. Did Chloe tell you the tragic news? Fiona was murdered outside in the alley behind my shop. We're closed for business until Detective Barrett says otherwise." Izzie had popped through the back doorway and now paced the kitchen. "I'm trying to be civil and understanding and sensitive to what happened to poor Fiona, but learning I have no grand opening for the foreseeable future, which means no income to pay the rent and utilities, sort of puts me in a foul mood." She waved her phone. "Adding to that, I've lost a thousand dollars for an ad that won't be placed because the date to get a refund has passed. Any questions?" She broke stride and sank into the chair across from me and Willow, blinking her watery eyes.

"That's just—is there anything I can do to help?" Willow hurried around the table and sat close to Izzie. Her chin trembled as she squeezed her employer's hand. "I'm so sorry."

"Me too." Izzie nodded and eased out of Willow's grasp. "The only thing you, that is, all of us, can do is hope Detective Barrett finds who murdered Fiona as quickly as possible. Then we can get back to our lives and Paint with a View can open like I planned."

I shivered at the fierce tone in Izzie's voice. Complicated only began to describe her personality. She had layers that took time to understand. Right now, I recognized the part of her that felt threatened. When her plans tumbled like a tall stack of Jenga blocks, she lost confidence, which could lead to total chaos.

"You know what? I think we should make a list of as many ideas as we can for future painting events."

"I already have those." Izzie hiccupped. "Fifty of them, which will take us through December, if we do two a week. That is, if we ever open." She sobbed and leaned her head on Willow's shoulder. "I'm a hot mess."

"Then we think of fifty more, or sixty to start next year." I snapped my fingers. "What about a suggestion inbox? People submit their ideas for an event theme. We pick one every month. The winner gets to bring a few guests for a private party."

"Sure." Izzie sniffed. "We can do that. Great idea, Chloe." She managed a warm smile that didn't reach her eyes.

I scrambled to think of another way to perk up that pretty face. My shoulders sank. "Okay. I'm done playing cheerleader. Should we make another kind of list? One with all the most likely suspects? We can give those names to Detective Barrett."

"Gwen. She's the only one I can think of." Izzie shrugged.

"What about Sammy Peale?" Willow suggested. "Chloe, didn't you say Fiona made some awful remarks about her during our paint event and that Sammy was shooting murderous looks at Fiona?" She shrugged. "Sorry. Murderous is a poor choice."

"Yeah, but Sammy couldn't have heard those comments. She was too far away." I thought for a moment. "How severe was Fiona's column about Sammy?"

"I know where you're going with this. Like I said, plenty of shop owners had a grudge against Fiona and her column. That's not a reason to kill, is it?" Izzie tilted her head and paused, as if waiting for one of us to answer. "If it is, then the Chautauqua County authorities should question every person she's written about."

"You're right." I threw up my arms. "We need to dig deeper."

Both Willow and Izzie widened their eyes.

"What? You want to sit back and let fate take its course, which, let me tell you, will mean either you or most likely I will end up charged with murder." Fear and imagined scenarios darkened my mood, and, all at once, the weight of that exhausted me.

"How about we stop playing detective and let the real one do his job?" Izzie stood. "I'm sure he can manage."

"Yes, but—"

The doorbell rang again to interrupt me.

"I'll answer it. I need to go, anyway. Date with my hair stylist." Willow tugged at her hair and laughed. "My purple has faded to pink." She nodded at the envelope. "That was in the shop mail."

"Thanks. I'll let you know when we can open back up," Izzie said.

Within seconds, Willow returned, carrying a covered dish. She pointed at the attached sticky note. "Mrs. Bixby sends her condolences and offers to help in any way she can." She raised her head with peaked eyebrows.

Izzie took the dish, lifted the lid and sighed, and then placed it in the fridge next to the other containers. "I swear, you'd think we were the ones grieving. This makes three dishes delivered this morning, all from our neighbors who must think we're starving. If one more tuna casserole comes to our door, I'm dumping it down the disposal."

"Izzie." I swallowed my response. "Thanks, Willow."

"No problem." She waved, then sprinted down the hallway.

"I know." Izzie pursed her lips. "I'm sorry. I'll try harder to be . . . what's the word?"

"Kind? Sensitive? Or maybe keep those mean thoughts to yourself." I chuckled.

Izzie opened the envelope and studied the contents. With a shake of her head, she folded the paper and shoved it in her pocket. Looking at me, she smiled. "Yeah, I can try, but right now, I'm making no promises. Once this . . . situation passes and we can reopen, I'll be back to my usual sweet, adorable self."

I skirted the table and gave her a hug. "Sweet and adorable is so much better."

"Yoo-hoo? Is anybody here?" Megan clip-clopped in her heeled sandals across the hall. Standing in the kitchen doorway, with oven mitts covering her hands, she held out a Crock-Pot. "Mom and I made too much clam chowder. We thought you might like some, in case you don't want to cook this evening because of, well, you know."

Izzie rolled her eyes. "Thank goodness it's not a tuna noodle casserole."

"Huh?" Megan blinked.

"Inside joke. Thank you. We love clam chowder. Please, place it over there on the stove. I need to make room in the fridge," Izzie said.

Megan passed by me to get to the stove. Her arms shook as she held onto the handles of the Crock-Pot. I stepped toward her. "Here, let me help you. I bet it's really heavy."

She pulled the pot out of my reach. "Trust me, you don't want to touch. Way too hot without mitts or potholders."

After setting the heavy cookware on the stove, she pulled off the mitts.

At once, I caught sight of the scratch marks, tiny threads of bright red stretched across her wrists. "Oh my gosh. What happened to your arms?" I spoke before thinking how intrusive the question sounded. Guess I couldn't follow my own advice to keep my thoughts to myself.

Megan quickly lowered both arms to her sides. "Would you believe gardening gone wrong?" She blushed. "Prickle bushes aren't something you want to tangle with."

"Seriously, since when do you garden? I thought plants and grass made you sneeze," Izzie teased, then lifted Megan's arm. She stared at the wound and cringed. "Oooh, that's looks bad, Megs. You should have a doctor take a look."

"It's fine. I decided to try a new hobby, and I take allergy medication nowadays. I thought I told you."

Megan's words carried an edge, as if Izzie's remarks irritated her. Or maybe she was offended Izzie didn't know those details about her. After all, they were best friends. Either way, her reaction seemed angry and out of place to me.

"I've got an idea." Izzie snapped her fingers. "Why don't we go to Jamestown for the afternoon? Do a little shopping and visit some sights. Now's a good time for a distraction, right? What do you guys say?"

Megan shook her head. "Sorry. I need to open up the store and sell candles to pay the bills."

The shop, Light Your Scent, had only been in business for a year. Megan's parents had owned the building, but then offered to transfer the deed to Megan, if she promised to make a serious commitment to running her candle business. Friends knew Megan had been wild during her teen years and all through college. She never stuck to one plan or interest for long. The candle shop was her chance at a do-over, and she was determined to prove herself to her parents and friends.

Izzie shifted her gaze my way.

I gave a thumbs-up sign. "Give me ten minutes to change and find my comfortable shoes." I headed out of the kitchen. "See you later, Megan."

Max followed close behind me, his nails clicking on the floorboards.

"Sorry, little guy. I can't bring you along this time." I gathered him in my arms and rubbed my nose in his fur. "You guard the house while we're gone. Okay? That's a good boy."

Once inside my bedroom, I pulled a sleeveless top and shorts out of my suitcase. With all the chaos in the past couple of days, I hadn't taken a moment to unpack. Slipping my feet into sandals, I skipped down the stairs where Izzie was waiting.

"Okay, we're off." Izzie led the way outside. "Your car or mine?"

"I filled up the tank right before I got to town." I stared at the powdery layer of dust covering my car. "Plus, we can hit the carwash on the way back."

The trip to Jamestown took less than a half hour, yet I couldn't stop those disturbing details of murder from worming their way into my head. Like a broken record, images punctuated with dramatic captions repeated, again and again. Maybe my brain was trying to tell me I'd missed something about that evening. An important detail that might help solve the case of whodunnit. What I did know was that plenty of people had both opportunity and motive to kill Fiona, and the authorities wouldn't stop until they got their man or woman. I glimpsed Izzie for a second. My heart ached for her. The feeling of having a dream crushed or broken was familiar. At least her dream of a successful business could be mended and put back on track. A temporary setback wasn't fatal. All we needed to do was find the killer. I gripped the steering wheel, thinking how in the blink of an eye life could derail and become something you never expected. In this case? Something scary and dangerous.

Chapter Five

While Izzie slept in, Max and I took a morning walk along the lakeshore to get some fresh air and watch the sunrise. Sailboats and fishing boats glided along the scenic view, manned by those, including Mom and Dad, who took to the water at the crack of dawn. I grew more relaxed watching the slow-moving action that became commonplace for those who lived and breathed the lake life. After taking a Sunday break from all tasks involving the shop and thoughts about murder, I was refreshed and energized for the start of a new week.

Max bounced on his hind legs, barking at the flock of purple-headed grackles overhead. They flew farther inland, probably on their way to some field where they'd nibble on sprouts and ripening corn.

Hearing someone shout my name, I turned. Izzie was standing on the front porch, waving her arms.

"Come on, Max. Time for breakfast." I tugged at the leash and jogged with him to the house.

"We're going shopping." Izzie pulled me inside.

My brow arched, and I tapped my watch. "At seven in the morning? Even the most ambitious retailers won't open that early." I unhooked Max's leash.

"We'll eat breakfast, sit on the back porch to drink coffee, and chat. Two hours will fly by. You'll see." She skipped down the hall, and Max trotted close behind her.

"Slow and easy lifestyle. Gotta get used to it." I shrugged.

The noisy hustle and bustle of New York City was quite the contrast.

"Scrambled or poached?" Izzie held up her arms, an egg in each hand.

I grinned at the unkempt hair piled on top of her head, with curls fighting to stick out here and there. She pulled off her own style of chic, wearing a faded T-shirt with an NYC logo and ragged-edged cutoffs.

"Scrambled is quicker, but then again, we're in no hurry." I pulled juice out of the fridge.

"Poached it is." She hummed a tune while working. Her phone rang, then dinged a couple of times, but she ignored whoever called.

"You're not going to answer that?" I poured juice into glasses and set them on the table.

"Nope. He can wait. Besides, I won't be able to tell him anything yet. So what's the point?"

I narrowed my eyes. "Him who?" Just then, my phone vibrated. I glanced at the screen. A short message appeared. "Ah, I see. Our detective on the case wants to speak to you. You know avoiding him won't work. He might even show up at the house."

"I'll call him, but not yet. Maybe tomorrow." She set a plate in front of me and piled on eggs and toast. "Stop worrying about it."

"I'm not worrying. I'm stating the obvious." I shoveled eggs into my mouth to keep from saying more. When to talk to Detective Barrett was her decision, not mine.

As our breakfast and coffee time passed, I almost forgot there was a world outside, where horrible things could happen.

After finishing her third cup of coffee, Izzie checked her watch. "I have time to take a quick shower before we leave."

"Now, what exactly are we shopping for?"

"Maybe some artsy deco for my store shelves? Pottery would be nice."

"Sammy's Quaint Décor." I squinted at her in a pointed stare. "You have an ulterior motive in mind, don't you?"

"Not exactly." Izzie shuffled her bare feet before a smile eased across her face. "Well, maybe I do."

I heaved a sigh. "I hope you have a plan on what to say . . . or ask. When put on the defensive, you know Sammy is like an F-five tornado. You'll need to tread softly."

Izzie pointed to her head as she turned to walk away. "Plan's all in here, word for word. I've got this."

*   *   *

Quaint Décor sat halfway between the string of shops along Artisan Alley and next to Penny Swenson's aromatherapy shop, The Healing Touch. The wood exterior needed a fresh coat of paint, but the shale roof held up well against the beating it received from sun, water, and inclement weather. Many of the businesses in Whisper Cove were run by family, handed down from one generation to the next. That was how Sammy had come by hers. A favorite aunt, who never married, decided to make Sammy her heir, which pleased her parents. After all, they already owned a screen print T-shirt business in Mayville, passed down by Sammy's maternal grandparents. On the other hand, Izzie was the rare local merchant who was starting from scratch. Of course, Izzie's paint party event shop was a fairly new concept in the craft world. Focusing on younger generations who looked for entertaining venues, paint parties allowed customers to create their own art rather than buy someone else's.

The chimes hooked to the door jingled as we entered. I gazed at the shop from one end to the other. Sammy had added some new touches to the place since I'd last been inside, more than a year ago. A section devoted to Native American art sat near the front. I lifted a clay pot decorated with red and turquoise paint from the shelf. The quality was exceptional, and the product was authentic, with the craftsman's signature scrawled across the bottom. During my stay in Paris, I'd worked part-time for an art collector and learned quite a lot about that part of the art world, especially how to recognize fakes and the seedier side of sellers and buyers.

"Hi, Sammy. How's business?" Izzie greeted.

"I'm not complaining." She shrugged. "Wouldn't help if I did, right?"

She skirted Izzie to give me a hug. "Nice to see you again. I want to apologize for hogging the conversation the other night. We should catch up sometime soon. You plan to stay awhile, I hope?"

"I'm here to help Izzie with the shop. So yes. At least until something comes along to pull me back to New York." I gave myself a mental slap for even suggesting New York, which had already taken a nosedive as far as my plans went.

"Great! What brings you two here today?" Her eyes brightened with anticipation as she clasped her hands.

Izzie tapped her lip and turned side to side. "I was hoping to buy something decorative to place on the shelves or walls of my shop. You know, to give it a more artsy feel?"

"Let's see." Sammy hesitated then pointed to the back corner. "I unpacked a collection of figurines and wall art shipped in from Milan this morning. Why don't we start there?" She led the way to the rear of the shop.

"I absolutely love wall art. Are those made out of brass? Would you look at that detail." Izzie rambled excitedly while she fingered a piece molded into the shape of a beach scene with the ocean waves, the sun, and birds flying over the water.

I left Izzie to gush over the Milan collection and browsed the aisles. Sammy had a variety of items that, from the price tags, provided something for anyone's pocketbook, big or small. I gasped as my attention landed on a Swarovski crystal figurine of a swan. They could range in price from hundreds to over a thousand dollars. This item was worth at least five hundred or more, and I guessed not many customers who shopped here could afford such a purchase. I couldn't guess why she'd carry pricey items with almost no chance of selling them. I tapped the shelf with my fingernail, then, after a second, I lifted the figurine to peek underneath. The Swarovski swan logo was printed on the bottom, and next to it was a price sticker. My eyes widened. "How in the world?"

"Those are beautiful, aren't they?"

I gasped and clutched my throat at the sound of Sammy's voice. "Oh! You scared me. Yes, they certainly live up to the Swarovski name." I carefully set the swan on the shelf.

"Hmm. You know your crystal." She smiled.

I tipped my head at the display. "A year working for an art collector in Paris will teach you a few things, especially about what items cost on the market." My eyes narrowed.

"I'm all set." Izzie approached, carrying a basket filled with her choices of wall art.

Sammy smiled and led the way to the cash register to ring up the purchase. "If you aren't done shopping, I can have these delivered."

"Thank you. That will help. We still need to make a stop at the *Gazette*." Izzie nibbled on the tip of her thumb while Sammy finished the sale. "Unfortunately, I'm taking a hit on the ad I bought for my shop's grand opening. You know, since we're now considered a crime scene."

I rolled my eyes at Izzie's poor attempt at subtlety, bulldozing her way into the topic. However, the bait worked.

"Yeah, no matter how despised Fiona was, she didn't deserve to end like that." Sammy shook her head.

"Such a shame." Izzie clucked her tongue in the same way our great aunt Mimi used to.

I snorted but quickly covered the sound with a cough. "Sorry." I pointed to my throat. "Tickle got to me."

Izzie glared at me, then turned back to Sammy. "That detective told us he plans to speak with all the merchants because of Fiona's column and her scathing comments." She scribbled her name on the credit slip, then looked up. "Has he spoken to you yet? I mean, Chloe told him about those vicious words Fiona had to say about you at our paint event that evening."

I groaned. Nothing like being snagged into Izzie's attack without a warning. "He insisted on a blow-by-blow account of the evening. I had to tell him."

Sammy slammed the register drawer shut. "Why? What did she say? Probably nothing I haven't already heard." She scowled.

The deepening red tint in her face made me stiffen.

"I . . . ah . . . probably like you said. Nothing you haven't heard before."

"She said you were lazy and would never make it in business." Izzie stabbed the counter.

"Oh, boy," I mumbled under my breath. Besides lack of subtlety, my sister had no filter.

Sammy stared unblinking for an uncomfortable minute. "Well, I'm not the only one. Did you know your friend Megan is barely hanging on to her candle shop? I heard from someone at the bank she's gone in three times to beg for extensions on her loans. Maybe her parents deeded Megan the building without charging her a penny, but how about that pricey car she drives? Why, that lakeshore condo she lives in must cost more than she can manage on her own. Who pays for all that?" Sammy's voice grew louder with each word.

Izzie grabbed her bag and my arm. "I think we overdid it," she whispered in my ear and hustled out of the shop, dragging me along.

"*We?*" I pulled my arm free and stopped as we reached the sidewalk.

Izzie waved an arm. "Don't worry. Sammy's temper is like a boiling teakettle. Once the stopper pops, all the steam lets out. She'll be fine in an hour."

"Let's hope." I worried about more than Sammy blowing a fuse.

That price sticker bugged me. The swan figurine would retail for at least five hundred U.S. dollars or more through a legal dealer. Sammy's item was marked at one hundred dollars. There was no way she'd make a profit off that amount. Unless she wanted a quick sale or . . . she was doing something illegal. What if Fiona had stumbled on a story? Could she have confronted Sammy with her discovery? I had to think this through, whether or not to discuss the issue with the Quaint Décor owner. I wasn't a legal authority or an agent for the IRS. Plus, she might be totally legit. Maybe the item was damaged and I just hadn't noticed. However, if what Sammy was doing was somehow connected, even loosely, with Fiona and her murder, I couldn't look away.

"I think she's spreading wild rumors," Izzie said.

"Hmm? What do you mean?" I snapped out of my rambling thoughts.

"About Megan. No way would Megan take on more than she can handle. She knows this is her last chance to prove she's responsible and not that flaky girl from college. The idea she's a suspect is ridiculous." Izzie puffed out her cheeks. "I'm telling you this. Sammy wants to point fingers so she looks less like the guilty one."

I clenched the strap of my bag and couldn't help picturing the scratches on Megan's arms. When Izzie questioned the idea of her gardening because of allergies, she'd seemed defensive.

"Aren't you forgetting? You said Fiona's vicious columns aren't enough of a motive to kill the poor woman."

Izzie threw up her arms. "Then I shouldn't be a suspect either. You, even less. So why are we worried?"

I pressed my lips together. "Back to time, place, and physical evidence, I guess. Wait until Detective Barrett's crime team manages to find all of that. Then we'll see if we have something to worry about." I glanced sideways.

The lines of worry deepened on her face. "Watch out!" Izzie's eyes popped as she called out.

"Oh!" I slammed face first into someone's chest. I extended my arms and splayed my hands against a firm torso to keep from falling. "Sorry, I . . ." Lifting my gaze, I stared at blue eyes and a smile that stretched across a handsome face. I swallowed and shuffled my feet backward. "Sorry."

He had to be nearly six and a half feet tall. With that full head of blond curls, he looked like one of those Greek gods.

"My fault, entirely. I was reading a message on my phone and not paying attention. I would never purposely run into such a lovely woman as yourself." He winked.

"Oh, please." Izzie mumbled under her breath.

I cleared my throat and managed a speedy recovery. "What my sister means is please don't apologize. I was just as much at fault."

"How about we start over?" He extended a hand. "My name's Grayson Stone."

I wiggled my fingers, then shoved my hand in his to shake. "Glad to meet you. I'm Chloe Abbington."

We both shifted our attention to Izzie, who shrugged. "Izzie Abbington, and right now my sister and I should get going. Lots to do this morning." She tugged at my sleeve and jerked her head sideways.

"Well, have a great day, Abbington sisters." He tipped his hand. "Maybe we'll bump into each other again, and soon."

"That was rude." I hurried to keep up with Izzie.

"I've seen him around town a couple of times, like he was lurking."

"Lurking?"

"People watching, I guess. Megan thinks he's creepy."

"Oh, well, if Megan thinks so, then it must be true." I couldn't help the sarcastic tone but got the classic Izzie eye-glaring stare.

"She also said he acted squirrely when he came into her shop."

"So, he's creepy *and* squirrely, according to Megan. Anything else?" I shook my head. When had she become such a fan of local gossip?

"All right. You made your point. I don't know anything about him. He might be a great guy. A real prince charming." She tapped her watch. "Do you think we can stop talking about him and finish what we started? I want to stop by the *Gazette* and settle my bill with Theo before the day is over and wasted."

I scrunched my nose and pointed at the sky. "It's barely ten. Plenty of daylight left."

"Oh, for—you can be so annoying." She threw back her head and laughed, then squeezed my arm. "I've missed this, you know? You and me spending time together."

"Yeah, me too." I leaned my head against her shoulder.

"Great girl talk." She stepped away. "Now, let's go."

We practically jogged for the next three blocks to reach the far end of town and the entrance to the *Whisper Cove Gazette*. I bent over to grab my knees, gasping for as much oxygen as I could get. In New York, we didn't drive or walk. We took taxis, Ubers, or the subway, even if the destination was close. That was my routine anyway. First thing tomorrow, I'd check into finding a reasonably priced fitness center to join. At least I'd think about it.

"Well, if it isn't my favorite customer. Morning, Izzie." Theo shoved the bill of her visor back, making the wiry black and gray mop of curls look like a Chia Pet. A blazing red apron covered her from her chest to her ample thighs. The sleeves of a tie-dyed T-shirt popped with orange and pink, while a cute fluorescent green miniskirt barely covered her hips.

Not exactly age-appropriate for the sixty-something *Gazette* owner, but somehow she managed to pull it off. Very hip, to use the lingo of her generation.

"Hi, Theo. It's been a long time." I waved.

"Hey, Squirt!" She slapped me on the shoulder. As she grinned, wrinkles feathered at the corners of her eyes and across her cheeks. "How's New York?"

I rolled my shoulder. She might be past middle age, but her strength and energy kept her youthful. "I'm taking a break and helping out my sister with her new business venture. How've you been?"

Theo pedaled into a ten-minute recap of her ups and downs from the past year while Izzie tapped her foot, faster with each minute, until Theo must've gotten the hint.

"I guess you're here to pay for the ad? Don't worry. Since I'm feeling kind of sorry for you because of the dead body of my employee in your backyard, I'll give you a break. You pay for the ad, and I'll post it in the *Gazette* whenever you're ready. How's that sound?" She wiggled her brows.

"Why, that's—" Izzie clasped her hands and bowed her head slightly. "You're a saint. Thank you, Theo. Thank you so much."

"The least I can do, considering." She nodded, while scribbling details on a receipt.

"Considering?" I asked.

Theo tugged at her ear. "Fiona was my responsibility *and* my worst headache. I hired her to write that editorial column. Lord knows I should've stopped her when I saw things going south, but I couldn't. Too late now."

Izzie's lips curled. "Why couldn't you? I mean, if things went south and she was a headache, as you put it." Her eyes shifted my way for a quick glance.

I agreed. Theo's choice of words did raise a few questions.

"By going south, I mean a few folks complained. Just a few, mind you. Others actually called or wrote to say they enjoyed her column. Of course, those people weren't on Fiona's hit list. Easy to laugh at something that's not targeting you. As for my headache? Fiona was one of the surliest, most undesirable employees I've ever hired. Trust me. I've had plenty come and go. She couldn't step one foot in the door without complaining to me. First, she argued the column should move to the front page. After that, she squawked that she didn't have enough space in the paper. Then she demanded I give her an office because who could concentrate on writing when people kept coming into the building?" Theo snorted. "Such a pain."

I inched closer to the counter and Theo. "You say some complained. Did they call? Write? Ever give their names?"

She tapped a pencil on her cheek. "Let me think." The pencil stilled and silence took over.

The exasperating pause was long enough for me to wonder if she planned to answer or had dozed off, eyes open.

All at once she pointed the pencil at me. "Yes! I mean, no. That is, most were calls from folks who refused to identify themselves. One, though . . ." She chuckled and wagged her head. "That woman darn well has guts. What she said? Didn't hold back, I tell you. Spouted off how Fiona should be behind bars for all the garbage she wrote. What's worse, she warned that if somebody didn't do something to stop Fiona, she'd take care of it herself."

Izzie gasped. "Oh wow. That sure sounds like a threat."

"Can you tell us who? I mean, maybe his or her name should be given to the authorities." I shifted my weight from one foot to the other.

Complaining about Fiona was one thing, but threatening to stop her was taking words to a whole other level of anger.

"Sure can. It was Gwen. Angrier than I've ever heard her. Why, that woman is like Mother Teresa, gentle, never having an unkind word to say." Theo wobbled one hand back and forth. "Maybe a little weird at times. Talks to herself a lot, you know? But never mean, never violent."

Gwen? I choked on my breath. How could someone who was soft-spoken, giving, and always looking for the good in people take matters into her own hands, overpower Fiona, and stab her with a paint knife? I tried picturing the older woman sneaking up behind an unsuspecting Fiona and plunging the weapon into her neck.

"Uh, uh. No way." I muttered to myself.

Gwen must've been angry and frustrated when she called. After all, she'd taken a huge hit in sales. Who knew for sure whether it was the fault of Fiona's column, though? Besides, lots of people said things they never intended to act on.

"Wait." I frowned and turned to Izzie. "Didn't Dad say something about Gwen's letter to the editor?"

"I'm getting to that," Theo added. "The following week after our call, I received an email. Gwen requested I put her letter in the paper. I hesitated, suspecting what a storm her words would stir up." She lifted her chin. "Still, I believe in the First Amendment. Free speech is the backbone of democracy. So I printed the darn thing."

Great way to handle a sticky situation. Just pass the problem along to others. In this case, the others being the good people of Whisper Cove. "By the way, how did readers respond to her letter?"

Theo scoffed. "Pick a side. That's what folks do. Some called to complain Gwen was too harsh, others to praise her courage. A couple of people even went so far as to say if they were her, they'd give Fiona what she had coming."

"But Fiona had to have the last word, didn't she?" Izzie asked.

"Yeah, you probably read her response in the following week's column." Theo scratched her curly mop with the pencil. "Boy, did I get heat from that decision. Again, made a mistake I can't take back."

Disturbing thoughts made me tremble. "When was this?"

"Her column about Gwen, you mean? Why, the week before last. Boy, you should've seen Gwen and Fiona go at it the day after. Right here in front of me. They threw words back and forth like they were shooting darts and arrows at each other. I was ready to call nine-one-one but then, all at once, Gwen stormed out of the building. If I were to judge, I'd say Fiona won that battle, hands down."

I rubbed my arms to take away the chill running through me. One thing was for sure, Gwen had plenty of motive to make her the number one suspect in Fiona's murder.

Chapter Six

I poured a scoop of kibble into Max's bowl and filled another dish with fresh water. "He said to come to the shop right away? Maybe he's finally going to let you open for business." I combed fingers through my messy bed hair, then tightened the belt of my robe.

Izzie had popped into my bedroom to wake me, then chattered on about her phone conversation with Detective Barrett. She must've grown tired of avoiding his calls and finally answered. I heard her grumble something about this one being the tenth since last night.

Izzie plopped in a chair. "Nothing like getting up before sunrise to hear his voice. The man barks orders like a commander in the army."

I chuckled. "No please and thank you?"

She lowered her lids to stare daggers at me. "Obviously not. He pushed until I told him I had a perfectly good alibi for that night and a speeding ticket to prove it."

"Oh? You never told me about that." I leveled my gaze at her. Yet another secret. "It's been six days since the murder. Why did you wait this long before telling him?"

"It's embarrassing and not something I felt comfortable sharing. Anyway, time-stamped at eight forty and about twenty minutes from Whisper Cove puts me in the clear. At least he seemed satisfied with that bit of information because I refused to tell him where I'd been or who I'd seen." Izzie gave her head a firm nod.

"Yes, I know. You made a promise to whoever." I sipped my coffee. A queasy feeling unsettled my stomach, and it wasn't from heavy doses of caffeine. Adding thirty minutes to the time she got the ticket meant Izzie would've returned to town between nine and ten after. That was twenty to thirty minutes before I discovered Fiona's body. That ticket wouldn't prove anything to Detective Barrett, other than Izzie had been out of town at some point before the murder.

"You should get dressed. I promised we'd meet him in a half hour."

I snapped out of my meandering thoughts. "*We*, huh?" Receiving another disapproving stare, I tapped my forehead with the side of my hand in a salute. "Yes, ma'am. Sergeant ma'am."

Swinging her arm, she tossed a dishtowel at me, but Max jumped up and caught it between his teeth, growling. "Ha. The pooch scores with a quick interception." Izzie grinned and pointed toward the hallway. "Now go."

I sprinted across the kitchen floor and out of her reach while Max trotted ahead of me, towel hanging from his mouth. Izzie and I hadn't talked much about our visit with Sammy. The situation with Gwen was a different story. Mom and Dad wanted to hear all the details about the weeks-long feud that had crescendoed into the blowout argument between her and Fiona.

We all agreed the authorities would take a closer look at the Go Fly a Kite owner when they learned the details about her and the columnist. Small-town news traveled quickly. No doubt, Detective Barrett had already heard the story. Maybe that was another subject he wanted to talk about. Gwen's shop was next door to ours. Of course, she hadn't attended the painting event that evening. As was the case with Izzie, though, not attending didn't mean much. In fact, almost anyone could've called Fiona to meet behind the shop. Townsfolk, outsiders, anyone.

At a little after eight, Izzie and I pulled into a parking space along Whisper Lane and around the corner from the paint party shop.

Detective Barrett's vehicle sat out front. With both arms crossed, he leaned against the car door, eyes closed, head tipped toward the sky.

To the left of Paint with a View, a closed for business sign remained in the window of Go Fly a Kite. No details as to when Gwen might reopen were posted. Given the disturbing account of Theo's story, I worried about our next-door retail neighbor's emotional state of mind. Maybe she needed help, but no one was close by to give it.

As I approached Detective Barrett, I got a better look at him. The other evening, dealing with a dead body and facing a barrage of questions, had left me too unsettled. The image of Fiona's body was stuck on instant replay, and I had struggled to keep focused on anything or anyone. Other than Barrett's brown eyes and hair and tanned skin.

I sized up the trim and well-built detective now. He most likely kept fit by working out at the gym or chasing down criminals on foot. Definitely, he wasn't a member of the donut-eating stereotype. I chuckled. This morning, he was dressed in casual pants, sneakers, and a short-sleeved, collared shirt unbuttoned at the top. I imagined there was a dress code, even for detectives, but maybe he liked to tweak the rules a bit, especially on a hot, muggy day in June.

"Good morning, Hunter." Izzie spoke first.

The use of his first name and the irritated edge to her voice made me curious.

A lazy smile crossed his lips, and he eased his eyes open. "Hi, Izzie. Long time no see."

"You two know each other?" My eyes widened as I stared at Izzie. "Why didn't you tell me?"

Her secrets kept adding up and made me nervous. I might be the impulsive type, but I liked to know what went on around me, kind of like my security blanket. People keeping secrets threatened to mess with my comfort zone.

She shrugged. "Nothing to tell. Hunter and I graduated together. Don't you remember him? Scrawny, short, Coke-bottle glasses, and a serious case of acne." She shot Detective Barrett a smug look.

"That's harsh," he said.

"Can't take a little teasing? I remember you and your friends loved to dish it out." Izzie threw back her head and laughed.

I puckered my brow, searching my memory. Being a year ahead of Izzie in school hardly qualified me to recognize any underclassmen, which, in this case, didn't matter. Detective Hunter Barrett in no way fit her description.

"Yeah, this is Hunter Barrett, all grown up." She smirked as she rummaged through her bag and pulled out a ring of keys. "Are we going inside?"

Something told me high school wasn't the most recent encounter they'd had, but I left my questions for another time when Izzie and I could be alone.

"Actually, we'll be going around back." He led the way alongside the shop.

I followed right behind him, while Izzie shoved the keys back in her bag and hurried to keep up. My heart pounded. This would be my first time visiting the crime scene since that night.

"What's this all about, Hunter? Is your team close to collecting all of whatever it is you expect to find so I can reopen my shop?" Exasperation filled Izzie's tone.

Detective Barrett shook his head as he stepped through a narrow doorway leading to the area immediately behind the building.

Walls made of weathered hardwood, measuring several feet high, bordered both sides of the property, allowing for a bit of privacy. The compact dumpster sat along the back, flanked by tall shrubs. I wrinkled my nose. Odors of paint and turpentine, mixed with the pungent, musky smell of lake water and plant life carried inland by the breeze, filled the air. I gave myself a mental slap as the image of Fiona lying on the concrete flashed in my head.

Barrett pulled out his phone and swiped the screen. "Here. Take a look at the photo." He handed the device to Izzie.

I stepped closer to look over her shoulder at what appeared to be the image of a food wrapper and a bottle. "What's this? Besides somebody's lunch trash."

He read from his notebook. "One empty soda bottle labeled Fizzy Orange and a sandwich wrapper from Bob's Barbecue Pit." He lifted his head to stare, waiting.

I shrugged. "Is this supposed to mean something important?"

Izzie squinted. Spreading her finger and thumb on the screen, she enlarged the photo. "The bottle and wrapper are sitting on top of my dumpster."

"Actually, one of my team members found the wrapper sticking out from under the lid. Looks like someone was in a hurry to get rid of the trash, or maybe was interrupted." He stuffed his notebook back in his pocket. "Do either one of you take lunch breaks out here?"

"Why would we?" Izzie tapped her heel. "What are you implying? Fiona's killer had a craving for barbecue and Fizzy Orange soda right before they stabbed her in the neck? You think one of us did it? I'd never eat such a heavy meal while at work, and soda of any kind is poison."

I winced as her voice screeched. Out of control Izzie was back.

"Look, Detective Barrett, anyone could come back here at any time. No reason to assume one of us is the fast-food junkie, right?"

"We need to collect all the evidence." He nodded and his jaw grew rigid. "Just as I need to ask questions, no matter how you might take them. It's procedure, Miss Abbington. I take a look at all the information and create the possible scenarios, hoping one of them will stick."

I scratched my chin and pointed. "Like the killer decided on a late-night snack from Bob's Barbecue while waiting for his victim to show up?"

"That's one of them." He lifted a pair of sunglasses from his pocket and put them on. The act was slow and deliberate, as if to give himself time to think. "Don't suppose you know who likes barbecue and could've hung around here that evening? Maybe even done so more than once?"

"Don't look at me. I only got back in town a couple of days ago," I said. "The other night was the first time I came out here, period."

"Maybe you should talk to Bob," Izzie suggested. "Although I'm sure he doesn't keep track of everyone who stops by."

"Already did." Barrett pushed his sunglasses farther up his nose, then plucked a toothpick from his pocket. He chewed on one end.

"Since we're standing here and you're asking us, I'm guessing Bob was no help." Izzie clicked her tongue. "Seems the theory of a killer with a craving for barbecue isn't working for you."

He held up his hand. "I don't give up that easily. I'll keep asking around. Somebody might've noticed a trespasser entering your property. Maybe your neighbor next door? We haven't had a chance to talk."

His innocent look with widened eyes didn't fool me.

"She's probably at home." I pointed. "As you already noticed, her shop is closed. We have no idea when she'll reopen, do we, Izzie?" I shifted my attention.

"Nope. No idea." Izzie emphasized with palms turned up and a shoulder shrug.

Barrett rolled the toothpick in his mouth. "Then I guess we're done here."

"What about opening my shop?" Izzie stepped forward.

"I'll be in touch." He waved as he walked to his car.

"Dammit. That man still fumes me." Izzie screwed up her face and huffed.

"I'd say so." I gawked at her. "Something tells me there's more to your story."

"Maybe, but I don't care to talk about it. I have other worries on my mind." Izzie faced me and bit on her thumbnail. "Megan loves Fizzy Orange and Bob's Barbecue."

"Lots of folks do."

"True." Her head tipped back and forth. "But not the way Megan does."

I blinked. "What other way is there? You either like a food or you don't."

We reached the jeep and Izzie opened her door. She rested her chin on the top edge. "Whenever Megan is upset, nervous, or depressed, she eats. If Bob's is open, she's there getting her usual order."

"Fizzy Orange and a barbecue sandwich." I tapped the hood of the car. "Still . . ."

"Barbecue with lots of yellow mustard." Izzie hiccupped. "You didn't notice, but I did. Maybe Hunter said nothing on purpose. Maybe he wanted me or you to mention it. Or who knows? Maybe he's not as great a detective as he thinks. I saw the yellow mustard stains on the wrapper, Chloe. Who else eats barbecue with mustard? Nobody." She slid behind the wheel.

I buckled in. "Yeah, sure. It looks bad, like she was the one hiding behind the shop." I held up a finger. "However, maybe the killer staged the scene to make her look suspicious. Think about it. Lots of people witnessed that argument between Megan and Fiona. What if one of those people is the killer?"

Izzie made a U-turn to head toward home. "And the killer saw an opportunity to steer the focus of the investigation on Megan." She swerved to miss a cat darting into the road.

"On us, too. Remember, the weapon used was a painting knife. Plus, the crime scene is in our backyard. This killer is pure genius." I rubbed my arms to fend off the chill running through me.

"Pure *evil* genius, you mean." She held the wheel in a fierce, white-knuckled grip. "We have to do something."

My gaze caught the cat's image in the side mirror. Now situated on a bench near the bus stop, the feline licked one paw, oblivious to passersby, as if it had no interest in anyone or anything. I shifted sideways to gaze at Izzie. "I thought we already were. Isn't that what the visit to Sammy was all about? You playing wannabe sleuth?"

"Sort of, and what we learned from Theo at the *Gazette* was an added bonus. I'm talking about doing whatever we can to make sure Hunter doesn't spend one second thinking Megan is the killer."

I picked a piece of lint off my pants. "Hmm. I hate to tell you, but the man you call a geek and a mediocre detective already has Megan's name in his little notebook, listed under most likely to commit murder."

Izzie slammed on the brakes, and my hands shot out to grab the dashboard before my forehead beat them to it.

"Hey! What the heck?" I grumbled under my breath.

"Don't be so negative. Megan is my best friend. I know her better than she knows herself. No way in this universe or any other could she commit murder. I don't care how much she hated Fiona or what kind of financial trouble she's in, Megan wouldn't do such a terrible thing." She drove her words home with force.

I puckered my lips and whistled. "Now that we've settled that issue, what's your plan?"

She eased off the brakes and the jeep continued down Sail Shore Drive and closer to home. "I'm not sure yet. I'll think of something." She turned into the driveway and killed the engine. Resting both hands in her lap, she tilted her chin and fixed her gaze on me. "This will sound strange, but I sort of feel violated. You know? My business becoming a crime scene is a lot to take in, but I've got to do everything I can to erase that heap of misfortune and set us back on track."

"Izzie," I started.

She held up one hand. "I'm sorry for focusing on what this has done to my shop and for worrying about my friend and my sister rather than grieving for the victim. I know that sounds selfish." She hiccupped and swiped away tears that escaped and trailed down her cheeks. "On the other hand, the only way I can think of to make all of this right and clear our names is to become—what did you call me? Oh yeah, a wannabe sleuth with an agenda to find the killer." She leaned closer. "What I want to know is, are you with me?"

I raised my arm and stuck out my hand with the palm facing her. "You had me at 'I'll think of something,' because you know I'm the brains of this sister team and you'll need my help." I smiled.

Izzie grinned and sealed the deal with a high five. "To the sisterhood."

Despite the serious nature of our situation, we managed to laugh. I led the way up the sidewalk. A slight drizzle fell from a cloudy sky and dotted the cement with dark gray spots. I covered the top of my head with my bag.

"Whose car is that pulling up front, I wonder?" Izzie asked with a head tilt as she caught up to stand next to me.

"What car?" I pivoted on my heel to face the lake. My breath hitched, and I flushed with heat. The black Mercedes and the man who stepped out of it were all too familiar. He wore a three-piece suit, buttoned shirt, and his signature red tie, despite the summer heat, which wasn't a surprise. But the fact he stood here in front of my family's home was.

"This isn't good," I said as he waved and walked toward us, allowing the rain to dampen his head of dark curls as if he knew it wouldn't ruin his appearance.

"Who is he? Why isn't this good? Please explain." Izzie tugged at my sleeve.

"Hi, Chloe. How are you? You left in such a hurry and with no proper goodbye." He leaned in for a hug. As he pulled away, his mouth brushed my cheek. "I've missed you." The words came in a soft whisper.

Arms crossed and foot tapping, Izzie cleared her throat.

"Sorry." I shook my head. "Izzie, this is Ross Thompson. My ex."

"Not for long, I hope." He winked. "Glad to meet you, Izzie." He held up one finger. "Almost forgot. Be back in a sec." He sprinted across the lawn to his car.

I raked fingers through my hair, my blood pressure spiking and heartbeat racing. *Not for long?* What was that supposed to mean? I glanced sideways at Izzie. How was I going to explain this?

Izzie murmured from the corner of her mouth while keeping her eyes on Ross. "I thought he broke up with you?"

"I lied." The smile pasted to my face hadn't changed.

"Why?" The word sang out in a drawl.

"Because I didn't want to hear the lecture from Mom and Dad claiming I should've known better than to jump into a relationship so fast. How was I to know he'd love his job more than me? It's not like he wore a warning sign." Out of frustration, my smile dropped.

Ross returned. As he rested on the bottom step, his chest rose and fell. All at once, the rain poured harder. "Maybe we should go inside." He pulled the jacket of his smoothly pressed suit over his head.

After a slight hesitation, I gripped the doorknob and led the way in.

Max sprinted across the floor, barking in a high pitch. He hopped up and down in front of Ross.

"Hey, little guy. You miss me?" He scooped Max in his arms and laughed while sloppy kisses wet his cheek.

"So, Ross. What brings you to Whisper Cove?" Izzie asked as we stood in the foyer.

Ross set Max on the floor, then discarded his jacket, draping the damp garment over one arm. A warm smile lit his face, deepening the dimple on his left cheek. "I'm here to win back this lady and bring her home."

Chapter Seven

I drummed my fingers on the side of my coffee mug. We'd finished breakfast and remained in total silence. I guessed all three of them were in shock. I couldn't blame them. Turning away, I faced the window, snuggled deeper in my chair, and entertained myself by watching two squirrels chase each other. They scurried around the tree trunk, weaving a coiled path, until one leaped to the ground and climbed over the neighbor's fence.

After way too many hours of what could only be described as awkward and embarrassing, Ross had left late last night to check into a hotel. Mom and Dad had done their best to act like gracious hosts, but Izzie only sulked and glared, mostly at me. Keeping secrets hurt. Growing up, we used to share all our thoughts and every detail of our lives. Maybe being adults had taken some of that closeness away. Maybe without saying so, we both wanted to remove some of that distance between us.

"I just don't understand." Mom repeated the same phrase for the umpteenth time.

"Maybe that's not what's important, Katy."

I pushed my mug to the side. My chest heaved as Dad squeezed Mom's shoulder. I knew I shouldn't be jealous of what they had together—a bond that only grew stronger with time, a love so unconditional and caring that it knew no boundaries. Maybe one day I'd find that kind of soul mate.

"Some details about my life I need to keep to myself, the deeply personal ones, especially the painful ones." I fixed my gaze on Izzie. "I admit, those are too hard for me to talk about." I smacked the arms of the chair and pushed off to stand. "But you're right. I shouldn't have lied about Ross. I should've said I didn't want to discuss my relationship. That's what grownups are supposed to do."

"It's fine, Shortcake. You'll meet the right guy someday and be as happy as your mom and I are." Dad skirted the table and stood close as he planted a kiss on top of my head.

"You can talk to us about anything. You know that, don't you?" Mom nodded. "We're here to help. No judgment. No lectures. We'll only listen, if that's what you need."

That promise was questionable, but why argue? "No. I'm fine. Ross and I worked out our problem. He understands I won't get back together with him. We're looking for different things in life. I can't be with a man who thinks, eats, and breathes only his job and has no time for a personal relationship." I shrugged. "I want what you have."

"Of course you do." Mom flanked my other side and wrapped her arms around me.

"Okay then. Are we done with the *Leave It to Beaver* moment? Chloe and I need to put our brains to work and figure out a new schedule for Paint with a View's future events."

Izzie worked her mouth into a half-decent smile and motioned to me with a wave of her arm.

I guessed that meant she was no longer miffed at me. Good thing we hadn't forgotten the forgive-and-forget part of our relationship. "What a relief Barrett called this morning to announce the shop could open. I don't think you'd have lasted another twenty-four hours."

"Not even that many. See you at dinner, loving and wonderful parents," Izzie called over her shoulder as she pulled me down the hallway. "We have so much to do. Fill the calendar with events, write descriptions, set up links so guests can register, and customize our supply list for each event. Oh, and can't forget to send out emails reminding those who signed up for the Paint Your Pet night to send in those images of their fur babies." She squealed and clasped her hands. "I'm so excited. Aren't you?"

I reared back my head and blinked. "Wow. How much coffee did you have this morning?"

"Why? What's wrong?" She threw open the front door and skipped outside.

"I . . . Nothing." I patted her shoulder. "Let's get to work."

The rain had stopped sometime during the wee hours of the morning. I sucked in several breaths of fresh air, with its rich earthy scent. Morning sunlight spread a glistening sheen on the wet grass, and lake water lapped against the shore. "Would you look at the day?" I sighed. "Isn't everything beautiful?"

"Uh huh. You've been in the city too long." Izzie clicked the remote and her vehicle answered with two beeps. "I figure we can have everything done by noon. Then I'll have Willow type up all the events with details and add them to our website. Easy as can be."

In minutes, we were cruising along the lake on Sail Shore Drive, headed for Artisan Alley. We stopped at the intersection at Whisper Cove Boulevard to wait for a red light. The stray cat stretched lazily across the bus stop bench.

"Some have it so easy."

"What was that?" Izzie glanced sideways.

"Never mind. Hey!" I pointed at the corner across the street. "Isn't that Gwen?"

An older woman with tinted brown hair, wearing a bright yellow dress and shoes to match, stood next to the street lamp. She clutched a bag to her ample chest. Gwen might be on the other side of middle age, but she certainly wasn't frail. She carried a large frame, though I'd stop short of describing her as heavy or fat. Despite her gentle, loving personality, I'd bet she could handle most anyone who crossed her, if necessary. I frowned at where I realized my mind had taken me.

"I bet she's decided to open her shop. Good for her." Izzie slapped the steering wheel. "We can celebrate our openings together, right? Let's invite her over for a drink. I'll send out for a bottle of wine. Doesn't that sound nice?" Izzie's smile beamed with excitement.

My enthusiasm, however, was dampened with worry. Detective Barrett would certainly come around to question Gwen. I only hoped she was ready to answer questions and able to defend herself. She was such a sweet lady and one of Mom's dearest friends, having known her for over twenty years. I'd hate to see her put under Barrett's magnifying glass. Gwen had been through enough. Then again, she .certainly didn't hide the way she felt about Fiona. The editorial letter had proved that much. Not to mention the phone call to Theo, with its threatening message, and the final blowout at the *Gazette*. I sank in my seat and pictured the detective, smug as could be, slapping handcuffs on his new prime suspect, the little old lady with the kind, generous heart. I gave my head a firm shake to dismiss the image.

In the next instant, Gwen disappeared through the doorway of Pick Your Poison, the local wine and beer store.

I laughed. "I think Gwen might be way ahead of you on having that celebratory drink."

"See? Creative minds think alike." Izzie steered into a parking spot and got out. Walking to the rear of her vehicle, she popped the trunk and hefted the box filled with her purchases from Sammy's shop. "Time to kick this operation into gear, big sister." Her keys dangled from the fingers of an otherwise occupied hand that held on to her cargo. "Take these."

"Love how you fail to say please." I opened the door and waved her inside.

"Sorry." She shoved the box onto the front counter and turned. A pink flush crept across her cheeks. "I am kind of pushy, aren't I?"

"Like I said earlier, you've been barking out orders since you were four, but after many, many years, I've grown to accept you." I winked.

"Funny you." Izzie pulled out the pieces of wall art, then swiveled. "Now, where will these look best?"

We finished hanging the six pieces on the side walls and sat chugging bottles of spring water. Several sheets of paper were spread out in front of us, one for each event covering the next several months. I did a mental count of how long this would all take.

"Please tell me Willow is coming in soon to help with all this." I waved an arm over the counter and the blank sheets of paper.

"Yep. In a couple of hours." Izzie tapped my hand with her pen. "Don't worry. When she gets here, you can take a break and go do whatever."

Izzie tapped the sheet titled Light the Night—Launch Event. "We don't have enough time to use the Paint Your Pet theme for our opening. Emails with images of pooches and felines are rolling in slowly. At least half of those who registered haven't responded yet, which is understandable, after all that's happened. Anyway, I'll have to move pet night to next week, maybe Wednesday or Thursday." She slid a flyer out of her folder. "I've been thinking up new ideas. I talked to the committee that's raising money to renovate the lighthouse and ferry. They're scheduled for the annual sailboat race, but they need more fundraising events to reach their cash goal. Lucky for us, they promised to advertise our painting event. In return, we donate some of our profits to the lighthouse project. Neat, huh?"

"The guests will paint the lighthouse. That's genius. You never cease to amaze me." I squeezed her arm. "Have you picked a date?"

She squirmed in her seat and swigged her water while holding up one finger. With a huge sigh, she nodded. "Day after tomorrow?"

My chin dropped. "This Friday? Are you kidding? You sure that's enough time for people to sign up?"

Izzie's enthusiasm could venture into the impossible on occasion. This might be one of those moments.

"Yes, and I've also scheduled the beach fireworks event for the following Monday."

"Izzie." I shook my head. Two events in the next few days seemed impossible.

"Don't worry. I have a plan." She batted her eyelids with that familiar look.

I stiffened and shook my head with a lot of force. "Oh, no." I wagged my finger. "No, I won't agree to whatever crazy scheme you've cooked up. Nuh, uh."

"Oh, come on. It will be fun. I promise." She punched her arm in the air. "One for the team?"

I groaned and mumbled as she explained her idea, which involved costumes and human billboards. "Let me get this straight. You want me to stand on a corner, in front of traffic and people, wearing a costume of a cartoon character, with a sandwich billboard shaped like an easel hanging from my shoulders, while I hand out flyers for our event? That's your best idea to sell admission?" My forehead hit the counter with a thud.

"What happened to the daring and impulsive sister I know? I come up with this crazy idea, which, by the way, isn't in my comfort zone, and you sit there all grumpy and critical. I'm trying to save my business the best way I can."

As my lips touched the countertop, I mumbled incoherently.

"What was that?"

I rolled my head sideways. "I said I'm not critical. I'm . . ." I smacked the counter. "Do we really need to stand in public wearing costumes so people can laugh at us? Why not be ourselves and pass out flyers like normal people?"

Izzie chuckled and patted me on the back. "This isn't high school. No one is going to make fun of you, Chloe. Costumes and billboards grab people's attention. You stand out by being different. That's what will work."

"I did promise to help you launch your business." I twisted my neck and opened my eyes to stare at her anxious face. "Fine."

"You will? Really? Chloe, you're the best." She jumped out of her seat and ran to the storage room. When she returned, she held up two costumes. "See? I'll be joining you and covering the other side of town."

I scoffed. "Which one am I? Minnie or Mickey?"

The door creaked open and the chimes overhead tinkled.

I turned and smiled. "Hey, Gwen. How are you?" I scooted off my chair and hurried across the room to give her a hug.

Izzie draped the costumes over the counter and came around to Gwen's other side. "It's so good to have you back. Mom's been asking about you every day since you disappeared. We all missed you."

"My goodness." She blushed and waved a hand to fan her face. "You sure make a lady feel wanted."

"Are you opening up the shop? It would be nice to have my neighbor back," Izzie asked.

"Absolutely. I've been away too long." She gripped the bag tighter. "Don't misunderstand me. I'm no slacker. I never let the dust settle. Time's too precious for that, you know. I did some gardening and knitting and came up with some new designs for my kites. Spent a couple days in the Finger Lakes and then stopped on my way home to visit with my sister-in-law, Tressa. She hasn't been feeling well." Her eyes widened.

"Come to think of it, that was the evening of the Paint Your Shop event. I'm sorry I had to miss it, Izzie. I'll be sure to come to the next one." Gwen heaved her chest and smiled. "But I'm back now and ready to work. Yes, I am. Ready and anxious and—say! Would you two girls like to join me?" She lifted a bottle of wine from the bag. "I hope you like semisweet. It's the only kind I drink, you know."

I blinked. Her chattering raced so fast, I barely kept up. I couldn't recall her talking at any pace but slow and calm. Her fingers wouldn't stop fidgeting, either.

"Sure! Hold on a sec." Izzie slipped behind the counter and pulled out a box filled with plastic cups and utensils.

"How nice is this? Three business ladies celebrating our successes." Gwen poured a generous amount into each of our cups. "I hate to confess, but these past few weeks have been stressful. Why, there was a moment I worried I'd have a mental breakdown." She tipped back her cup and drank then poured more. "But that's over now, thank goodness. Our town has returned to the peaceful place we all love. Don't you agree?" She arched her brow as she took another sip of her semisweet, her eyes peeking at us over the edge of her cup.

I blinked, speechless, and totally confused. I didn't recognize the nervous, flighty woman in front of me.

"Well, it's certainly nice to have you back." Izzie slid the bottle behind her and to the other side of the counter. "I'm sure you have plenty to keep you busy. Why don't I walk with you back to your shop? I'd love to see those designs." She skirted around me and whispered. "Call Mom. Tell her to come here, ASAP."

"Oh, I thought . . ." Gwen knitted her brows and wiped her lips with the back of her hand. "Yes, I do have a lot to prepare. Thank you, Izzie. Maybe you can visit another time? My new work needs a bit of tweaking, you understand."

"Absolutely." Izzie wrapped an arm around her shoulders and walked Gwen to the door. "You have a great and productive day then." Izzie waited on the outside step while Gwen walked toward her shop, then pivoted on her heel to face me. Her jaw dropped. "What the heck? She's never acted this way or drank so much. I'm calling Mom."

I held up my phone. "Already texted her. She's on the way." I hiked my rear back onto the stool. "Maybe she did have a breakdown. I mean, the story Theo told us was pretty disturbing. A gentle, easygoing person like Gwen might not be able to handle such trauma."

"I don't know if you remember, but Mom told us how she'd worried about Gwen during her divorce." Izzie poured more wine in her cup. "Hard to believe Gwen's been single for more than twenty years. Anyway, Mom claimed Gwen held it together, as sane and strong as anybody through the whole ordeal. No breakdown. No hysterics. Not even I could be that calm and collected. Although the younger Gwen might've been stronger than the one we saw today." Izzie tipped her cup forward and pointed. "I heard from others besides Mom that the ex is a real loser. His reaction to the divorce was to cause an angry scene in court. Said he'd make her pay somehow."

"Funny." I traced my finger around a ring of sweat from the bottle on the counter. "Why would Gwen stay in touch with her ex's sister?" I thought about Ross and the group of friends we had hung out with on those rare occasions he agreed to take a break from work to socialize. Actually, they were his friends, buddies from college and their spouses, and sort of like his family. I'd feel strange doing anything with them now.

"I certainly can't understand." Mom entered the shop, flushed and bright-eyed. "Since Gwen and William divorced, she hasn't mentioned her sister-in-law, Tressa. She'd tell me if she visited her. I'm sure of it."

"Maybe she didn't want you to know?" Maybe Gwen kept it a secret because she didn't want a lecture.

Izzie and I weren't the only ones showered with Mom's words of intended wisdom. She dished out advice to her friends and anyone else who would listen. Well-meant intentions weren't always welcomed.

"She could've kept it secret for a good reason."

"Where is she, by the way?" Mom circled the shop and peeked inside the storage room. With hands hitched on hips she gave us one of those looks with a chin slant and squinty eyes. "You didn't let her leave, did you?"

"Don't worry, Mom. She went to her shop. I watched her go inside."

"Still." Mom marched to the door. "I'll go visit to make sure she's okay. See you girls later at dinner." She waved and cut across the lawn to Go Fly a Kite.

"Never changes." Izzie swung a leg over the stool and scooted on the seat.

"Yeah, but Mom is a great friend that way." I studied the spread of papers for the events.

"You think it's only us who are bothered by all the attention and advice and coddling?"

"Nope. Not in the least." I rolled my eyes and laughed.

"She's the best, right?"

"Absolutely the best Mom we could hope for." I scribbled notes on one sheet of paper.

"Make sure you include the exact time, date, and price in the description of each event." Izzie tapped her pen.

"Yes, ma'am." I wrote more details while letting my mind wander.

Gwen wasn't herself. That much was obvious. The question was why, and what had caused it? Could her behavior involve Fiona's murder, or was there some other reason she behaved this way and kept quiet?

"Okay, how's this sound?" Izzie straightened her paper and cleared her throat.

"Wait!" I held up one finger. "I want to close my eyes and visualize your words."

"You're such a tool. Shut up and listen."

I squirmed in my seat, placed my elbows on the counter, and cradled my chin in upturned palms. "Ready when you are."

Before Izzie could speak, the door chimes jingled again. "Oh wow. Look who came to visit, again."

I pushed off the counter with my hand to turn the stool around. "Don't tell me you're done checking on Gwen already? Mom, you should know we—Oh!" I hopped off the stool and scratched behind my ear. "Ross. I figured you'd be halfway to New York by now. What gives?" That alarm ringing in my head to tell me something was off made me wary and tense.

"Ha. Funny thing. I, um, my car wouldn't start this morning. Turns out I need something or other fixed, according to the local mechanic. I guess that means I'll be sticking around for the next couple of days, maybe more." He avoided making eye contact and shifted his gaze around the room. "Nice place."

"Days, huh?" I whistled under my breath. My alarm scaled up several decibels. Fate sure had a twisted sense of humor.

"Yeah." He ran his tongue along his upper lip. "He doesn't carry parts for a Mercedes, so he called in a rush order from a dealer in Buffalo. Any recommendations for good places to eat?"

"This is *so* great." Izzie crept up behind me and gave my arm a squeeze.

"No, it isn't," I hissed at her. "There's a diner around the corner on Whisper Cove Boulevard. Millie's." I bit the inside of one cheek as my brain worked to make sense of his story. "I don't understand. Why don't you rent a car to drive home? I'm sure you could arrange for somebody to drive the Mercedes back to New York."

He shook his head. "I don't trust strangers driving my car. You know that. Besides, I took a few days of vacation. The office doesn't expect me to return until next week."

I did a mental countdown to cool my temper. "You don't take vacation time."

"I do now. I'm sure we'll run into each other again." He tapped his hands against his thighs. "Yep. Couldn't pick a nicer town to get stuck in, right?"

My lips pressed together. I raced to think of a response that didn't involve something I'd regret later on.

"This doesn't have to be awkward, Chloe. Nothing's changed. I wanted to give you a heads up, is all. See you around." He swung the door open wide and disappeared down Artisan Alley.

"Wow. That's a surprise," Izzie said.

"Not a good one." I rolled the pen between my fingers, while staring at the door as it slowly creaked closed.

"Why should you care? You broke up, right?"

I snapped my head around. "Would you want your ex, someone who begged to get back together and caused an embarrassing situation when you said no, to hang around like some wounded puppy dog?"

"Oh boy. Yeah, that does sound awful." She rustled papers in her hand. "But he's old news, and life goes on. We have an agenda to complete."

"You're such a bossy boss." I grabbed another sheet and studied the title. "Lego My Ego?"

"Yep. The group will paint self-portraits in the shape of Lego blocks." She wiggled her brows.

"Huh." I stuck out my lower lip and nodded. "You might make a go of this after all."

"Thanks for the confidence. Now, let's finish as many of these event descriptions as we can before Willow gets here. Then, after dinner, we're putting on those costumes and hitting the streets to promote our event. It's sink or swim time, Chloe. Sink or swim."

* * *

Izzie was right about one thing in particular. The sooner the killer was found, the quicker life in Whisper Cove could return to normal and clear the innocent, including her and me. I worried Detective Barrett had kept me at the top of his list of suspects. That time, place, and opportunity fit my unfortunate situation perfectly, which had my insides tied in knots. No matter how many pieces we added to his Clue game board, the detective would still keep me, and most likely Izzie, in play until the real killer was caught.

I walked along Artisan Alley past several shops to reach Quaint Décor. Izzie and Willow stayed at the shop to finish putting all the event info on the shop's website, so I was free to carry out my own agenda. Our visit to Sammy yesterday and what I'd discovered had me curious. I couldn't shake loose the notion that she was hiding something important. She'd been quick to point our attention to Megan, planting the seeds of why Izzie's best friend would have reason to kill Fiona. Distraction to throw us off seemed like a guilty person's move.

However, what I really wanted to learn more about was the story behind that underpriced crystal swan. I pushed open the door and stepped inside. Sammy stood at the front, unpacking boxes. With head touching shoulder, she pressed her phone to one ear. I waved to catch her attention, then I took casual steps farther into the shop to browse the aisle where the crystal collection was displayed. Comfortable hearing Sammy's voice on the phone, I lifted the swan off the shelf and examined it more closely. Seeing no nicks or scratches marring the piece left me puzzled. The price tag was the same as I'd noticed yesterday. I glanced over my shoulder. Sammy continued to chat. I ran my finger along the shelf, searching for another Swarovski I would recognize. My gaze landed on a lady figurine dressed in a full-length gown. I tipped the item on its side and tensed. Again, it was lower than market price. Not wanting to fall into the trap of making assumptions, I grabbed the swan, turned, and walked toward the register and Sammy. A heart-to-heart talk was the fair way to handle the situation. That was the least I could do for a friend.

Sammy nodded at me, then said a quick goodbye over the phone. "Hi, Chloe. You're back so soon. Is something wrong with the wall art Izzie purchased?" A frown of concern creased her brow.

"Quite the opposite. Izzie is gleaming with pride and so happy with the results. Good choice." I tapped fingers against my thighs. "Browsing. That's why I came back." I set the crystal on the counter. "Swarovski crystal figurines are beautiful, aren't they? I have a couple items in my collection. Knockoffs, of course. I couldn't afford the real deal. Way too pricey."

"Hmm. Yeah, they can be." She cleared her throat, then bent down to grab more items out of a box piled on top of several others.

I lowered my gaze to examine the stack. At once, my heartbeat picked up speed. I stared at the name stamped in bold, black letters on each box. Infinity Collectibles brought back unpleasant memories. I remembered my employer, the art collector in Paris, complaining about unscrupulous players in the art world. He'd been cheated in dealing with those who were prominent in the black market, like Infinity Collectibles. Up front, the business appeared totally legitimate. However, Infinity fell into the group known for gaming the system, as well as their clients, by using ruthless tactics, sort of like those mafia characters you found in movies like *The Godfather* and *Goodfellas* who never seemed to get caught or arrested. They would purchase stolen merchandise to sell to merchants rather than buy legal, and that was just one of their crimes. Maybe my view was extreme, but those were the kind of people you were smart to stay away from.

In any case, this bit of news amplified my concern over what Sammy was doing, and I was determined to push until I got answers.

"Are you interested in buying the swan?" She stood straight and pushed a stray curl out of her eyes. "It's a genuine Swarovski and a steal at that price."

"Yeah, about that." I rubbed my bottom lip, working out what to say next. This heart-to-heart approach was harder than I thought. I pointed at the box. "You do much business with Infinity Collectibles?"

She nodded. "All the time. Why?"

I detected the slight twitch in the corner of her eye as she clutched a ceramic candle holder to her chest. I waved an arm. "Oh, I've just heard some things."

"Things like what?" The eye twitch stopped, replaced by a glare.

Going immediately on the defensive was another bad sign. I sighed. "Infinity Collectibles is a dummy corporation known worldwide, but you probably already knew that. Did you also know it has a shady reputation as a black-market dealer? Infinity buys stolen merchandise, so they can easily sell to clients at cheaper prices. In fact, some in the art industry suspect the company has shipped merchandise with contraband hidden inside objects. I know this because I worked for an art collector who had trouble with Infinity. He lost money and even took heat from the authorities when their investigation of stolen merchandise led to his collection. The inspector had explained to him he wasn't the only victim and Infinity was clever enough to avoid any charges against them. They hid their tracks, and their victims were afraid if they said anything, Infinity would retaliate. The company was known for threats, too."

I reached across the counter and laid my hand over hers. "Sammy, are you in trouble with them? You can tell me. I know a great lawyer who can help." The corners of my mouth curved in an attempt to give her an encouraging smile.

She sniffed and lifted her chin. Her eyes grew moist. "I can't. It's too . . ." She cleared her throat. "Would you like to buy the swan? I'll throw in a coupon from Penny's shop next door. Mood therapy is the latest trend in medical cures, you know?" She swiped her eyes and bent down to look behind the counter. "I know I put those coupons in here somewhere."

"Sammy. Sammy, please." I skirted around to stand next to her. "They will keep pulling you in, deeper and deeper, and you will never escape." I squatted until we were face to face.

Tears filled her eyes, and she broke into heavy sobs.

"I, I was so desperate." She grabbed my hand. "More than desperate. I had to do something or he'd be put away forever. I couldn't let that happen."

"Who, Sammy? Who will be put away?"

She nodded. "My dad. My dad was arrested for embezzling. Now, I owe a lot of money."

Chapter Eight

Sammy sat on the floor. "My dad's only chance at getting a lighter sentence was for us to hire a good lawyer, and I wanted the best, you see." She heaved a sigh. "I don't have that kind of money because all of it has been sunk into this shop. I heard about Infinity from another business owner—no one from around here—and how the seller has connections to purchase merchandise at way below market price, but totally legal. Or at least that's what I thought. Gullible, naïve me, right?" She shrugged. "Anyway, my plan was to buy cheap and sell at a high enough price to still make a huge profit."

I eyeballed the crystal swan and the hundred-dollar price tag. "Just how deep of a discount did Infinity give that you made a profit?" I shook my head. "Never mind. I guess you found out too late the true nature of Infinity."

"Yep. When I approached them the first time about discontinuing my orders, things didn't go as planned." Sammy shivered. "My designated contact promised there would be serious consequences if that was my decision."

"Maybe asking the bank for a loan would've been an easier option." I gritted my teeth. Kate Abbington's behavior in giving advice that wasn't asked for didn't fall too far from that proverbial family tree. "I'm guessing you already tried that first. Sorry, I don't mean to judge."

"It's fine. Yeah, I tried but was turned down before the ink on my application had a chance to dry." She picked at the flap of one box. "I've already saved up enough for a retainer to hire one of the top criminal defense lawyers in the state. Unfortunately, that's only a small portion of what I'll owe him by the time the trial is over."

"Debts to the black-market dealer *and* to the lawyer. A double whammy, as my granddad used to call it." I whistled. "You're in a pretty tight squeeze with no wiggle room. Better watch out."

Sammy stood and brushed off her bottom. "Trust me. I'm careful. My dad and my business are all I care about. I can't afford to lose either one."

I considered, for a moment, what lengths I'd go to to help a loved one in trouble. Circling around the counter, I picked up the crystal swan and handed it to her. "Ring me up. It's the least I can do to help out a good cause." I grinned and pulled out my credit card.

"You always were my favorite underclassman." Though her lips trembled, she managed to wink.

While she covered the swan in layers of bubble wrap, I thought about her troubles and how she had managed to keep them a secret. What if someone found out, though? Like Fiona? I didn't know the woman well enough to say whether or not she'd resort to something as devious as blackmail. However, I'd been friends with Sammy since high school. I struggled to accept her as capable of murder.

"Here you go." She slid a gift bag with my purchase across the counter. "Your credit card. Don't forget that."

I took the card and tucked it inside my wallet. "You know your secret is safe with me. I only hope you'll do the wise thing before Infinity burns you."

"Thanks." She fingered her necklace while her gaze drifted for a second. "Chloe, I know what Izzie meant by her comments. She suspects I might have killed Fiona. Maybe that detective thinks so too. But I didn't. I couldn't. You believe me, don't you?" Her eyes pleaded as tears filled them again.

I pressed fingertips against my chin. "My gut tells me you don't have a murderous bone in you. However, what I think doesn't matter. It's Detective Barrett you'll have to convince." I turned to walk toward the door but paused and glanced over my shoulder. "Have a good afternoon, Sammy. Stay safe. I meant what I said earlier. If you want to get out from under Infinity's thumb, I can help. I happen to know a great criminal defense lawyer who's in town this week."

I stepped outside and glanced at my watch. Dinner was in twenty minutes, followed by my showtime debut as Minnie or Mickey. Izzie and I hadn't clarified that detail. A fine mist of rain fell and dampened my cheeks, so I sheltered my head under my bag. Clutching the Quaint Décor purchase to my chest, I sprinted across the front lawns of several shops to reach Izzie's. The windows were dark, with no sign of anyone inside. "Figures."

I remembered my grandmother's advice that running got you just as wet as walking. By now, the mist had turned to a steadier rain. I gave in to the situation, lowered the bag to my side, and stuck out my tongue to catch the raindrops. I grinned at the childlike behavior, then stomped in a puddle of water, splashing my legs. Two more blocks and I landed on the front porch of our family home.

The door swung open. "About time." Izzie eyed me head to toe. "You're soaked."

"Really? I hadn't noticed. Are you going to move or do you expect me to climb over you?" I was too wet to care how I sounded.

A smirky grin curled her lips. "Go around back to the mudroom. Mom would kill the both of us if I let you puddle up her wood floor."

I did a double eye roll. "This is like childhood all over again. Fine. Is dinner ready? I need to take a quick shower." I held out a hand, palm facing skyward. Not a drop.

"Make it a quick one because if you're late to the table, Mom—"

"I *know*, Izzie. She'll be mad." I puffed my cheeks and blew out air. Hopping off the porch, I ran to the rear of the house. Being home certainly had its perks, but downfalls as well.

Max met me at the door, tail wagging. His tongue hung to one side of his mouth as he panted.

"Hey, boy. You anxious for dinner, too?" I scratched his head, then kicked off my shoes and grabbed a towel hanging from the rack. I rubbed to dry my soppy wet hair and body. "We should sneak upstairs before your grandma Kate catches us like this. Okay?"

Max hopped on his hind legs in a circle, then led the way to the back stairs.

"Smart pooch. Nobody can claim otherwise." I followed Max to climb what we as kids had called the secret getaway.

Whenever either Izzie or I got in trouble, those stairs bought us some time before the lecture and punishment. As youth passed into the teen years, Izzie waited until late evening, then tiptoed down the back way and out the door to meet with friends, sometimes a boy. Mom and Dad figured out her scheme at some point because one day a bolt lock was installed on the door at the top of the stairs. Izzie searched and searched but could never find the key. Once we graduated, the bolt lock was gone and the stairs were free to use again. I admired their ingenuity. They didn't need to lecture her or say one word. All they needed was a bolt lock. As for me, I was the geek in high school, without dates or a nightlife. Pathetic as it sounded, my evening companions had been textbooks and the classics.

I snatched a bath towel from the linen closet and turned on the shower. While waiting for the water to warm, I sat on my bed. Max hopped up and rolled on his back for me to give him a belly rub.

"You can be my best guy, okay?"

Max sneezed then wagged his tail.

"Agreed." I slid off the bed. "Romantic relationships are overrated, Max. Remember that the next time you meet a cute little poodle who bats her eyes at you." I stepped in the shower and dismissed my problems, at least for a few minutes.

*　*　*

"Would you hold still? I can't button the back while you're squirming like a five-year-old." Izzie tugged at the costume with some extra force.

"I can't help it. The material is itchy and hot." I clenched my fists and willed myself to remain calm.

Truth be told, my restless act had more to do with the dinner conversation than the scratchy fabric. When Mom casually mentioned she had bumped into Ross at the general store and invited him to dinner some evening, I choked on my broccoli and needed a full glass of water to wash it down. My protest only resulted in her claim that friends shouldn't have to eat out every night when there was a perfectly good home-cooked meal available.

I thought we'd covered the whole breaking-up issue, but the category of ex-boyfriend hardly mattered to Mom when it came to feeding the needy. Or something to that effect. I was fuming too much to pay close attention to the conversation after the initial bomb was dropped.

"There." Izzie touched up the rouge on my cheeks, then grabbed my shoulders and turned me around. "You look so adorable! A cute little Minnie Mouse." She grinned and clapped her hands. "This will be so much fun."

I stared in the vanity mirror, tipping my head side to side. "Maybe. Although I have a hunch people will be asking if I'm lost and why I'm not at Disney World."

"Not when they see this." She placed the sandwich bill-board over my head.

I admired the artwork. Willow had created the design, and Izzie had taken it to a local print shop to finish up both boards and make copies of the flyer. I gestured with a thumbs-up. Details on the board included the name of the event and a message stating tickets were going fast.

"Now, my turn." Izzie slipped into the Mickey Mouse costume.

"What's your take on Mom's invitation?" I fidgeted with Minnie's bow. "She should've run the idea by me first, right?"

She tugged on Mickey's gloves then turned. "Does it matter? Not like she can take it back now. Button me, please."

"Yeah, she can't. It would be too awkward and too rude. Oh well, maybe Ross will decide not to come."

Izzie snorted. "I doubt it. He'll come with a smile, carrying flowers and maybe a box of chocolates."

I scoffed. "He can't bribe me with presents."

"Not for you, dork. The flowers and candy would be for Mom. Remember, the way to strengthen a relationship is to make nice with the parents." She poked my shoulder. "Face it. You're on the losing team."

I pressed a gloved finger to her lips. "Shut it. I don't want to hear any more from you."

"Just as well. It's time to work that corner, Minnie. Just don't take any rides from strangers." She threw back her head and laughed as she stepped out of the room.

"You're a hysterical guy, Mickey. Keep it up." I adjusted my billboard, then followed her down the stairs and outside.

To make the most of advertising our Disney parade of two, we took our trip to the center of town on foot. We answered whistles and howls and beeping horns with cute arm waves and curtsies. I had to admit, the Abbington ladies were good sports when it came to humiliation.

I took my post on the corner of Sail Shore Drive and Whisper Cove Boulevard. At six thirty in the evening on a weekday, traffic in town was at its peak, both by car and on foot. I waved bye to Izzie as she walked farther down the block, toward the east end of Whisper Cove. Licking my lips, I glanced back and forth and finally at the sidewalk. The funny looks I got didn't help calm my nerves. I felt about as silly as anyone would, dressed like Minnie Mouse, wearing a billboard.

Clearing my throat, I held out the flyers. "Come visit Paint with a View for an evening of fun and painting. We have Light the Night on Friday. A portion of our sales will go toward the lighthouse project, and if you like fireworks, we'll be painting those Monday evening."

"I'll take one of those, miss."

I pivoted on my heel and the billboard rocked sideways, nearly knocking me off balance.

A hand reached out to grab my arm and steady my wobbly steps.

"Oh! Ross, it's you." Heat rushed to my face. "Why are you here?"

He laughed. "I thought we covered that this morning."

"I mean, why are you *here*?" I pointed to the sidewalk and the space between our feet.

He pointed behind me. "The diner. Stopping by to grab a meal before heading back to the hotel."

I studied him for a quiet moment. He'd changed into khakis and a polo shirt. Ross's idea of dressing down never went too casual. I'd yet to see him wear a pair of jeans or a sweatshirt. I pressed my lips into a tight line and shoved a flyer into his open hand. "Not sure why you want one. You don't paint."

"Always open to try new things." He folded the paper neatly and tucked it in his pocket.

"Since when?" My eyes narrowed. Taking vacation time was surprising enough. "I don't believe you." I wagged a Minnie Mouse finger in his face. "You're up to something."

He widened his stance and crossed arms. "I'm making the best of an awkward situation. On top of my plans being ruined, I'm stuck here. No point in holing up in my hotel room, is there?"

I gawked and batted my fake eyelashes. "Well, I'm sorry. This is awkward for me, too. You're welcome to join the paint party Friday evening. And dinner, sometime before you leave town. Mom told me she invited you." I could be civil about this breakup too.

His shoulders relaxed. "Thank goodness. I was worried you'd blow a fuse when you found out. I told your mom I'd take a look at my schedule. I'll get back to you about our date."

I bit my tongue to keep quiet. Our date? With one tiny remark, he had turned the situation into something it wasn't. Well, I wouldn't ask again. Mom would do that.

A sly smile spread across his lips. "You look adorable as Minnie, by the way. I don't suppose you'd let me take a selfie of us?"

Before I had the chance to say one word, he whipped out his phone and snuggled close to me.

"Say Disney!" He snapped the picture then scowled at the screen. "You didn't smile. How about we try another?"

When he raised his arm, I batted it away. "Stop. I have a job to do, and you're interfering. Now, shoo." I waved toward the diner. "Go grab your bite to eat."

He winked. "See you Friday."

"Looking forward to it." I smirked, then turned to face the street and waved flyers in the air. "Come join us at Paint with a View. Enjoy an evening of painting and help save the lighthouse."

"We'll take a couple. Sounds like fun."

Two ladies remained while they pored over the flyer. I stood quietly, waiting to answer any questions they might have, and used the time to people watch. I recognized a few passersby, but most were strangers, likely visitors to Whisper Cove. We had lots to offer—the lake for boating, swimming, and fishing, lots of places to shop, and for evening entertainment, a very unique theater. A floating stage situated on the water provided a venue for tribute bands to perform. Several concerts were scheduled each year, starting in May and wrapping up in early October, weather permitting. The only attraction not available at present was the ferry. Several times a day, drivers and their vehicles loaded onto the ferry that puttered to the other side of the lake. Until the overpass bridge was built, the ferry ride was the only shortcut across. Unfortunately, both the ferry and the lighthouse needed repairs.

I shaded my eyes against the evening sunlight with one hand and studied a familiar profile exiting First Federal Savings and Loan. She was covered neck to knee in a beige, trench-like raincoat. A floppy hat covered her head and shaded her eyes, but the thick blonde curls and stocky figure gave Megan's identity away.

"Excuse me, but will you serve wine with the event? I heard one of those party businesses in Cleveland does the paint and sip deal."

I snapped to attention. The taller and older woman spoke. "Yes. I mean, no. You can bring your own beverage, but right now we aren't serving wine. Sometime in the future, we might." I stretched my neck to get a better look at Megan.

She dabbed her eyes with a tissue and power-walked to the corner to sit on the bus stop bench. With a headshake, she pulled out her phone and slapped it to her ear.

"Sounds great. Can we buy tickets from you?"

"Hmm?" I volleyed my focus from Megan to the ladies in front of me, not exactly giving them the spirited pitch Izzie would've hoped for.

"Tickets?" Her eyebrows shot up.

"Oh! Sorry." I pointed to the flyer. "Online is best."

"We can't buy from you? That's inconvenient." Her eyebrows inched together, forming a scowl. "What if a person doesn't have internet?"

By now, Megan's arm-tossing and head-shaking hinted that her phone conversation wasn't going well. I stepped sideways to get a better look.

"Let's go, Sarah. We can use the Wi-Fi in that diner to sign up." The younger one tugged at her companion's arm.

"How can you promote a business with that kind of attitude? Seriously, Mira, the younger generation needs to learn some manners."

I opened my mouth to apologize, but they'd disappeared into Millie's Diner. "Great. You're doing a fantastic job, Chloe."

"I'd say the costume and billboard are doing the job for you. No need to worry."

I jumped. The billboard swung and slapped against my chest. "Ouch." I turned to face Detective Barrett.

My mood soured even more. That dream where a person landed in a public place, maybe at school or work, dressed in pajamas, with curlers in her hair, and looked like a total loser came to mind.

I waved. "Hi, Detective. What brings you to this corner this evening?"

He pointed. "Making a stop at Spill the Beans for some coffee before heading home. Care to take a break and join me?"

I gave him a cursory stare to decide whether he was serious. I shrugged with arms outstretched. "No animals, especially cartoon ones, allowed inside."

"I really wish you would." He dropped the amused expression.

I gripped the sides of the billboard, my armor made of card stock, and hugged it closer to my chest. "Oh, is this more like an official invitation from the Chautauqua authorities? If I'd known, I would have dressed for the occasion." My snarky behavior didn't match Minnie's friendly-with-a-smile attitude, but I couldn't help how he irked me. Maybe under different circumstances, when I wasn't the subject of a murder investigation, my disposition would improve.

He scratched the stubble on his chin. "No. It's more like me welcoming you back to Whisper Cove. A friendly gesture."

I yanked on the hair bow itching my head and told myself to play nice with the detective. My suspicious nature remained on high alert. He was investigating a murder that had happened under my watch. Suggesting I join him for a cup of coffee didn't seem like a friendly gesture. This was a fishing expedition.

"In that case, I'll pass. I'm working." I held up the flyers in one hand and stabbed the billboard with my other. "You're welcome to attend. Tickets are forty dollars. Consider that *my* friendly gesture."

Detective Barrett made a sucking sound with his lips. "Miss Abbington, you are a challenge. I'll give you that."

"Always have been. Ask anyone who knows me." We locked gazes for an awkward moment, then I glanced away, waving the flyers over my head. "Come visit Paint with a View! Paint party fun and a chance to help out the campaign to save our lighthouse."

"Have a good evening, Chloe. I'm sure we'll be talking soon." He jogged across the street.

I grunted with some effort at a goodbye. Whatever mood he'd put me in, mostly irritated and flustered, I wouldn't let him get to me. Scanning the street, I witnessed the bustle of activity as shoppers and tourists filled the sidewalk, some carrying armloads of purchases, others chatting with friends. I stopped to fix my gaze on the corner bench. Megan stuck her phone in the pocket of her trench coat and tugged at the brim of her hat to shade her eyes. Looking side to side, she stepped away from the bench. In seconds, a man wearing a panama hat, a Hawaiian flowered shirt, and white linen pants approached her. His garb shouted misplaced tourist who belonged in some tropical vacation spot and not Whisper Cove. The two of them carried on a brief conversation before Megan marched away. The whole scene—the trench coat disguise, the phone conversation, and the mystery man—gave me pause. Sammy's comment that Megan had financial problems came to mind. Could she be right? If true, Megan had reason to be angry with Fiona. Tearing apart her reputation that already teetered on the edge of failure could've been enough to push Izzie's dear friend over the edge.

On the other hand, Izzie swore that if Megan was in trouble, she'd know. Maybe I was grasping for clues where none existed.

Obviously, desperate measures called for me to fall apart and act like an idiot who trusted no one. "Well, what do you know, Detective Barrett? Guess we have more in common than I would ever imagine."

I waved at Izzie, who jogged across the street, clutching her sandwich billboard. One way or another, this crime would be solved. Right now, my guessing as to whodunnit was like spitting in the wind, and nothing backed my claim but speculation and suspicion. Like the cop show detective would say, evidence solved the case. At least I had one thing right. No matter who the killer turned out to be, life in Whisper Cove was changed forever.

Chapter Nine

"What are you up to this morning?" I skewered a chunk of pineapple and eyed Max, who lay on his back, panting.

The ceiling fan hummed while a slight breeze drifted in from the kitchen window. Both offered relief from the morning heat, with feeble success.

Izzie checked her watch. "I arranged a meeting with the supplier to sort out the delivery snafu. Somebody somewhere needs to answer for a shoddy performance because now we don't have the paint colors we need for tomorrow. Gotta love these moments." She raised her arm to give the chain of the ceiling fan several pulls until the blades picked up speed. "Let's hope the repair guy comes today to fix the AC. I don't know how much more of this sticky, hot weather I can take. Do you have any plans?"

"Oh, I thought I'd take a walk into town and visit some friends, maybe do a bit of shopping." I hadn't divulged the entire story about Sammy's situation. With the opening event scheduled for tomorrow evening, topped off by this morning's delivery mess, Izzie was a tangled bundle of nerves. I didn't even tell her about Megan's odd behavior, how she was sneaking around dressed in a trench coat. Adding more worries to her full plate didn't seem fair, at least until after the opening.

"How many do we have so far? I counted twenty sign-ups before I fell asleep."

"Thirty. We hit the maximum number allowed by the fire department. Even your ex is coming." She winked.

"Yes, and your dear classmate from high school, Hunter Barrett." I exchanged my empty fruit bowl for a plate of scrambled eggs and returned to the table.

"He's not my dear anything," Izzie huffed while gathering her bag and sweater.

Max licked my ankle, grabbing my attention. I scratched the top of his head, then stood to walk over to the pantry. "Beg to differ, but let's move on. Willow called to say she'll be at the shop this morning to prepare sketches and organize materials for the event but then plans to leave by noon." I poured kibble into the bowl.

"That's fine. I should be back from Jamestown by then to finish up the prep." She tied her hair in a ponytail. "Take over for a couple of hours afterward, will you? In case someone stops by to check out the place or maybe has questions about future events. You can close up by five. Mom's invited Gwen for dinner. She wants me to pick up a few items before coming home." Izzie whistled. "I can only imagine the table conversation we'll be listening to."

"Yeah, I bet. Okay. I'll be at the shop by three."

The hall clock chimed eight. I shoveled the last bite of egg in my mouth as I carried the plate to the sink and mumbled goodbye as Izzie rushed down the hall. Alone with Max, I let my thoughts ramble, thinking about Sammy and her situation with Infinity. None of her problems were my business, unless they somehow tied her to Fiona. Yet the caring side of me wanted to fix all things broken. Sammy might need rescuing from those goons she did business with, but I couldn't force help on her.

My phone rang, breaking my thoughts. I snatched it from my pocket and tensed at Sammy's name popping up on the screen. "Hey, Sammy. I was thinking about you. Maybe we—"

"Should talk, yeah I know. I . . ." She broke off with a quivering breath.

"You do? Boy, that's a relief." I sank into a chair. "I can make a quick call to my lawyer friend, and we can meet this morning."

"Oh! No, I mean, yes. I could use some legal advice, but that's not why I'm calling."

I rubbed my brow. "I don't understand."

"Listen." Her voice lowered. "I can't stand the idea of people believing I harmed Fiona, but you think I'm innocent, right?"

"I also told you the one to convince is Detective Barrett." I gripped the phone, not sure where this conversation was going.

"That's why I did some digging. Chloe, I figured out who killed Fiona."

My breath held for several beats. "You should talk to Detective Barrett then." I hoped my visit yesterday and our conversation didn't push her to do something foolish.

"I'd rather run it by you first. See what you think. Can you stop by the shop this morning?"

I twisted my arm to get a look at my watch. "How's eight thirty?" Truth be told, I was anxious to learn who she thought murdered Fiona and was excited for life to get back to normal.

"Thanks, Chloe. I'll feel a lot safer if someone besides me knows."

A ricochet of questions fired off in my head, but the call ended. I lost any opportunity to ask a single one. Debating whether to call Ross, I kept my finger on the phone keyboard. A second pair of ears to hear Sammy's story would help. Not to mention, having someone I knew and trusted to tag along would bolster my confidence, in case I was wrong. What if Sammy was the guilty one and this was a scheme to lure me into some sort of ambush? I gave myself a mental slap. If she planned to do me harm, she wouldn't ask me to meet someplace so public like her shop, would she?

I drummed my fingernails on the table, contemplating my next move. "There's always safety in numbers." I picked up the phone once more and made the call. I grumbled as his voice mail greeted me. "I know you're on vacation, but wake up. Meet me near the shop by eight thirty. You can hang out by the lake. Soak in some sunshine and get rid of that pasty-white New Yorker look. Oh, and I might have a new client for you." Nothing like the jingle of money to get a lawyer's attention. I hung up.

I pulled a biscuit treat out of the doggy canister. Max danced around me while he barked.

"You be a good boy and keep Mom and Dad company while I'm gone." I gave him a gentle pat on the head, then made my way to the front door.

Within five minutes, I parked along Whisper Lane leading to Artisan Alley. I was early, but Sammy had said to come as soon as possible. Grabbing my bag from the passenger seat, I hurried across the road and past Paint with a View. The darkened windows indicated Willow hadn't shown up yet. I shifted my gaze toward the lake and sighed. Neither had Ross. Pulling my shoulders back, I continued toward Quaint Décor. I tapped out a quick text to tell Ross I'd be at Sammy's and to meet us there.

Stepping up to the door, I read the closed sign that hung over the window pane. Of course, she wouldn't open for business until nine. Our meeting would be private. My hand lingered above the door handle for a second. I turned to glance at the lakeshore. No visitors had arrived, except for a flock of geese pecking at the ground. Facing the door, I grabbed the handle to give it a turn but without success. I knocked on the door, then peered through the front window. No sign of Sammy. She hadn't mentioned if she had called from the shop or home. Maybe she was running late.

Taking a seat on the stoop, I anchored elbows to my thighs, then cradled my chin in both palms. I had nothing better or more important to do. Like I'd told Ross, enjoying the lake view and getting some sun was a nice way to spend time. I closed my eyes and daydreamed of sailboat rides with Mom, Dad, and Izzie.

The cackling sound of chatter caught my attention. I turned to find Sammy's neighbor, the one she had called Penny, standing outside her aromatherapy shop. A shingle hung sideways over the door, etched with the title, The Healing Touch. Today, Penny had her hair curled and cascading down her back. Dressed in a denim dress that touched her sandaled feet and with chunky turquoise jewelry on her neck, wrist, and ears, she paced the short length of her front stoop with her arm waving chaotically. "I don't care if you want to change the date because of your appointment. Talk to your therapist. She can reschedule. People have already committed their time to our Karma Knows Best event. Flo, I love having you as a partner, but you can be a real pain in the—" Penny paced in my direction, then brought her steps to an abrupt halt. She stared at me with a dropped jaw and widened eyes. "Oh! Hello there." She shrugged an apology and pointed at her phone before dashing inside.

No doubt the karma event would be the perfect healing solution for plenty of folks in Whisper Cove, myself included. I tapped my heels on the wooden step, then checked my watch. The second hand ticked forward. Eight thirty had passed ten minutes ago. Maybe Sammy was in the back room and hadn't noticed the time because she was busy doing shop stuff. Anxious to move, I sprinted around back and knocked on the service door. After a minute of feeling frustrated, I trudged to the front once more.

"Hey!"

Ross stood near the lake, waving to get my attention. At least somebody had bothered to show up.

I waved back and jogged across the alley to meet him. "Glad you could pull yourself out of bed, even though you're late." I skidded to a stop. My grin dribbled into a puzzled frown. Dressed in cargo shorts, a bright green T-shirt screen-printed with "I love Chautauqua Lake" across the chest, and flip-flops on his feet, his attire screamed tourist. "What the heck, Ross. Who *are* you?"

With arms lifted, he pivoted side to side. "Don't you approve? You always said I should step out of my comfort zone and try new things."

"Yeah, but . . ." I blinked, then gave my shoulders a dismissive shrug as I sat on the ground. "Thanks for coming, but, other than enjoying the view and sunshine, I'm afraid I asked you here for nothing."

"Is this about the new client you mentioned?" He chewed on a piece of grass.

I nodded. "My friend Sammy is in deep trouble. Maybe more than I imagined." I explained the shop owner's dealings with Infinity Collectibles and how she'd already attempted to cut ties with them. "They dished out their usual threats so she backed off and continued her business arrangement. Really sad situation."

"As I see it, she's got two choices. Give testimony about Infinity's criminal actions or continue to run and hide." He leaned back and, with eyes closed, lifted his face to the sky.

My jaw dropped. "That's the best you can offer? Seriously, I could've come up with that idea. She's scared, Ross. Going to the authorities with what she knows could be dangerous, and leaving Whisper Cove, her family, her *dad*, who might go to jail for the rest of his life, her friends, and give up the shop she worked so hard to keep?" I shook my head. "I can't see her doing that."

"Better than dying." He shrugged.

I threw up my arms. "Would you stop being so dramatic?"

He opened one eye to peer at me. "Just being honest. Besides, if I don't tell the truth, I'm giving her false hope." His voice grew sober.

I cursed realism, but he was right. Sammy needed to be scared straight.

I sat up and faced him. "There's more to the conversation I had with Sammy, but I need to catch you up to speed on what happened right before you came to Whisper Cove. There was a murder, you see."

Ross turned on his side and rested his head on one arm. "I wondered when you'd get around to telling me."

I bit down on my thumb, then stabbed him with a glare. "How did you find out?"

"Your mom told me. After I promised not to squeal, that is. Guess she figured you'd be mad." A grin stretched his face. "You're not mad, are you?"

"Don't joke. This is serious, and I'm worried. Sammy swears she's figured out who killed Fiona but refused to say anything else over the phone. That's why we were supposed to meet." I stuck my wrist in his face. "Twenty minutes ago. She's not here and I'm worried."

"You said that already."

"Well, I *am* worried. More than worried, I'm terrified. What if someone overheard our phone conversation?" I shuddered. "I'm imagining all sorts of horrible outcomes."

"Twenty minutes is nothing. I have clients who are notoriously late, sometimes by as much as an hour. Never bothers me because those are billable hours, but I understand you're worried." He stood and brushed off grass and dirt from his shorts. "Which is why you need to take a break, even if it's only for a few minutes, and enjoy the beautiful morning. If Sammy wants to talk, she'll come." Lifting his legs high, he ran straight toward the water.

"What are you doing? Come back here." My jaw dropped as he plopped his rear on the dock and scooted to the edge.

He took off his flip-flops and stuck both legs in the water, then stuck up his thumb. "This is so great. You should try it."

I threw back my head and laughed. "You're such a nut." The warm, fuzzy feeling of the familiar tingled down to my toes, which lasted until I reminded myself we were finished. I'd told him so, hadn't I? I turned away and tucked my knees underneath my chin. I scanned the alley and each of the shops, quaint and cheerful in appearance, until my gaze rested on Paint with a View. Willow walked around the corner and stepped up to the entrance. As she turned to face me, I waved, and she returned the gesture. Izzie was lucky for many reasons. She had a business that held promise, a great support system, and plenty of customers.

Lifting my face, I stared at the clouds. They drifted over and across the sun until they disappeared, as if leaving the sky undressed. The June day delivered on its promise to be hot and muggy. I tugged at my shirt, sticky with sweat already, and came to a decision. Though I hated to admit such a thing, Ross was right. If Sammy was that desperate to talk, she'd be here. Maybe the time had come to give Detective Barrett a call. Let him handle Sammy's news about who had killed Fiona.

When Ross hollered for me, I wheeled around to face the lake. Though my heart wasn't in the moment, I gave a weak smile. He stood waist deep in the water, splashing his arms. I couldn't stop bad things from happening, just like I couldn't save the world. It took no more than a few seconds, and I ran toward the lake.

Hopping on one foot then the other, I pulled off my sandals and tossed them in the grass. "Move over, Mr. Attorney. I'm coming in."

Sammy never showed, but the quick dip in the lake improved my spirits. I'd called and left a message for Detective

Barrett. Twice. The first was to ask him to call because I had some news. The second was to cancel the first and suggest we should talk in person. I'd added I'd be at the shop until five.

After lunch, followed by a quick cat nap on the sofa next to Max and a relaxing hour on the back porch while I read another chapter of some cheesy romance Mom had bought, I drove to the shop. Nearing the parking area, I spotted Izzie beside her jeep.

"Hey! I'm here." I thrust my arm out of the window and waved.

"Oh, good. I was about to send you a text. I locked up the shop, but the spare key is under the welcome mat. We need to get a third set made so all three of us can carry them." She hiccupped and took a deep breath. "Sorry. Just a teensy bit flustered, worrying and all." She tossed her bag in the car. "The delivery people were so helpful. They agreed to make the order right and promised the goods the day after our event." Another hiccup ended in a sigh.

I blinked. "Well, that blows. Is there somewhere else you can pick up the paints we need?"

"Absolutely. I made a call to an art supply store in Buffalo. We can get all the colors we want if we go pick up the order. In person. That's over an hour, one way." Her shoulders sank. "Guess what I'll be doing tomorrow morning?"

"Sorry, Izzie. I'm sure this won't happen again, or at least not all the time, right?"

"Spoken like a true believer in happy endings." She slid into the driver's seat, then fanned a list at me. "I'm off to collect all the groceries Mom needs. Wish me luck." She eyeballed the paper. "Seriously, who uses mango powder? Mom said it's for some Indian dish she wants to try. Let's hope this meal doesn't give us heartburn, or worse, food poisoning." She pulled out onto the road and winked as she stopped alongside me. "*Namaste!* See you at dinner."

"Hmm. I don't know. Maybe I'll stop at Bob's and bring home barbecue," I teased.

She wagged a finger. "Don't you dare. Mom will get even and feed you quinoa every day for the next month to clear your digestive system of impurities. Her words, not mine."

I tapped my lip. "Decisions, decisions." In the next second, I busted loose with laughter. "Go on. Get your shopping finished. I'll see you at home in a couple of hours."

She waved and sped out of the alley.

Grabbing the cheesy romance novel and a thermos of tea from the back seat and my bag from the front, I clicked the remote lock button. Hardly any vehicles were parked nearby. Besides that, I counted only a handful of people near the lake and boat dock, lingering to catch the afternoon sun or a last boat ride before sunset. The row of shops looked vacant, with no sign of customers going in or coming out, which worried me. Summertime was the retail bonus season for merchants. By winter, most visitors vacationing in western New York flocked to ski resort towns like Ellicottville, leaving Whisper Cove almost deserted until late spring.

Of course, tomorrow might turn out to be another story. Shoppers and retail proved time and time again to be fickle. I shoved the paperback in my bag, then bent over to flip the mat and retrieve the key. Once inside, I switched on the lights. Every station was set up, just like the other evening. I shivered. This was the first time I'd been alone in the shop since Fiona's murder. A cold and clammy sense of dread slid through me. How could anyone do something like that to another human being? I set my things on the counter and forced my thoughts to go elsewhere. Rubbing my arms melted the chill that nipped at me.

The sketches Willow had made were hung on the wall. She'd even captioned each with a bullet list of steps and tips, then taped them underneath each canvas. Izzie had snagged a real gem when she found Willow. Whatever she paid her probably wasn't enough. I moved down the length of the wall and stopped to run a finger along the grooves of a sunflower painting, layered perfectly to give the flower and background a two-dimensional look. Moving closer, I could make out the signature. Izzie. I smiled, then moved around the room, checking out the other paintings. A couple of them were from the Paint Your Shop event. Sammy and Penny must've agreed to let Izzie display their work.

"Knock, knock."

I startled and pivoted on my heel. Gwen stood in the doorway with one hand clutching a package and the other giving me a finger wave. My gaze traveled from her head to her toes. She was dressed in a pink-and-green-flowered kimono with a white orchid tucked behind her ear. Pink bangles covered her wrist, while a beaded necklace hung in layers over her chest. Polished toes peeked out from beneath the hem of the kimono, and lime green flip-flops completed the ensemble.

"Hey, Gwen. What brings you here? You look fantastic."

"Thank you. I want to drop off this gift. My way of apologizing for acting like such a loon yesterday. I've been so out of sorts lately. No excuse, though." She shoved the package in my hands. "Not much, but it's the thought that counts, right?" She giggled nervously.

"Oh. Why, thanks, Gwen. No apologies needed." I gave the box a gentle shake. "I love surprises, but maybe we should wait to open it at dinner? You're still coming, aren't you?" I set the box on the counter and waited while a puzzled frown puckered her brow.

"Dinner? Yes, I'm going to dinner." She blushed and patted her curly hairdo with one hand. "I have a date, but how did you know?"

I blinked. "I'm confused. Izzie told me Mom invited you to dinner."

Gwen fussed with the orchid while remaining quiet.

"Maybe I misunderstood." I rushed to cover the awkward moment.

Her eyes glazed with confusion as she ran her tongue over her mouth.

"In fact, it probably was a mistake. Sometimes, my ears tune out when Izzie talks. Blah, blah, blah." I chuckled. "She's a real chatterbox. So, hey! You have a date. How wonderful is that? Who's the guy. Someone I know?" I clamped my lips and winced. Right now, I was the chatterbox who needed to shut up.

"Hmm?" She came to attention then smiled. "Oh, yes, it is wonderful. He's such a nice man. You know . . ." She cupped one hand to the side of her mouth and lowered her voice. "I haven't been on a date in twenty years. Isn't that awful?" She straightened her shoulders. "Never too late, I say. Well, I should be going. You have a good evening and enjoy your gift." Gwen pushed open the door and flip-flopped across the lawn.

I froze and gawked at the colorfully adorned Gwen as she hurried down Artisan Alley. My concern for her state of mind leveled up several notches. Either I had truly misheard Izzie's comment or Gwen was having a senior moment. I'd like to think the blame was on me. I debated whether to follow her but grabbed for my phone instead.

After three rings someone picked up.

"Mom. Hi. Hey, did you invite Gwen to dinner this evening?"

"Yes. Why? Is something wrong?" Mom's words clipped with an edge in her voice.

"Ah, no. I don't think so. I'm not sure." I tapped the phone, thinking. "Did she mention anything to you about dating someone?"

A loud fit of laughter burst through the receiver. "That's absurd. Gwen doesn't date. After her divorce, she swore off men. Told me so dozens of times, even when I tried to play matchmaker. Why? Chloe, what's going on?"

I shrugged, though she couldn't see. "Gwen stopped by a few minutes ago, dressed up and ready for her date. Or so she told me. The strange part is she seemed totally unaware of your dinner invitation. Should we be worried?"

"Worried? Obviously. I'll give her a call and see what I can find out. Honestly, though, there's not much we can do other than to keep an eye on her." She sighed. "Love you, sweetie. Don't be late for dinner."

I gripped the phone and chewed on my lip while my mind carried on about Gwen. I'd read that traumatic events often brought on strange and disoriented behavior. Traumatic like committing murder.

I shuddered. "Stop it, Chloe. You're speculating again. Gwen has earned the right to have those senior moments." I paced the room. "And to keep certain things like dating to herself." I stopped at the front window to stare out at the lake. A boater docked and cranked down his sail. He pulled something from his pocket as he stepped onto the dock. In the next second, he lifted his arm and held his hand close to his ear.

I gasped as my phone rang and vibrated in my hand. Without glancing at the screen, I clicked to open the call. "Hello?"

"Hi, Chloe. It's Hunter Barrett. I got your message."

The deep growl of his voice made me shiver. An authoritative rather than friendly tone hardly put me at ease.

"Yes. I have some news to share." I grabbed the nearest chair and sat, giving my wobbly legs a break.

"Are you still at your shop?"

"I'll be here until five." All at once, I had doubts. What if he scoffed at my story about Sammy? Then again, I didn't know any details about what Sammy knew. The news could be important.

"Good. I'll be right in."

I heard the click to end the call and frowned. "Right in?" Bouncing out of my seat, I turned toward the window. My eyes widened. Detective Barrett was jogging across the dock and up the lawn toward the shop.

"Huh. How about that?" I opened the door and waited as he approached.

His face was tan with a blush of red from too much sun. He wore frayed khaki shorts and a faded Lollapalooza T-shirt.

I pointed. "You ever been there?"

He lowered his chin for an instant then smiled. "Yep. Two thousand ten."

"Hey, me too." I nibbled on the tip of my thumb. "I'm surprised."

"Why?" He tilted his head.

"You don't seem the type. Green Day? Soundgarden? I mean, Lady Gaga? Seriously not you." I chuckled. Were we having a moment, one that didn't include crime interrogations and finger-pointing?

He crossed his arms and widened his stance. "I can name the first album and first hit released by Soundgarden and by Green Day. Can you?"

"Too easy. I bet you can't tell me what Lady Gaga wore to the Grammys in two thousand eleven. Now, that would impress me." A smile teased the corners of my lips.

"Black leather and thigh-high boots." He winked.

My eyes widened. "You're a true groupie, Detective."

I couldn't believe I was having fun. His authoritative tone had mellowed, nearly coaxing the tension right out of me, until I remembered why he was here.

I cleared my throat. "Much as I'd like to continue playing music trivia with you, we should probably talk about why I called."

He pulled back his shoulders and tensed his jaw. "Is this about Fiona's murder?"

I gestured to the chair next to mine. "I think so."

"Go on." He pulled out a notepad and pen from his back pocket.

I walked behind the counter and opened the mini-fridge. "Would you like a bottle of water? Or soda. We have that too." I retrieved a bottle of water.

"None for me, thanks. Now, you were saying?"

I took a couple of swigs from the bottle and returned to my seat. Something stopped me from revealing what Sammy had told me in confidence about her problems with Infinity. Most likely, Hunter and his team had found that information while investigating. At least the thought kept me from feeling guilty about not sharing those details. "Sammy called me early this morning. She claimed to know who killed Fiona and wanted to meet with me."

"I see." He tapped the pad with his pen while his gaze bored through me.

He was probably calculating time in his head. The next question would be why I waited until almost noon to call.

"I suggested she call you, but she refused. I think she wanted to see how I'd react. Sort of like taking a test drive. Anyway, I decided if I met with her and listened to her story, then I could persuade her to come to you." I chugged the rest of my water to quench my dry throat. The tension in me rushed back at full throttle.

"I'm guessing you couldn't convince her. What happened?"

"Not exactly." I explained how Sammy never showed. "Makes no sense, does it? I'll admit, I'm sort of worried. She hasn't tried contacting me since her call this morning. And before you ask, my calls to her went straight to voice mail." I shoved both hands under my rear to stop from chewing on my nails or engaging in any other nervous habit wanting to take over. Saying those things out loud deepened my concern.

Barrett's steely glare with its hint of judgment didn't help to calm me. "Maybe she had an emergency and couldn't meet you." His expression softened with the slight upturn of his mouth. "Before I go back to the office, I'll stop by her shop and her house, if need be, to make sure she's okay. How's that sound?"

"Thank you." I stood and scratched behind my ear, puzzling over his gesture of what? Sympathy? Caring? "Um, yeah, that would be nice."

He shrugged and rose from his seat. "I need to check out her story anyway. Just doing my job."

My smile slipped. The detective who was all business and without a trace of empathy resurfaced. Not a big surprise.

I gave a quick glance at my watch and jumped. "Crap. I'm late." I juggled my bag, book, and thermos. "I'm sorry to push you out, but I need to go."

He stepped to the door. "One more question?"

"Sure." I fished for my keys, then remembered I'd left them on the counter. Retracing my steps, I snatched them. "Can we talk while walking?" I gestured toward the door with my chin. "Will you? My hands are full."

He held the door open with his backside. "Have you seen Miss Finch lately? I've been trying to get in touch, but she never returns my calls."

I set down my load and fiddled with the lock while deciding what to say. He might have noticed Gwen leaving our shop. The view of Artisan Alley from the lake was mostly unobstructed. Only a few trees blocked parts of what a boater could see. In any case, there was no point in lying to him, and Gwen would have to deal with him sooner or later.

"I spoke with Theo, the owner of the town *Gazette*." He moved closer.

"Oh?" The lock clicked, and I skipped away from both the door and the strong scents of coconut sunscreen and musky cologne that were rather enticing.

"She had an interesting story to tell about an argument that might move Gwen Finch to the top of my list." He shoved his hands in his pockets.

"Yeah, that Theo. She loves telling stories. Embellishes a bit to make them more entertaining." The top of his list, his suspect list. My stomach curdled. I couldn't help my impulse to protect fragile and broken creatures, like our neighboring shop owner. "All I know is Gwen stopped by earlier to drop off a gift. I think she mentioned meeting someone for dinner." I kept my head down as I inched closer to pick up my things.

"Okay. Thanks. I'll catch up to her sooner or later. You have a good day."

I straightened, hefting the gift, my bag, book, and thermos once again. He hadn't waited for a response. I studied the tan, well-built form of Detective Barrett as he jogged across the lawn and toward Quaint Décor.

"You too, Detective," I whispered with a shrug. No point in expecting he'd call to let me know about Sammy, which was fine because I could learn that information without his help. This was a small town, where most everybody knew what everyone else did.

I made my way across Whisper Cove Boulevard and arrived home, only fifteen minutes late to dinner. Mom would give me the pouty, hurt look then quickly forgive me because that was how she was. I dropped everything in the foyer and power walked down the hall to the kitchen. Max pranced around me while everyone sat at the table, waiting. I had one ace of an excuse up my sleeve and planned to use it. "Sorry. Detective Barrett paid me a visit. I couldn't get away." I scooted my chair closer to the table and spread a napkin across my lap. "How was everyone's day?"

"Well, not as interesting as yours, I bet." Izzie leaned against her chair. "What did Hunter have to say? More accusations about how we killed the victim with a painting knife while munching on barbecue?" She snorted.

"Izzie Abbington. No point in being disrespectful about the authorities," Mom said while passing the green beans to Dad.

"Yeah, stop being such a smart . . ." I caught the other look Mom always gave us and stopped what I intended to say but threw Izzie an impish grin.

"What did he have to say, Shortcake?" Dad forked a slice of seasoned beef off the plate.

"Wow. I can smell the spice from here." I waved a hand in front of my tearing eyes.

"It's the mango powder." Izzie nodded. "Wait until you try some. Yummy."

The scrunch of her nose told me otherwise. "Before I tell you why Detective Barrett came to the shop, I need to give you guys some backstory." I debated on sharing the account of Sammy's dealings with the black market. Instead, I dove straight into her claim she knew who the killer was and wanted us to meet but then never showed up. Obviously, I left out the part about my lake swim with Ross. No good would come of feeding the gossip mill.

"Wow. Do you think she really knows? I mean. I figured she fit under the column of most likely suspects." Izzie pushed away her plate.

"Let's hope so. Then life can return to normal. Izzie, you shouldn't waste food." Mom pointed to the plate.

"Whatever she has to say, she can tell the detective." I pushed the beef to one side of my plate, then took a tiny nibble of the potato dish.

"Maybe I should call her. See if she's okay." Izzie pushed away from the table.

"I doubt you get to answer. I've already tried." I shrugged.

The house phone rang. Dad usually answered. As leader of the neighborhood watch, he was first on the call list whenever there was a problem. "Be right back. Don't eat all of the key lime pie while I'm gone." He winked.

"Can we talk more about Sammy?" Izzie began and gave me a pointed stare. "What do you think she knows? Did she say something on the phone that seemed off?"

"Well—" I stopped when Dad returned to the kitchen.

He rubbed his jaw while standing next to the table.

"Dad? Is everything okay?" I swallowed.

"Detective Barrett. He wants to speak with you, Chloe."

My heartbeat raced while I hurried across the room. "Maybe he spoke to Sammy and wants to let us know she's okay." There. I'd shoot for one of those happy endings Izzie talked about.

I reached the living room. My hand hovered, then I picked up the receiver. "Hi, Detective."

"Chloe. I followed up on what you told me. Sammy isn't at her shop or at home. In fact, no one—not her neighbors or anyone on Artisan Alley—has seen her since early this morning."

"Oh." I dragged out the moment, sorting out what he'd told me and searching for what it meant. "She's missing then?"

"I don't know yet, but Sammy's next-door neighbor, Nell Simpson, saw her leave the house. She wasn't alone."

I tensed. If this had anything to do with Infinity and those thugs Sammy did business with, my hunch was Detective Barrett had more to worry about than a missing person's case.

"The odd part of Miss Simpson's story is her description of the woman leaving with Sammy. Shorter than average, curvy figure, dark hair cut above the shoulders. Sound familiar to you?"

I ran my tongue over my lip. His words stabbed me like daggers, quick and sharp.

"Chloe, did you have anything to do with Sammy disappearing?"

Chapter Ten

I snuggled under the throw blanket and stared at the lake from the front porch. The sun's crescent-shaped form peeked above the horizon, changing from a pale, ghostly yellow to a bolder shade as it inched upward. I squinted, narrowing my eyes to concentrate on the scene. Like one of those slow television broadcasts from Norway where viewers watched an ordinary event for hours, I could sit here all day until sunset. Maybe that was what I'd do. Anything to avoid my reality. If only the phone conversation I'd had with Detective Barrett would stop playing in my head.

At first, I thought I had a chance to avoid blame, to cry foul. I didn't have anything to do with Sammy's disappearance. The person fitting my description wasn't me. However, when he informed me that Penny claimed I was snooping around Quaint Décor, peeking in the window, sneaking around back, I knew how my behavior looked. After that, I caved. My confession about knowing Sammy's business arrangement with Infinity only made things worse. Without seeing his face, I cringed, imagining that steely-eyed, accusatory stare. My goose was more than cooked. The bird was on fire.

I wasn't worried about myself, though. My problems would get sorted out. I had faith in that outcome. What churned my insides and weighted my heart with guilt was Sammy. If only I'd gone to Detective Barrett right away, but I hadn't. I needed to own up to that mistake. He agreed to follow the trail of bread crumbs of Sammy's whereabouts by talking to the people at Infinity. I was grateful, but my worries would linger until Sammy returned safely home. I shivered and pulled the blanket to my chin. Safe *and* unharmed.

Despite the tailspin of events putting me in a funk, there was an ironic twist to the situation that almost made me laugh. Ross, in a roundabout way, was the only one who could back up my story. Of course, Detective Barrett planned on talking to him. Ross would love to help, which meant I'd be indebted to him. He'd love that part even more. Yep. I should've called Detective Barrett at the first sign of Sammy's troubles.

"I thought you might need this." Izzie handed me a mug of tea, then sat in the wicker chair close to mine.

"Thank you." I sniffed and worked my mouth into a smile.

"Just so you know, I called Hunter and scolded him for even suggesting you had anything to do with Sammy's disappearance." She slid her sunglasses down an inch and glanced at me. "You didn't, did you?"

"Oh, for—really, Izzie?" I set the mug on the floor and buried myself deeper in the blanket.

"I'm sorry." She stroked my arm. "I had to ask. You haven't said a word since you woke up this morning, and last night was kind of a confusing ramble of he-said-you-said summary of your phone conversation." Her eyes narrowed. "Hunter told me about his talk with Sammy's neighbor. Why didn't you tell us?"

"I don't know who Nell Simpson saw, but it wasn't me, which is why I didn't mention it. Look, you shouldn't worry about Sammy or me. You have this evening's event to think about."

Mom and Dad had already doled out more than enough sympathy and concern. I couldn't handle Izzie's too.

"Which is exactly what you should be doing." She smacked her thighs. "I'm keeping the shop closed until later this afternoon. Why don't you come with me to Buffalo? Call it a sister bonding opportunity. What do you say?" She wiggled her brows.

I fiddled with the fringe of the blanket and gave the sunrise another glimpse. "Rain check? I need some alone time to think. Maybe I'll go for a walk along the lake."

"Whatever makes you happy makes me happy, big sister." She rose from the chair and stretched, then twisted side to side. "Beautiful day for a walk. You enjoy, and I'll see you when I get back." She ruffled my hair. "Maybe comb out this tangled mess of bed hair, first? Don't want to scare the neighbors."

"Ha. Little sis makes a joke." Despite my downer mood, I grinned.

Her pep talk was extra special since underneath that happy, confident demeanor was a nervous, terrified little girl who worried about all things, all the time. Izzie was trying her best for me. I could do the same for her.

I threw off the blanket and pushed out of my seat. With an eye roll, I pulled on a fistful of hair. "In some parts of the world, this is a fashionable look."

"Where exactly?" She tickled her chin with her fingers. "I so want to go there. Do you think they'd style mine?"

I poked her in the side. "I'll make you a special appointment. Now, go fetch those paint colors, Miss Izzie. Daylight's ticking away."

She kicked her heels and patted her rear as she hurried inside. "Giddy up!"

I laughed. "Goofball." I folded the blanket and tucked it under one arm. After a quick shower, I'd take the back stairs and sneak out before anyone noticed. I loved Mom and Dad and all their caring and concern, but I needed a break. I'd go for a walk in town, grab a bagel and coffee from For Sweet's Sake, and then sit beside the lake to enjoy my breakfast.

*　*　*

Claire's bagel shop sat in the center of town. The envy of most shop owners, this location reaped the rewards of continuous foot traffic and a cash register that was always full. No doubt, Claire had enough tucked away in her bank account and mutual funds to take an early retirement, but she loved her job and swore to keep the place running forever. Though the claim was an exaggeration, I had to love her spirit.

I stood on the sidewalk, admiring the white and coral exterior. The windows dressed with scalloped canopies were a throwback to an era that favored natural shade over air-conditioning. The scents of dough baking and coffee brewing filled me as I sniffed the air, then hurried inside.

"Hi, Claire." I waved.

The whirring drone of the dough mixer and the ding of the oven timer welcomed me, along with the baker's wide grin.

"Why Chloe Abbington, I heard the rumor you were back in town. Come on and show this girl some love." Her brown eyes sparkled as she wiggled her fingers and scurried around the showcase. Her skin, the shade of chocolate, glistened with sweat from the kitchen heat. Her muscular arms hinted at days spent kneading dough and lifting heavy trays of bagels and donuts. She brought me in for a hug, then planted a kiss on my cheek.

I managed to break loose. "Always great to see you. I would have dropped by sooner, but things got a little crazy right after I arrived."

The deep-throated laughter broke as her shoulders and chest quaked. "A little? More like a tidal wave hit the shores of Whisper Cove. How you holding up?"

I teetered my head. "As well as anyone who finds a body with a knife sticking out of her neck." My eyes widened. "I can't believe I said that out loud."

"Speak your mind, I always say. Truth doesn't waste folks' time." She tucked a stray lock of hair under her hairnet. "Not to shovel more dirt on anyone's grave, but that woman had venom on her tongue whenever she opened her mouth to speak or scribbled a word in that column of hers. I still have the bite marks from the time she put a target on my shop." Claire wiggled her shoulders. "Maybe it's not respectful to speak this way about the dead, but respect goes both ways."

Thinking about truth and Fiona's death steered my attention to Sammy again. "I don't suppose you've seen Sammy lately?"

Claire puckered her lips. "Can't say I have. Which is odd, come to think of it."

My brow inched higher. "How so?"

"Sammy stops by every Thursday morning for coffee and her usual asiago cheese bagel. We chat for a while about our respective high school days on the track team. We might've graduated a couple of decades apart, but things haven't changed much, only the coach and the uniform. Lots of great laughs and stories."

The timer dinged again.

"Hold on." She skirted around the counter and to the kitchen. After a minute, she reappeared, carrying a huge tray with mitted hands. "Why you asking?"

"Oh my. Those smell so delicious. I'll take one of those blueberry bagels and a large coffee with cream to go." Not wanting to start rumors, I made a quick decision to explain as little as possible. "I was supposed to meet with her yesterday, but she never showed. Guess maybe she had something more important to do."

Claire set a bagged bagel and the coffee on the counter. "She's a sweet lady. Always comes in with a smile and some kind words to say. I'm sure she'll give you a call when she can."

I handed her money for my breakfast purchase. I thought of Sammy that way too. All the more reason to worry about where she'd gone and why. Even more puzzling, who was the woman with her that looked like my twin? Was the neighbor a reliable witness? Maybe she wore glasses and without them couldn't see clearly more than five feet in front of her.

After exchanging goodbyes, I retraced my steps to head for the lake. Sammy might have skipped her weekly cheese bagel because she was distracted by thoughts of who had killed Fiona or because we'd arranged to meet that morning. I gave myself a mental scolding for overthinking the situation.

This morning was for relaxing and getting my chi back, as my yoga instructor would say, then maybe I could think rationally about Sammy.

I chose the perfect spot underneath a shady oak and sat cross-legged, facing the lake. As if the rustle of my paper bag was a cue a feast was coming, a goose waddled closer. I picked off a few pieces of bagel and scattered them across the lawn. Three more birds scurried on webbed feet, pecking at the ground to gobble up the treats. I laughed, then waved an arm to shoo them away.

In less than twelve hours, Izzie, Willow, and I would be greeting guests for the shop's grand opening. We were beyond prepared. The list of supplies we needed had been counted and checked off numerous times. We had divided the program tasks among us and rehearsed from step one to the last. The only way this evening could go wrong would be if a storm knocked out the power or some other act of nature plagued us. We were ready, and I knew I shouldn't be nervous.

I stood and walked to the trash canister and tossed in my bag and empty cup. Izzie would argue the cause of my behavior was Ross. She was wrong. The one who worried me was Detective Barrett. I had my doubts he would be attending the event for the entertainment of painting a lighthouse. If I had money to gamble, which I didn't, I'd swear his agenda for this evening was to check out the crowd for plausible suspects.

I picked up the strap of my bag and marched along the lake and away from Artisan Alley. "He's such a tool. Nothing like making our customers feel unwelcome. They'll probably never come to another paint event. Such a pain in the— Oh!" I clutched my throat and nearly collided with a large dog who, by now, had planted his front paws on my chest while licking my face.

"Sorry! Major is just excited to meet someone on our walk. He really loves the ladies."

I managed to unlock Major's paws from my chest and petted the top of his head. Glancing ahead, I spotted someone familiar jogging in our direction. Blond curly hair and six plus feet of handsome. This was the Greek god I'd run into a few days ago near Sammy's shop. At once, I straightened and used both hands to smooth the loose strands of my wind-blown hair. I hadn't bothered with anything but shampoo and soap when I had gotten ready this morning. Not even a dab of makeup. Well, the fresh and natural look was in style. Yeah, I could go with that.

"Thanks for not freaking out. Major and I appreciate it." He smiled while clipping a leash on the dog's collar. "You a dog lover?"

"Little ones." I gestured by holding my hand a few inches off the ground, then rushed to add, "Big ones are nice too."

His forehead creased. "Have we met? You look so familiar." He whistled. "Boy, did that ever sound like a pickup line. Sorry."

Heat warmed my face with embarrassment. "Now that you mention it, I think we might have. Maybe along the alley? I was shopping there with my sister, Izzie, the other day." I twisted the hem of my shirt. Being coy was definitely not one of my talents.

He snapped his fingers. "The Abbington sisters! You're Chloe."

"Yep. That's me. Are you staying in Whisper Cove?"

"For the summer." He pointed behind him. "A friend offered accommodations at his condo while I finish a sculpting project. How about you?" He stroked the top of Major's head.

"I live here. At least for the time being. I'm readjusting to small-town life after two years in New York."

"Well, seems we have something in common. I have a place in New York and spend as much time as I can there. Say, how about we do dinner one night? Or go out for drinks? We can talk about big city life. People say I'm great company, and you can count on me to make you laugh. I know lots of jokes. Tons." He clasped his hands together in front of him.

I laughed. "Are you sure Major won't be jealous? Leaving him alone while you take someone out for dinner or a drink is a bold move."

"As long as I bring him the leftovers, he's happy. What do you say? Tomorrow evening?"

I shook my head. "Maybe after I get settled. Right now, I have lots to do. I'm helping Izzie launch her new business." I struggled to believe he was a lurker or a creep, as Izzie and Megan thought of him, but living in New York had branded me with a cautious, wait-and-learn attitude.

He let out a sigh and laid one hand over his chest. "You break my heart, Chloe Abbington. I'll tell you what. I'm planning a beach cookout next week for the folks of Whisper Cove. My way of getting to know the locals. I want you to come. Bring your sister. Bring your whole family! Please say you'll be there."

"I'll think about it."

"You will?"

"Yeah." I pointed behind me. "I should go. We're having our opening event this evening at Paint with a View. It's a joint venture with the committee to raise money for the lighthouse. We were planning to have Paint Your Pet as our launch, but things got complicated and we had to reschedule it for next week and—" I shook my head. "Listen to me. I'm sure you have no interest in the details of what we paint."

"Not at all. In fact, the pet painting sounds like fun." He rubbed Major's fur. "Count me in."

I gave a thumbs-up. "Sure. Okay. See you around, Grayson."

"Ha. You do remember." He grinned.

I waved as I walked back toward the shop. With a bounce in my step, I hummed a tune. Whether I was interested or not in Grayson Stone, his flirting made me smile and renewed my confidence I was someone worth a man's attention. Ross could take a few lessons from the Greek god.

Passing by Quaint Décor, I slowed to take a quick glance, maybe hoping to see lights and Sammy's familiar profile. My shoulders dropped. The darkened windows were depressing and pricked my balloon of optimism. The longer she was missing, the more worried I'd become. Detective Barrett and I had talked about what might have contributed to her disappearance—her claim she knew Fiona's killer and her business dealings with the black market. Right now, one other reason popped into my head, which brought me right back to where I started. What if Sammy had killed Fiona and was worried the authorities were close to arresting her? Izzie's comments probably hadn't helped put her at ease. Nor had all the accusing looks from people in town. That kind of pressure could've pushed her panic button, so she decided running was her best chance.

I jumped at the blare of a car horn and snapped my head around. Without realizing it, I'd reached the intersection of Whisper Cove Boulevard and Sail Shore Drive and nearly stepped into oncoming traffic. I shaded my eyes from the sun and watched the light turn from red to green. Only one thing stood in Sammy's way. She'd never abandon her dad. Nothing, not even the threat of being arrested for murder would drive her away when she knew he needed her help.

I walked along the front sidewalk and entered the house. Sammy's dad was the key, the catalyst that dictated her every move. "That's it!" I snapped my fingers and ran straight into Izzie. "Lord. You scared the heck out of me." I skipped backward.

Izzie took a bite out of her apple. "Aren't you the jumpy one? I thought you were having a relaxing walk on the beach to calm your nerves. Doesn't seem to be working."

"Sorry. I can't seem to turn off my brain. Not when it comes to Sammy." I tipped my head. "You're back already?"

"Yeah. After picking up the order—that store is fantastic, by the way—I decided to skip brunch and head home." She stuck out her bottom lip. "Since my big sis deserted me."

I sucked on my tongue and jabbed her with my finger. "The restaurant was closed, wasn't it?"

"Yeah." She winked. "For remodeling." She sat on the foyer bench and patted the empty spot next to her. "What's your brain telling you about Sammy?"

I slid next to her. "I can't think of a possible reason why she'd leave and abandon her dad when he needs her."

"Unless she didn't go willingly. If she knows who killed Fiona, the killer might know she knows. You know?"

I blinked. "Somehow, I understood that, but I'm trying not to think in those terms. Let's put that scary scenario aside."

"Okay, but then what? She left because . . ." Izzie counted on her fingers. "One, she's scared the killer will find out she planned to tell the authorities. Two, she's running from the black-market goons who've threatened to bury her six feet in the ground. Or three, she's the killer and is running to escape arrest."

"I've hit a snag with that last one. Her dad is in jail and needs her help. She can't do anything if she's behind bars."

"Exactly!" Izzie bounced off the seat. "Sammy ran away to keep from being arrested because she doesn't have to be nearby to help dear old jailbird dad. Assistance is only a phone call away, and who needs in-person visits when there's Zoom? Or Skype. Or Google Hangouts. Or . . . you get what I mean."

I screwed up my face. "You're so determined to be right."

"About Sammy as the killer?" She lifted her chin. "When you're right, you're right."

"Geesh." I plucked at my shirt and sniffed underneath. I smelled of dog slobber and sweat. "Okay, I'm taking another shower before lunch. You can share more of your infinite wisdom at the table." I climbed the stairs.

"Sarcasm and jealousy are not attractive." Izzie called after me.

"Got it." I waved an arm and retreated to my room.

*　*　*

"This place is fantastic. I wish I'd thought of the idea first." Joanna Bixby, our next-door neighbor and one of Mom's best friends, winked. "You know I'm kidding. I'll stick to my little knitting projects."

"Are you serious?" I asked. "You're the Etsy queen of craft sales. Why, Izzie told me she overheard some customers at the art supply store in Buffalo talking about you. You, Joanna, are a national celebrity."

"You're embarrassing me." Joanna blushed and patted her perfectly coifed hair. "I'm sure that's an exaggeration." As if giving the notion some thought, she chewed on her fingernail. "Did they really say my name?"

I raised three fingers on my right hand. "Scout's honor."

Paint with a View was bustling with people and chatter. Izzie played the perfect host while Willow hurried from station to station repositioning materials and giving the big screen a final check to make sure it worked. Nothing was left to chance. We were ready to go. While Izzie and I teamed up as instructors, Willow's job this evening was to circulate among guests, offer help with their projects, and refill paint palettes.

Charlie Wales, leader of the committee to save the lighthouse, circulated to shake hands with guests. Animated and glowing, she laughed and rattled on about Whisper Cove's history and the importance of preserving the lighthouse. At seventy and, despite her tiny size, she still ran on full steam, keeping up with most anyone half her age.

I got the nod from Izzie and weaved a path toward the stage. I tossed my emotions from sad to relieved then over again as I hadn't spotted Ross. He had either bailed or found something better to do, like taking another swim in the lake. I covered my smile with one hand at the thought. Even the local detective was nowhere in sight.

Izzie flashed the lights to grab everyone's attention. "Hi, everyone. Thank you for attending this evening. My name is Izzie Abbington and this is my sister, Chloe Abbington. I recognize several of you from town—fellow shop owners, neighbors, and a couple of friends. We really appreciate your love and support. You being here means everything. For those guests who are strangers, our parents have lived in Whisper Cove for years, decades actually. We come from a long line of artists, several generations of painters, sculptors, and, if we go back far enough, there was a blacksmith who made metal art in his spare time. Or so Chloe and I have been told."

I laughed, along with others, at the mention of our great-great-great-uncle who had lived in Vermont and, at the age of fifty, gave up his smithy shop to spend the remainder of his life doing what he loved. The story grew more romantic with every telling. Dad had a true gift of gab.

My breath caught and I choked on a laugh as Ross and Detective Barrett walked into the shop together. I clutched my paintbrush. Both were smiling. No stern faces or finger jabbing or shouts, which was a relief. Two men having what looked like a pleasant conversation. I scowled. That bothered me even more. I didn't want Ross to be chummy with the detective. In fact, the safer choice was for them not to talk to one another.

"Psst." Izzie jabbed me in the side, then raised her voice. "Chloe, would you like to say something to our guests?"

"Yeah, sure." My gaze shifted from the stations where everyone sat to the front door where a best bro bond was being formed that I couldn't stop. "Welcome. Have a great time. Holler if you need help." I glanced at Izzie before stepping off the stage. "Take over, will you? I'll be just a minute." I ignored the grumbles annunciated with plenty of colorful adjectives followed by the squeak of a hiccup.

"Okay then. Painting a lighthouse. We're going to start by outlining with our pencils," Izzie instructed.

I whipped through the center aisle toward the two men, hoping the conversation, particularly what Ross had to say, hadn't gotten too personal. When it came to sensitive topics, like breakups, Ross would talk to anyone who'd listen and share every detail. I hardly knew Detective Barrett, but if my fear was real, he was learning a lot about me.

I skidded to a stop and attempted a casual posture, as if that was possible. "Hey, you guys. You came."

"Wouldn't miss the grand opening of my girlfriend's business," Ross said.

I sucked in air. "Not right on either count, but moving on. Detective Barrett. How are you?" I nodded.

"Same as I was when we talked less than twenty-four hours ago." He tipped his chin. "Nice place. Good turnout."

"Yes, and you should both take your seats." I turned. "Ross, you're at this end. Detective, you'll find an open spot up front near Izzie." Satisfied I'd put out the fire of Ross revealing my soap-opera life to Barrett, I worked my way back to the stage.

"Rinse your brushes thoroughly and wipe them dry with the paper towel. You'll be using the white paint next." Izzie cupped one hand around her mouth. "You take over the next step, will you? The sky and water background shouldn't take long. I'm going to sneak outside for some fresh air."

"Sure thing, boss." I saluted.

"Goof." Izzie hopped off the stage and walked out of the shop.

"Now, let's put a dab of white on our brushes, then add a tiny amount of blue. Using wavy strokes, fill in the bottom third of your canvas."

I concentrated while adding water and waves to my canvas, ignoring the low rumble of conversation coming from the front of the room. My gaze strayed, and I nearly dropped the brush. Detective Barrett leaned over to speak with Joanna Bixby, and, from her frown, she didn't appear to be overjoyed by whatever he had to say. I laid my brush in the tray, then inched toward the edge of the stage. Giving the situation no more thought, I stepped into the aisle. "Willow and I are going to circulate around the room. If any of you have questions, raise your hand."

I made a straight line to Detective Barrett's station. "Detective, is there a problem? You haven't added anything to your canvas." I clucked my tongue like my third-grade art teacher would have done to show disapproval.

Barrett straightened. "Sorry, Miss Abbington. I was distracted." His smirky grin hinted he wasn't sorry.

"If you don't keep up with the instruction, I can't be responsible for the results." I spoke through gritted teeth, but Joanna's relaxed expression gave me a sense of victory.

He gestured with fingers touching his forehead to salute. "No problem. You've got my complete attention."

That was even worse. I dropped the teacher act and moved around him to lean over Joanna's shoulder. "Sorry, he won't bother you again."

"It's okay. He's just trying to do his job," Joanna whispered close to my ear.

I patted her arm and scowled at Detective Barrett, then returned to the stage. "Now, when you've finished, I want you to rinse your brushes and—"

Izzie broke through the doorway, clutching her chest. "There's—oh, my God. There's a fire." Her words came in sketchy breaths followed by a series of hiccups. "Sammy's shop. It's, it's, oh my." She plopped down in the closest chair.

As if an alarm went off, everyone got up and stampeded toward the door. I shoved my way through and straight to Izzie. "What happened? Are you hurt?" My hands traveled up and down her face, shoulders, and arms.

She wobbled her head and sobbed. "I'm fine. It's just . . ." Her chest heaved. "Sammy's shop is on fire. I heard the sirens and followed the sound. The firefighters are there now." She gripped my arms. "Chloe, what if Sammy is inside? What if she dies?"

I shook my head. "Stop. She left town. Remember?" My brain worked to keep me from panicking, but thoughts of black-market thugs and knife-toting killers pushed their way in, and I worried right along with Izzie. What if Sammy *was* inside?

Chapter Eleven

Smoke rose from the roof of Quaint Décor, but the backdrop of an inky sky made the trail barely noticeable. The smell that teared my eyes and the crackling flames, though, told the story. I stood next to Izzie, several yards away from the sight. Detective Barrett had gone to assist in whatever way possible. Ross joined him. The scene left me both sad and terrified. Firefighters hosed the roof while others broke the front window glass to search inside. I shuddered at the thought of what they might find. Or who.

"Is that Penny?" Izzie pointed to a spot directly in front of her shop, The Healing Touch. "And is Hunter right next to her?"

I blinked to relieve the sting in my eyes. Penny stood with her arms tightly crossed while shaking her head. Izzie was right. The detective stood next to the shop owner. In the next instant, he walked away. After a brief pause to say something to one of the firefighters, he headed our way. I could see beyond him as men came out of Quaint Décor. My knees weakened. They weren't carrying a gurney or a body bag, thank goodness.

"I'm heading back to the office. Everything's under control here, and I need to file a report." He paused. "Thank you for inviting me to your event. Sorry things didn't go like you planned."

I bypassed the pleasantries and zoned in on one tiny detail. "File a report? Why do you need to file a report?"

"Well, seems the men found traces of a flammable liquid, and rags soaked in kerosene were left by the door."

My heartbeat skipped. "The fire wasn't an accident." I played connect the facts, and it took me down a path I didn't care to go down. My head shot up and my eyes widened to stare at Detective Barrett.

His look told me he was thinking the same thing.

"Oh wow. Do you think the guys from Infinity did this?" Izzie's voice squeaked.

I bit my lip. Make that three minds thinking alike.

"Until I have the evidence to prove it, I can't say." Barrett stroked his jaw. "Just in case, I'll ask the sheriff to have a couple of his deputies patrol the alley. If this was the work of an arsonist, he or she might return and set fire to more shops."

Izzie hiccupped. "I think I'm going to be sick."

I wrapped my arm around her waist while shooting Detective Barrett a steely glare. Even if it was unintentional, his suggestion about a crazy arsonist had set off Izzie's panic button. "Let's go close up the shop. I doubt anyone will come back to finish their paintings this evening."

"The paintings!" Izzie dug her nails into my arm.

I winced and detached her fingers, one by one. "Don't worry. We can email the guests and reschedule the event. You'll see. Everything will be fine."

"Chloe's right. Safer to close up shop and go home," Detective Barrett said.

"Yep. That's where we'll be as soon as possible. Come on, Izzie." I tugged at her sleeve to hurry away. "Thanks, Detective. You've been a big help," I called out as we gained distance. If we'd stayed another minute, no telling what else he'd have said. "Stick the other foot in his mouth, no doubt."

"What was that?" Izzie stepped onto the walkway in front of the shop.

"Nothing. Let's clean up and get out of here. I'm tired and need a bath to cool down." I threw open the door.

"Wow. Would you look at this? You're an angel. Thank you." Izzie smiled.

Willow stood behind the counter. She'd collected all the used supplies and cleaned the stations. The unfinished canvases were placed along the walls to dry. Each one had an attached sticky note with the name of the guest artist. "Just thought I'd get a head start on clean-up rather than wait for you to come back. Is everything okay? I mean, is Sammy's store all right?" She paused from wiping the counter, and her face wrinkled with concern.

"They put out the fire before the place burned to the ground. I don't know for sure, but my guess is everything inside is toast." Izzie flopped down in a chair.

"She's right. We don't know. We don't really know much of anything." I picked a dropped paper towel off the floor and tossed it in the trash can. "Looks like you've done a great job. We owe you." I smiled at Willow, who shrugged.

"Okay, then. Let's lock up and go home." Izzie paused to glance at her phone that lay on the counter.

"It rang once while you guys were outside," Willow said. "Beeped, too. Maybe whoever called left a message."

"Probably Mom or Dad. I'm sure by now the whole town has heard about the fire." Izzie talked while she held the phone to her ear. Seconds passed before she pressed another key and made a call.

"Izzie should pay you extra for all the cleaning." I scanned the shop. Everything had been put back in its place and even the floor shined.

"Just doing my job." Willow shoved the mop and bucket behind the counter. Turning, she grinned. "Guess I'll be going. See you tomorrow? A few of the guests stopped back to ask when we plan to reschedule. I can help send out email notices, if you like."

"Sure. We can talk about that tomorrow. Meet here at nine?"

"Sounds perfect." She grabbed her bag and waved as she ducked outside.

"I can meet you tomorrow morning around eight . . . Not a problem. You have a good evening." Izzie opened her bag and exchanged phone for keys, then swung around. "You ready?"

"Yeah, let me get my things from the back." I made the trip to the storage room, then quickly returned to the front. "So, you're meeting someone tomorrow morning?" I kept my voice even. "I thought we'd come here to talk about rescheduling the event and other shop stuff."

Izzie flipped the light switch. "I won't be long. We'll have plenty of time to talk shop."

Her eyes shined a little too brightly. I recognized the sign all too well. Call her Pinocchio and her nose would grow any second now. I bit down on my thumbnail. I didn't want to intrude. She had a life and a right to keep a personal agenda, but secret meetings twice in one week? I shivered, not wanting to think about what had happened the last time. The secrets and sneaking around were killing me with curiosity, though. I opened my mouth to ask more, but my phone rang. I groaned and stabbed the button to answer. "Hi, Mom."

"Well, don't sound so crabby. I wanted to make sure you and your sister are okay. We heard about the fire . . ." Her voice trailed off.

"I'm sure everyone's heard about the fire. We're fine, Mom. Be home in few minutes. Bye."

"That sounded rude." Izzie pulled open the door and stepped outside.

"Sorry. Too long a day that ended badly." I followed her to where we'd parked. Scanning the area, I spotted two men in uniform. Detective Barrett had been true to his word.

"You think Bob's is still open?" Izzie popped open the car door.

"Seriously?" I slid into the passenger seat. "It's nearly nine thirty. Your stomach is already queasy from all the excitement, and you want to add spicy barbecue to your digestive system? Unbelievable." I gave her a disapproving *tsk-tsk*, along with a sharp head shake.

Her brow puckered. "Yeah, but dinner was awful. I hardly ate, and right now barbecue with a side of—" She wagged her finger. "You. You are so mean."

I laughed. "I'll take a sandwich with extra sauce and a double order of cheesy fries, please."

Izzie started the engine and turned up the stereo. "Bob's, here we come!"

I lowered the window and stuck out my head. The evening breeze off the lake cooled the air, and a soft scent of pine mixed slightly with the smoky odor drifting from Quaint Décor. We were both making an effort to *not* think about what had happened this evening and the reasons why. Sammy was out there, somewhere, and right now, the best we could do was pray she was safe and be grateful no one had been hurt.

*   *   *

"See you at dinner," I called out to Mom from the foyer while juggling my bag and thermos of coffee. After waking up late this morning, I had opted for a shower and skipped breakfast, which was a plus since table conversation with Mom and Dad would involve reasons why I should reconsider my relationship with Ross and show him there were no hard feelings by doubling down on the invitation to dinner—he'd obviously made a great impression on Mom—or why Izzie and I should stay clear of Artisan Alley and the shop until the alleged arsonist was caught. Emphasis on the word alleged. Neither topic was appetizing. My plan to recover from the disturbing events of last night was to work, keep busy doing shop things, and avoid topics like Ross, arsonists, and murder.

"Wait!" Mom's flowered skirt billowed as she ran down the hall, waving a plastic container. "I made blueberry muffins with walnuts. Take them, since you don't want to have breakfast with us." Her lips turned down.

"I want to, but I don't have time to. Thanks." I stood on tiptoes and planted a kiss on her cheek. "You're the sweetest, kindest mom in all the world."

She smoothed the hem of my shirt. "Chloe, please be careful. You know your dad and I don't like to tell you girls what to do, but we worry."

I shuffled my feet in reverse, putting my hand behind me to find the doorknob. "Yes, and you do a great job worrying. I mean, caring about us. Bye." I finger waved, hopped outside, and closed the door. My chest collapsed as I released my breath, then hurried to my car. "That was close."

Tires squealed as I sped down the drive and onto the road. Izzie had left before I got up and placed a sticky note on my bedroom door. *Be back by ten or eleven.* That was all. Six words of practically nothing. Cavemen could express themselves better. Still, I had made that promise to not be the nosy, patronizing big sister, and I wouldn't break it. No matter how hard that promise was to keep. I triggered the windshield wipers to clear the fine mist. Clouds darkened the sky and predicted a gray and dreary day with intermittent showers. After a week of sun and heat, this would be a welcome reprieve.

The parking area, which was mostly grass and dirt, had turned into a muddy mess. Pulling my jacket over the top of my head, I tiptoed around puddles and reached the front of the shop. Willow stood in the open doorway, arms and ankles crossed as she stared at the lake. Seeing me, she waved and retreated inside.

I clutched my gear to my chest and followed her. "Morning. Izzie won't be in until ten or eleven, at the latest, so we're on our own." I dropped my bag in the closest chair, then sat on a stool to eat and drink. "You want one?" I mumbled and held up one of the three muffins Mom packed.

"No thanks. I had my morning dose of greasy food from Spill the Beans. Fried egg, undercooked bacon, and biscuits. Yum." She ran her tongue along her lips, then laughed.

At once, I felt grateful for the doting parent who baked. "In case you change your mind, I'll leave this on the counter." I slid the container to the side and picked up my thermos to pour into my favorite mug. Etched on the front were the words "I paint. What's your superpower?"

"I guess we could start with those emails. Do we know the schedule for events beyond next week?" As she sat next to me, Willow pulled up a window on the laptop.

"I have no idea. Izzie left before I got up this morning, and we didn't get a chance to discuss it last night." I sipped my coffee. "Maybe we start with something else on our list and wait until Izzie gets back to send the emails."

Willow tapped the screen to close the window. "What about the flyers for Beach Fireworks and Paint Your Pet? I picked them up yesterday from the office supply store. All the information is posted on our website, but we should get these flyers out ASAP. After all, the fireworks party event is Monday, and Paint Your Pet is only a couple of days after that. Each shop owner in town could take a few and hand them out to customers. How's that sound?"

"Love your enthusiasm." I smiled.

"I'm volunteering." She hopped off the stool. "I have an errand to run on the other side of town. I can start handing out the flyers there and work my way back here. Plus, this way I can get both tasks done."

"Perfect." I shifted my gaze side to side. The front room was spotless and organized. "Maybe I'll head to the storage room and inventory supplies." I stiffened and my stomach lurched. Sooner or later, I'd have to get comfortable working back there. Not yet, but eventually.

"Already done. I made a list." She patted a folded piece of paper sticking out of her pocket. "I got us a great deal on canvases. An order of fifty at half the price. That order should arrive in a couple of days. Not much else. Some paper products and more turpentine. We never got the second part of our order from the distributor in Jamestown, but I can stop by the general store and pick up enough to cover the beach fireworks event. Just in case, you know."

"You are amazing." I smiled. Relief washed over me. I could put off facing my fears a bit longer. In this situation, procrastinating hadn't hurt.

"Not really. Doing my job, is all." She blushed and grabbed her keys and bag.

"No, seriously." I pointed to the ceiling. "It's like Izzie called for an angel, and here you are."

"Well, this angel needs to deliver flyers." She flapped the thick stack at me. "Be back in an hour or less."

"No hurry. I'll just sit here reading this cheesy romance novel since you've left nothing for me to do," I called after her and got a dismissive arm wave in return.

I tapped my thighs and scanned the room once again. Willow had even painted the fireworks scene—three canvases in three different stages, and, as with the lighthouse, she'd added sticky notes. I couldn't compete, but there had to be something I could do. Wasn't that why I'd come here? Work. Keep busy. Avoid troubling and disturbing thoughts. I took a straight path across the room to the stage. Grabbing a couple of blank canvases from the stack and some sketch pencils, I sat at the nearest station. I'd checked online and three people had signed up and responded to the website post. They'd emailed headshot photos of their pets. We limited attendance to fifteen guests, since this event involved individual instruction. Sketching each headshot took time. We had four days to finish them, and, most likely, the majority of those signing up would email their pet photos the day before.

I tapped my phone and pulled up our business email account, then printed off the first pet shot. The printer whirred and spit out paper. I examined the image and grunted approval. I hummed while sketching a cute cocker spaniel on the canvas.

The jingle of the front door chimes barely registered in my brain. Artwork drew me in, as if my body had traveled someplace far away. Izzie always said she envied me that concentration.

The tap on my shoulder, however, startled me and brought me back to the shop. "Oh! I didn't hear you come in." I set the pencil aside and stepped away from the station. "Detective Barrett, what brings you here? Catch any criminals lately? That would certainly put my mind at ease." Maybe a tiny bit of sarcasm colored my tone, but I managed to stop a smirky grin to go along with it.

He stood with arms crossed. Not even a hint on his face showed my words bothered him.

"Sorry to interrupt." He nodded at the canvas sketch. "I do have some news. The forensics team finished their toxicology report on Fiona. No drugs were in her system, which rules out an attempt to poison her."

Now, the smirk rose to the surface. "Figured the knife in her neck would've given them that conclusion."

His expression didn't change. "More importantly, your blood type didn't show up on any of the samples. Neither did your fingerprints."

"Huh. Imagine that." I erased a smudge mark on the canvas then looked up. "That goes for Izzie, too?"

"Absolutely. Of course, the lack of prints or blood matches doesn't mean everything in a case."

"Mmhmm." I clenched my jaw and counted to ten, refusing to say words I'd regret later. "Would you like something to drink? Water? Tea?"

"Not right now." His face softened as he leaned against the table of the station next to me.

My brows arched. "Is there something else?"

"I spoke with your Ross."

"He's not *my* Ross." I grabbed the pencil and turned my attention back to the sketch. I outlined the nose and mouth. "What about him?"

"He confirmed your story about the visit to Sammy's shop and about her trouble with Infinity."

"Gee. Just like I told you." I scribbled the pet owner's name on a sticky note and slapped it on the canvas, then plopped down in the chair. Too much had happened in the past twenty-four hours. My nerves had splintered and frayed, making this conversation difficult to handle. "Why do you insist on thinking I'm lying to you?"

"A certain amount, or let's say, a lot of distrust comes with the job." He tilted his head. "Sorry if that offends you. It's nothing personal."

My eyes widened. I leaned back. "How can this not be personal? You think I'm a murder suspect. Me. Can't get more personal than that."

He held up both hands. "It's part of doing my job. I look at everyone as a possible suspect."

I snorted. "Even your mother? How about your wife? Is she a possible suspect too?"

His lips narrowed. "My mother lives in California, and I don't have a wife. So, no on both counts. Are you always this confrontational? I know Ross said you can be at times, but I figured he was exaggerating."

My heart hammered against my chest, and my face flamed with heat. "You discussed personal stuff about me with Ross? What is wrong with you?" The chair scraped across the floor as I pushed it away.

"I asked him to confirm what you'd told me. So yes, we talked about you. It's not my fault he wanted to go on and on about your relationship." He scratched behind one ear. "He's a real chatterbox, isn't he?"

I calmed a bit and sniffed. "Yeah, he is. That doesn't mean you should listen. My personal life isn't part of this investigation."

"You're right. I'm an idiot." He raked fingers through his hair.

I wiggled a finger at him while keeping a smile from showing. "Why, Detective Barrett, I think this is the first time we agree on something."

"I guess you're right." He shrugged an apology. "Do you think you could drop the detective title and call me Hunter? Your sister does, and she hates me."

I let go with a laugh. "I don't know what you did to her in high school, but I doubt Izzie holds that much of a grudge to hate you."

"How about we leave it at that? I don't want to add to the unfavorable image you already have of me."

"Deal. I promise never to ask again." I held up three fingers.

"A former girl scout, huh? I'll check off another item on that personal life list." He winked.

I rubbed my arms to rid the goose bumps. The conversation had taken a turn, and our roles of suspect and detective changed into something I wasn't comfortable with yet. "Okay, Detective Hunter. You need to go so I can get my work done."

"Detective Hunter. At least we're making progress. See you around, Chloe." He tipped his hand and whistled as he walked out of the shop.

Willow held the door as Hunter stepped past. "What was that all about?" She came inside and set a shopping bag on the counter.

"Nothing really." I narrowed my gaze.

Her complexion lacked its usual pink blush, and she moved like her energy of an hour ago had expired without notice. "You okay?"

"Yes. Why?" She blinked with widened eyes, then turned away to unload her purchased items from the bag. "It's a downpour out there. If you leave anytime soon, better carry an umbrella."

"Hmm. Thanks for the tip." I folded my bottom lip under my teeth. "How about some tea? I think there's some ginseng Mom included in the last care package she delivered. That'll perk you up."

"I said I was fine." She snapped the words, then immediately followed with a laugh. "Listen to me. I don't even know where that came from." She threw up her arms. "Oh wait.

Maybe it's the guy I thought was nice. We had dinner together. Twice. He was sweet and charming, you know?"

"Yeah, I'm familiar with the type." I lowered my head and winced. I hated playing Dear Abby, but the conversation seemed to be roping me into the role. "Maybe if you talked to him, told him how you feel?"

"Nope." She sniffed. "I'm done, moving on, and leaving him for the next stupid, starry-eyed girl."

"Okay. Good for you, but the offer of tea is still on the table. Or, if you want to take off and spend the rest of the day watching reruns of *Friends* and eating leftover pizza, that's fine too." I was horrible at this, and the look on her face proved it. My usual MO was to stop answering the phone after two or three dates. Except for Ross. We'd lasted two years, which probably amounted to over a hundred dates, and look how that ended.

"No tea. No going home. Keeping busy with work is my medicine." She piled supplies in her arms and headed to the storage room.

"Now that's a remedy I can relate to." I followed close behind her, then skidded to a stop. I gasped at the creaking of the back door as Willow hefted a bag of trash outside. I peered through the opening. Rain pelted the concrete pavement and pinged as drops hit the trash bin. Fiona lying outside the door as blood puddled and stained the pavement around her flashed into my head. Again. Not as scary as the last time, but still . . . I heaved a breath and retreated to the front.

"That wasn't too hard. Next time I'll try to stay put and not have a panic attack," I whispered in an attempt to avoid Willow overhearing.

The clock read a quarter before eleven. I checked my phone. No phone call or message from Izzie either meant she should be here within a few minutes or something else had come up. I refused to imagine what something else could mean. Like I'd told Hunter, too much had happened in the past twenty-four hours. As far as I could see, we'd maxed out our quota of unfortunate events.

Heavy footsteps sounded as Willow returned from the storage room. She slung the strap of her bag over one shoulder and held her phone in a white-knuckled grip. Her face had turned from pale to almost ghostly white. "I think I should go home. I'm not feeling well."

"Sure. Of course. You deserve some alone time, and rest. Plenty of rest. Call if you need anything." I followed her to the door and stood there with one arm braced against the frame as she barreled outside.

As she did, Izzie came around the corner and nearly collided with her. They spoke briefly. The exchange lasted only a few seconds as the rain fell harder.

I stepped to the side and Izzie rushed in. "Hey, little sis. Glad you decided to come visit your shop. You know, the business you decided to run? Hope you didn't have to ask for directions to get here."

"Emphasis on the sarcasm, Chloe?" She shook out her rain jacket. "I said by eleven and I've got ten minutes to spare."

"Jeez. Where's the clever comeback?" I nudged her. "Was your morning that bad? Maybe you should choose better company."

"My morning was fine. Do we have any coffee left?" Izzie frowned at the empty carafe, then rummaged through the cupboard and pulled out boxes of tea. "Would you look at all these? Mom is a true wonder. Ginseng, Earl Grey, and here's one called Rum Raisin Biscotti. Yum!"

That was my cue. No more talk about her trip to wherever this morning. "Hunter stopped by earlier."

"Hunter." Izzie chuckled. "Since when are you on a first name basis?"

"He wore me down. Anyway, good news. Blood evidence and fingerprint results put us in the clear." I retreated to my chair and picked up the pencil. Eyeing the unfinished cocker spaniel's ear, I resumed sketching.

"That's great. Maybe he'll stop coming around and calling to harass us." Izzie sipped her tea.

"Not so fast. According to him, we will remain on his list of suspects until told otherwise."

"Why?" She set down the mug.

"We could've worn gloves. We might be part of a murderous gang. Maybe we hired a hit man." I threw up my arms. "How do I know what goes through that obsessed, almost neurotic detective brain of his? I'm only telling you what he said."

"Well, that stinks." She sank in the chair. "So, Hunter, huh?" She winked.

"Stop." I avoided her teasing by staring at the canvas. Thank goodness I didn't have a mirror because my face must've turned tomato red.

She dropped the subject and hunched over the laptop. "I'm thinking we should push out the date to finish the lighthouse paintings after the beach fireworks and pet events. Sound good?"

"How far?" I cooled down and dared to look up. "Can't wait too long. Otherwise, we'll lose those from out of town who may only be here for a short visit. Refunds too. Don't forget that part."

Her shoulders sagged. "You're right. I did forget about refunds. Let me count." She tapped the screen. "I see four names I don't recognize. I'll reach out to them first and ask how long they plan to stay in town. If needed, I'll have to refund their money. By the way, what's up with Willow? She wouldn't tell me much, other than she didn't feel well."

"Boyfriend problems, I guess." I finished the ears and worked more on the eyes.

"Huh. Funny. She told me it was the greasy breakfast making her ill."

"Boyfriends. Greasy food. They both have that kind of effect." I snorted.

"Ha. Got that right."

We worked on sketches and schedules until my stomach began to growl. "How about I order takeout?" I tapped my watch.

"Sure." Izzie stood back from the canvas she was working on and stretched. "Chinese or Mexican food?"

"Mexican. I'll pick it up." I made the call and reeled off a list of the usual items, then grabbed my bag and keys. "Back in twenty."

I exited the shop and heard a loud, hysterical voice coming from next door. Gwen stood outside with a phone pressed to her ear. She paced in a circle and waved one arm. Hesitating, I tossed reasons back and forth for why I should or shouldn't approach her, maybe ask if she needed help, or stay out of business that wasn't mine. I cringed as her voice elevated.

"Don't do this. It's cruel and unfair, and you know it." She held the phone at a distance and sobbed. After a second, she spoke once more. The tone changed, edgier, angrier. "If you do this to her, I'll make sure you pay." With that, she marched back inside her shop.

"Oh, Gwen. What is going on with you?" I muttered aloud, then moved on to get to my car. Whoever she was speaking to, the conversation hinted she was unhappy. I had never witnessed any angry or threatening behavior from her before. What and who could push her to act that way? I opened the car door with a trembling hand. I didn't want to think of reasons why because, right now, all my thoughts were clouded by Fiona's murder and how Hunter would only find her behavior suspicious. Especially since he'd talked to Theo and heard all about the ongoing feud between Gwen and Fiona and had placed the usually kind and gentle woman at the top of his whodunnit list. Quite honestly, I wasn't sure his suspicions were wrong.

Chapter Twelve

"Mom, tell me more about Gwen and her sister-in-law." I spread butter on a bagel and carried my plate and coffee mug to the table.

"There really isn't much to tell." She pulled down the window shade. After an all-day soaker, we were blessed this morning with brilliant sunshine, and the temperature on the outdoor thermometer had already climbed to eighty. "After the divorce, Gwen stopped talking about William or anything relating to him. I assumed that included his sister. Tressa had never married. At least as far as I know. Gwen said she was strange. Shy, never talked much or left her house."

"Gwen mentioned Tressa was ill. I wonder if it's serious." I piled scrambled eggs on my bagel and took a bite. I'd spent a restless night thinking about Gwen's phone conversation. It sounded as if she was trying to protect someone. Maybe the person she had spoken with wanted to harm that person. But who? The unanswered questions were killing me. Besides, knowing the answers might explain why Gwen was acting so strangely. The bonus would be if I could help clear her name from Hunter's suspect list, or at least move her farther down the list.

"I don't know, but something tells me you're going to work on finding out, aren't you?" Mom sat next to Dad and patted his hand. "Drink your beet juice, dear. You need the energy boost."

I shuddered at the mere thought of beet juice and took several gulps of my coffee. "Maybe I will work on it. Hey!" I winked at Izzie as she entered the kitchen. "It's the slumber queen of Whisper Cove come to breakfast. I'm guessing from the Frankenstein hair and angry scowl you didn't have pleasant dreams."

She wadded a napkin and tossed it at my face, then turned to Dad. "Can you cut down the tree outside my window, please? Those baby robins squawking at five in the morning are giving me migraines."

"Sleep in the bedroom across the hall for now." Mom carried her plate to the sink.

Izzie sighed. "That was Granddad's room."

"So?" Mom turned.

"He . . . never mind. I'll put up with the bird noise." She shifted her gaze my way. "Are you going to the shop with me this morning?"

I munched on the last bite of bagel and egg. "I have a couple of things to take care of first, but I'll be in by this afternoon, if that works for you. We'll have plenty of time to prepare for tomorrow evening's event. Isn't Willow coming in?"

"Nope. Stomach cramps and a slight fever. I sure hope it's not contagious. This isn't the time for all of us to get sick."

Mom and I exchanged looks.

Izzie threw up her arms. "What? It's true. I feel bad for her, but I have to think of the business." She stretched then scratched her messy hair. "I'm going to take a shower, a cold one to wake me up."

"Hey, I know it's a challenge, but don't use up all the shampoo." I called out as she shuffled away in her bunny slippers. "What are you two doing this morning? Any sailing adventures?" I cleared my plate and Dad's from the table.

"Visiting your Aunt Constance in Mayville." Mom dabbed her lips with a napkin.

"She invited us to have lunch at her fancy club." Dad twisted his mouth into a frown.

"Joe. Not nice. She's your sister-in-law." Mom tapped his arm. "Family is important."

"You're right. Remember that, Shortcake. Even if one of your family members turns out to be an obnoxious, opportunistic snob who marries your brother to—"

"Joseph Abbington." Mom narrowed her eyes then smiled at me. "Would you like some quinoa? I made this batch with blueberries, strawberries, and walnuts. It will give you that pick-me-up when you need it this afternoon."

"I'm good. You have a nice lunch and give Aunt Constance my love." I hurried out of the kitchen before Dad tossed out another insult about family. I doubted Mom could keep her cool for long if he did. I didn't blame him. His older brother, David, passed away last year, but Aunt Constance insisted we all stay in touch. Of course, everyone mourned the death of a loved one in their own way, but Dad thought his sister-in-law should've grieved longer. As it was, she kept busy with her social agenda and spent money, mostly from the Abbington inheritance, like there was no end to it. Dad didn't like that behavior either.

As I reached the foyer, Max trotted out of the living room and into the hall with a slipper in his mouth.

I pointed. "Dad won't be happy if he catches you. That's his favorite slipper. Why don't we put it back before he notices?"

Max let the slipper drop and barked, his tail wagging.

"You already chewed the other one, didn't you?" I blew air out of my mouth. "All right then. Let's do some damage control. Where is it? Lead the way, pooch. I have lots to do this morning and little time for hunting slippers."

It took less than a minute, and Max pulled the damaged goods from behind Dad's chair. I examined the torn heel and sighed. "Guess I know what we'll be getting Dad for an early Christmas gift." I gathered Max in my arms, along with the slippers, and marched up the stairs to my bedroom. I planned to do a bit of web surfing and see what I could find out about Tressa Finch.

I was prepared to find the surname might be common enough to turn up dozens, maybe hundreds, even with a less common first name like Tressa. If I included a few filters, like location, approximate age, and marital status, that would narrow the list.

"Positivity." I flexed my fingers, then tapped the keyboard. Within minutes, I found three people with the name Tressa Finch within a fifty-mile radius. Sinclair was the closest to Whisper Cove, and the address belonged to a nursing home. If Tressa was ill, maybe she resided in one. I checked the addresses of the other two. One lived in Buffalo, and the other was a thirty-year-old from Belmont. I picked up my phone and dialed the nursing home.

"It's showtime, Max." I smiled at him and nodded.

"Sinclair Point Nursing Home. How may I direct your call?"

"Hello. I was calling to inquire how Tressa Finch was doing today."

"There's no change. Is this her sister-in-law, Gwen?"

I chewed on my lower lip, thinking fast. "Ah, yes. I hoped she'd be feeling better since my last visit."

"Pretty much the same. Nonresponsive, but at least there have been no other outbursts. Your visits seem to help. Would you like to speak with her nurse?"

"No. That's okay. I just wanted to see if she'd improved since I was there a couple of weeks ago. I think it was on a Thursday, wasn't it?" I gripped the phone tighter.

"I wish I could tell you when. Our records are a mess right now. Computer glitches have wreaked havoc."

"Yes, of course. Thank you for the information. Tell Tressa I'll be visiting again soon."

I punched the end call button and stared at Max. "Well, that got us nowhere."

Max placed his paw on my arm and barked.

"Yeah, you're right. Might as well try another lead, but where do I start?"

I hoped Gwen told the truth, that she was far away in Sinclair the evening of Fiona's murder and not hiding behind Paint with a View with a knife, but so far, I couldn't prove it. My rational side told me I shouldn't interfere in a murder case.

On the other hand, my heart convinced me I must. With Izzie and me as suspects, the threat to the Abbington name and the unstable future of Paint with a View pushed me to investigate whoever and whatever led to the real killer. I shivered. Even if the search was dangerous.

My phone buzzed and vibrated in my lap. Ross's name appeared on the screen. I cleared my throat. "Hi, Ross. What's going on with you?"

"Oh, not much. That's why I called. You want to come and have lunch with me? Or dinner. We could do dinner. Or even just meet for coffee and—"

"Would you stop sounding so needy?" I laughed. "Yes, I can meet you for lunch. How about the Blue Whale? Today's special is crab cakes with roasted veggies."

"How about I pick you up at twelve thirty?"

"How about I meet you there at one?" One lead that might be worthwhile involved driving to Sammy's neighborhood and having a talk with the neighbor, Nell, about her story of the mystery woman who looked a lot like me. After ending the call, I made a quick change into a skinny-strapped sundress, then sat on the bed next to Max. I scratched his mop of fur. "No worries. It's lunch and nothing more. No way am I getting back together with Ross. We've been there, and it didn't go well."

"Woof." Max laid his front paw on my arm.

"Exactly. Now, you hang out here, take a nap, beg Mom and Dad for treats, but don't destroy any more slippers. Deal?"

He answered with a sloppy kiss on my cheek.

I skipped downstairs to the front door and scribbled a note, explaining my lunch date and plan to meet Izzie at the shop afterward, then left it on the foyer table. "Going out!"

I hurried to my car and started the engine. The inside was like a sauna without the steam. I powered down all four windows and opened the sunroof while cursing the failed AC and how I had put off getting it fixed. I needed transportation, and tying up my vehicle in a repair shop for several days wasn't an option right now. I patted the dashboard. "Maybe next week."

I reached the east end of town and Sammy's neighborhood in five minutes. Boxwood hedges lined the front yards of brick homes built after the Second World War. You couldn't tell them apart, other than the personal touches added to some yards, like planters with colorful flowers or cute little gnome figures.

I pulled into Sammy's drive and spotted Nell working in her flower beds. According to Sammy, Nell kept to herself, limiting their conversations to an occasional hello or goodbye, except for the few times she peered out her window as if she were spying. Of course, Sammy thought it was funny and not creepy at all.

I exited my car and walked across the yard. "Hello."

At that moment, Nell stood and turned to face me. A frown creased her brow, then her eyes narrowed. "If you're selling something, I'm not interested." She gathered her gardening tools and placed them in a basket.

"I'm Sammy's friend. Chloe Abbington." I smiled and held out my hand.

Ignoring my gesture, she clutched her basket in both arms. "You're the one who was with her the day she left."

"No. You're mistaken. Maybe it was someone who looked a lot like me, though. Can you describe what you saw that day? Anything you might have heard Sammy or the woman with her say? I'm really worried about my friend. She could be in trouble. Really serious trouble." Maybe I was laying it on a bit thick, but the part about being in serious trouble was more than likely true.

"I already talked to that detective." She took a couple of steps back toward the porch. "Seems to me if he wanted you to know anything about Miss Peele, he'd have told you. Now, if you don't mind, I have work to do." She turned away and hurried toward the porch steps.

"Please!" I called out and held my breath as Nell stopped. I'd already told enough people about Sammy's troubles, but I was desperate. "Sammy is in serious trouble with some really bad men. They threatened her, and I'm worried she's hurt." I stepped forward. "Nell, think about it. You could help save her life by telling me what you know."

Nell chewed on her lip. "But I told the detective."

I took another step and now stood a few inches from her. "That's just it. I don't know if she'd trust any authority figure who confronted her. She might run and end up in even worse trouble," I whispered.

She stared without blinking. I felt as if she was trying to see inside me, to find out if I was telling the truth. "Maybe you've remembered something new since you spoke with the detective? Even a tiny detail might help me figure out where she's gone."

A long moment of silence passed. Nell set down her basket and tapped the side of her jaw with her finger. "You know, there was one thing I noticed the past few nights and found it odd." She nodded.

"Yes? What was it?" My breath hitched.

"No lights. Not one lamp on, not even the front porch lights. She programs lights to turn on in the house and on the porch anytime she's away on a trip. I notice these things. Not this time, though. It's like she didn't plan this trip. Must've been in an awful big hurry." Nell picked up the basket once more, then leaned in closer to me and squinted. "Now that I get a better look at you, maybe you aren't the one who was with her. You're much too skinny." With that, she turned and marched to her front door.

"Huh." I shrugged. "Guess I'll take that as a compliment." Popping open the door, I climbed back inside the car and pulled out of the drive. Sammy had left town in a hurry, which meant either she was running scared or there had been some kind of emergency. I knew she had family spread across towns in western New York. Perhaps someone, like her sister or her mom, had called for help. On the flip side, leaving town because she was scared could only be for one of two reasons. Either men from Infinity were after her or—and I prayed this couldn't be true—she had something to do with Fiona's murder. No other explanation came to mind.

I pulled along the curb to park in front of the Blue Whale. The lunch crowd would be heavy today, I suspected. Crab cakes were popular, and customers loved to take advantage of the special giving them three dollars off the regular price. I spotted Ross as he approached the front entrance. After stepping out onto the sidewalk, I shouted and waved. "Hey you. Over here!"

He turned and smiled. "You're on time."

I scowled. "As if I'm ever late. Tardiness is your habit."

"I'm teasing. Lighten up, will you?" His eyes shifted up and down. "You look great. I love the sundress. Brings out the color of your eyes."

"Would you stop? I'll turn around and get back in my car so fast, your head will spin." I pointed first at him then me. "You, me. Friends. Got it?"

He chuckled. "Just an innocent compliment, Chloe. Now, how's your day been? Mine's fantastic so far. I had the most delicious frittata for breakfast at a nice place right outside of town, and then I took a walk along the lake. Gotta tell you, I love this vacation gig. I should do it more often. *We* should." He wrapped his arm around mine. "Together. Maybe a cruise or a tour through Europe. That would be fun."

"Ross."

He patted my arm. "As friends, of course."

"You never stop." I sighed and stepped inside the restaurant ahead of him, but turned my head slightly to call over my shoulder. "Let's enjoy lunch and not talk about vacations together, okay?"

We were told we had a fifteen-minute wait for a table, which I expected. The place was packed and the chatter of guests and the tinkling of silverware filled the room. The delectable aroma of seafood wafted throughout the restaurant. My stomach growled.

"Since we have time, I'm running to the restroom." I wove through customers waiting to be seated. As I headed down the narrow hall leading to the restrooms, the sound of raised voices, one female, one male, came from near the back. I slowed my pace and paused in front of the ladies' room door.

All at once, steps pounded and someone rushed around the corner. A startled gasp escaped my lips as Megan appeared. She dabbed at her teary eyes with a tissue. "Megan?"

Her head jerked up. "Oh! I'm—I need to go." She passed by me in a rush.

Growing concerned, I turned to follow her, but she had already disappeared into the crowd of customers. I could think of many reasons why she was in such an emotional state lately. But because of Izzie and her belief in Megan's innocence, I wouldn't pursue those thoughts. Instead, I hurried to reach the end of the hall in time to see a tall man with blond curly hair push open the exit door and storm outside. "Grayson Stone," I mumbled under my breath.

Within seconds, I returned to the waiting room and Ross. I shifted my gaze from one side of the waiting room to the other. No sign of Megan.

"The hostess says we're up next." Ross frowned. "Hey, are you all right? You look worried."

I let go of a nervous laugh. "Leave it to you not to miss a detail. I'll tell you during lunch. The hostess is waving to us now."

While following her to our table, I deliberated over what to tell Ross. I trusted him. Even if he hadn't been a great boyfriend, he was the perfect confidant.

Ross pulled out my chair, then took his seat. "Now, what's the problem?"

*   *   *

I turned at the next stoplight onto Whisper Lane, thinking about Sammy and Megan. The one thing I had to face was that chances were someone we knew had committed Fiona's murder. And when Hunter caught the killer, we could likely lose a friend.

During lunch, I had explained to Ross the emotional scene between Megan and Grayson. I had no clue what they had argued about. In a typical male response, Ross had suggested they were having an affair. If that were true then why would Megan have called him creepy? Unless she was trying to hide the relationship from Izzie. I refused to judge him. Not yet. Not until I had proof. Even if it was a lovers' quarrel, that didn't make him a creep or someone I shouldn't trust. In the meantime, I wouldn't mention any of this to Izzie, who'd flip and probably hunt down Grayson to give him a verbal thrashing for making her best friend cry.

I walked around the corner to Artisan Alley. The shop was veiled in darkness and a closed sign hung on the door. I pushed sunglasses to the top of my head, then checked my phone. No calls or messages from Izzie. I tried her number, which went straight to voice mail. "Okay, Izzie. What's going on?" A call to Willow met with the same response.

Hopping back in my car, I sped home. Maybe Izzie had decided to wait for me before going to work. Not her usual behavior, but I couldn't think of another reason for her not to be at the shop. We had lots to do before tomorrow's event. I'd promised to finish the decorations we'd planned for the fireworks theme, hanging colorful streamers from the ceiling and shiny appliqués on the walls.

Pulling alongside Izzie's jeep, I killed the engine and climbed out of my seat. Taking wide steps, I sprinted to the front door. Once inside, I tossed my gear on the floor. "Izzie! Where are you?" I kicked off my shoes. At the silence, I headed down the hall. "Izzie, answer me." The kitchen was empty, as well as the screened porch. I circled around and checked the dining room, living room, and then entered Dad's study.

Izzie was hunched over at the desktop computer. Her one hand clicked the mouse while the other dabbed at her eyes with a tissue. Without turning, she spoke. "My life is ruined. First, it's the murder, then my shop is considered a crime scene and closed for days so I have to cancel the first event. Now? Oh, you'll love this." She swiveled the chair to face me. "Everyone, and I mean every single registered guest, canceled for the beach fireworks event tomorrow evening. You want to know why?" Her voice elevated to the ear-piercing screech of nails on a chalkboard.

For the second time today, I felt helpless to stop the train wreck coming at me.

"Someone—I can't imagine who—spread the rumor that Willow has some kind of contagious virus and our shop is closed until we have the premises fumigated. Can you believe it? Fumigated." She paced the room. "If I find out who started this nonsense . . ."

"You'll do nothing because, like all small towns, rumors happen. Somebody comments on seeing Willow at the doctor and the next person says she was taken to the hospital by ambulance. Before you know it, she's got a disease like Ebola, which everyone knows is highly contagious and fatal. See what I mean?" I shrugged and then approached her with caution, hoping she wouldn't jump or punch me in the face.

"Oh, Chloe." She sobbed and hiccupped as she wrapped her arms around me. "I'm so frustrated. This is not how I pictured my beautiful and wonderful business plan."

"I know, sweetie. I know." I patted and rubbed her back while thinking that the day had somehow managed to get worse, after all. The scary part? We had more than twelve hours to go before it was over.

Chapter Thirteen

"Paint with a View is open and ready for business! We have Paint Your Pet night later this week and Light the Night is rescheduled for Saturday afternoon to finish the lighthouse paintings. Beach Fireworks, Lego My Ego, Trick Your Pumpkin, and Glitter Autumn are just a few of the events to come. Something for everyone. Sign up online or stop by the shop." I distributed flyers to outstretched hands of passersby and kept a smile pasted on my face. After more than an hour standing on the street corner, all I wanted to do was to sit, on the ground if necessary. No chair required. My feet and back ached.

After sulking the rest of the day yesterday about having to cancel the beach fireworks event, Izzie had awoken with renewed determination. Her plan to do damage control involved handing out flyers with a detailed schedule of events. She would've included more, but we ran out of room on the page. Theo had agreed to print a huge and predictably expensive ad in the *Gazette*, but only after Izzie pleaded for an hour on the phone. Nothing got results like a persistent Abbington chewing your ear off. At least no costumes were involved this time.

As if Mother Nature was taking pity on us, the day brought plenty of sunshine, and a strong breeze off the lake tempered the summer heat. I examined my stack of flyers, which had thinned to almost nothing. On impulse, I walked into Millie's Diner. Millie's husband stood behind the counter. I placed the remainder of the flyers beside the register. "Please hand these out to your customers. You don't mind, do you? Thanks, Sal." Before he opened his mouth, I hurried outside and crashed into Ross. "Hey there." I anchored fists to hips. "You haven't left town yet?"

He tilted his head. "Come on. We had a nice lunch together yesterday, didn't we? And why would I leave without saying goodbye? Besides, I called the shop this morning. The car isn't ready yet. He ordered the wrong part and needs to start over."

I locked my lips to stifle a laugh.

"I guess he's not used to working on luxury models." Ross shoved his hands in his pockets.

"No, I suppose not." Jake Marino ran the only car repair shop in town. He wasn't high-tech, but he knew his way around a carburetor and could rebuild an engine in record time, as long as the make was domestic. In fact, I wouldn't be surprised if "Made in America" was tattooed on his chest. "Looks like you'll be sticking around a few more days."

"I guess I'll have time to come over for dinner. If the invitation's still open, that is. Is it?" The sheepish expression with that pouty mouth and the hangdog eyes pulled me in and softened my resistance.

"Lunch wasn't enough, huh? Sure. How about tomorrow evening? At six. Mom's a stickler for routine when it comes to meals. Something about keeping a healthy digestive system, which I'd rather not discuss."

"I'll be there. Should I bring wine? Flowers? Chocolates? For your mom, I mean, since she's the hostess." He wiped his brow.

An inward groan traveled from my chest to my gut as I recalled Izzie's comment. "Flowers would be nice. My parents have an entire wall rack in the basement filled with wine."

"Okay then. It's a date." He winked then jogged down the sidewalk.

"Seriously? It's not a date. We're just friends, remember?" Clenching my fists, I hollered after him, but he kept moving. "Unbelievable."

"What is?" Izzie leaned over my shoulder.

"Yikes!" I spun around. "Where did you come from? Never mind. Are we done? I need an energy fix, and Mom's quinoa mystery snack isn't doing the job."

"My lord. You're in a foul mood." Izzie hiked the strap of her bag over her shoulder.

"Ross."

"Ah, Ross. Got it." She nodded, then linked her arm through mine. "I have a handful of flyers left, but if we take a quick walk along the lake—"

"Or you could leave the rest in Millie's like I did." A sheepish grin popped out.

"Leave it to you to take shortcuts. Come on. Ten more minutes?" She split her flyers and handed me half. "We divide and finish in five. Please?"

"You're a cruel boss. Good thing I love you." I held up my hand. "Five minutes. If I have any flyers left after that, I'm feeding them to the ducks."

"Which I'm sure they'll enjoy." She pulled me along Whisper Lane, toward Artisan Alley and the lake, where we parted. "You start here. I'll head over to the north end of the lake and work my way back."

A dozen or so boaters were hanging out by a nearby dock. I jogged toward them. After a quick pitch of our event, I handed each of them a flyer. Eyeing the case of soda one of them placed in a cooler, I suddenly craved something to quench my thirst. Turning on my heel, I headed back to the shop, but took no more than a few steps. I recognized the man walking his dog along the path and smiled. "Perfect."

In seconds, Major planted his furry paws on my chest and licked my face.

I peered beyond the fur and wet tongue to gaze at Grayson. "Hey. Remember me? The New York runaway who returned home?"

He smiled and showed his perfect teeth. This time, I noticed the Cary Grant cleft in his chin.

"Chloe Abbington. This is becoming our spot, isn't it?"

"Our spot? Hmm, yeah. I guess." I scratched the top of Major's head, thinking of what to say next. Asking about his argument with Megan would be too abrupt and intrusive. I'd have to find another way, somehow. "Oh, here. You mentioned you might be interested." I shoved the last flyer at him. "Paint Your Pet night is Wednesday evening. Maybe you'll come? I mean, if you aren't busy, that is." Talk about awkward. I should swallow my tongue and never speak again.

"That would be great. Major loves the attention, and a portrait of him hung above the fireplace would stroke his ego." He snapped his fingers. "Before I forget, did you read today's

Gazette? I placed a full-page ad about my bonfire party. It's this Friday. I'm celebrating the finish of my sculpture. The commission I get will keep Major in dog kibble for the rest of his life and then some. Anyway, there will be plenty of food, music, and hopefully guests. Say you'll come."

"Come to what?" Izzie stepped next to me.

"Izzie!" I fixed an expression on my face that, with any luck, didn't show the emotions I was feeling, embarrassment being at the top of the list. "You remember Grayson. We ran into him in front of Sammy's."

"Sure do." Her lips narrowed, but at least they turned up at the edges in some sort of welcoming smile.

"He was telling me about his bonfire party Friday evening, and we're invited. That's nice. Isn't that nice?" I struggled to calm my heartbeat.

"Very, *very* nice." She tapped her watch. "We should go. Lots to do at the shop."

"Right. We'll be there Friday. I'm anxious to see that sculpture. Bye, Major. You be a good boy." I patted his head and then followed Izzie across the lawn. "You didn't have to be so rude." I wondered if Izzie knew more about Grayson than she was letting on. What if Megan had told her about the argument she'd had with him at the Blue Whale? I ran my fingers through my hair. I *so* hated keeping secrets.

"I was being polite. Not all giddy and excited like you." Izzie opened the front door to the shop.

"I was not giddy. I was genuinely polite, unlike your fake attempt." I stepped inside. "Hi, Willow." My eyes popped. "Willow! You're here."

"Where else would I be?" She stacked paper plates and towels on the table.

"For one, we thought you were still sick. According to the rumors, you should be in a hospital dying of some tropical disease," Izzie said.

"Stop. Be nice." I aimed a scowl at her, then turned. "Don't mind my sister. Too much sun and coffee. So you're better. That's a relief. We were worried about you."

"I think it was some kind of stomach bug. I feel great now. You want these set at the stations or should we wait until Wednesday?" She held up the plates and paper towels.

"Wednesday is fine." Izzie lifted her chin. "Sorry about what I said. Chloe's right. When I'm cranky, my sense of humor goes dark."

"No problem." She pointed to the lake. "I see you were handing out flyers. Did you happen to walk along the other end of the alley? I noticed Megan's shop is up for sale. Weird, right? I mean, isn't she your best friend, Izzie? You never mentioned anything." Willow sat in a chair and leaned back to take a swig of her water.

Izzie blinked. "I'm sure if she was selling her shop, she would've told me. You must be mistaken. Besides, I was down that way a few minutes ago. I'd have noticed a for-sale sign."

"The sign is in the front window. Maybe you didn't look closely enough." Her chin lifted.

"Chloe, go ahead and work on those pet sketches. I'll be right back." Izzie snatched her bag off the counter and marched out of the shop.

I kept my gaze on Izzie as she maintained her angry gait across the walk and angled right toward Megan's.

"She seems upset." Willow cradled the paper towels and plates in her arms.

I shifted my gaze and stared blankly at her. Naïve? Intentionally mean? Or maybe shallow? I didn't know how to explain Willow's behavior, although intentionally mean was a strong contender. Then again, we'd only met less than two weeks ago. "Why don't you pull out the paint colors we'll need for the event and set them next to the plates and paper towels in the cupboard while I work on the sketches. Okay?"

"Um, sure." She pivoted on her heel and stalked to the storage room.

Without meaning to, I felt defensive of Izzie. Scolding Willow for her comments wouldn't help. We had to work together. Besides, I counted on her apologizing to Izzie. If she was that clueless, I'd suggest the idea to her. Satisfied, I grabbed blank canvases from the cabinet and opened the laptop to find the pet photos. Staring at an image of a Maine coon cat twice or maybe three times the size of Max, I shuddered. "We're going to need a bigger canvas to fit this one."

Fifteen minutes later, Willow walked out of the storage room with a plastic tray. Finding the paint colors couldn't have taken that long. Intentional or not, I appreciated the timeout she'd given me.

"Did you finish handing out all the flyers? I could take another trip across town and hand out more, if you like." Willow set the tray of paints on the counter.

"No, we finished. People along the lake took the rest." I spied the *Gazette* on the far end station. I walked over and picked it up.

"Well, that's good."

"Yeah, it is. Ah, here's the ad he talked about." I spoke the thought aloud.

"What ad?"

"Hmm?" I looked up. "Oh, right. A summer visitor we ran into—he was walking his dog—invited Izzie and me to a bonfire this Friday. He mentioned putting an ad in the *Gazette*." I whistled. "When he said full page, he wasn't kidding."

"A bonfire?" She blinked, then lowered her head to stare at the tray of paints. "I've never been to one. Sounds like fun."

"You should go, then. Grayson is inviting the whole town. Nice, right?"

She glanced up and smiled. "Maybe I will. Who's Grayson?"

"Grayson Stone. He's staying at a friend's condo along the lake for the summer to finish his sculpture."

"An artist. How perfect." She turned to store the paints in the cupboard.

"How's the boy drama going?" I sat in the chair once more and searched through the box of sketching pencils.

"I've decided to take a break. Men can be such slime sometimes." She scowled and slammed the cupboard door.

"Huh. Well put. I'm in boyfriend limbo at the moment. Ross—he's my ex—decided to travel from New York to Whisper Cove and beg me to get back together."

"Ouch." She winced. "How'd that go?"

"Well, since I broke up with him in the first place, round two and my response didn't go the way he planned." I chose a pencil and drew the outline of the Maine coon.

"Poor guy." She wagged her head. "Probably sulked all the way back to New York."

I pointed my pencil at her. "Now, see that's where you're wrong. He's still in town. His excuse is he's taking a vacation. Ross Thompson never takes a vacation."

"How romantic. He wants you so much he won't give up." She winked.

"Maybe." I shrugged. "If that's the case, he'll be staying here until Christmas and beyond because the answer will still be no." I pictured his sad, puppy dog eyes when I'd told him we were still over and the giddy smile when he had jumped into the lake. I gave my head a hard shake and squeezed my eyes shut to erase those images.

The door chimes tinkled. I turned. Hunter shrugged out of his jacket, then raked fingers through his windblown hair. I didn't need that visual either.

"Detective Hunter. What brings you to our quaint and cozy little shop today?" I rested my elbow on the table and leaned my head against an open palm. "Care to try your talent and sketch cute puppies and kittens on canvases?"

He chuckled. "In another world, I'd love to. In this one, I have a murder case to solve." He held out his jacket and turned his head side to side. "Care if I hang this somewhere?"

"I'll take it. We have coat hooks in the back." Willow took the jacket and disappeared into the storage room.

"Seriously, why are you here?" I scooted forward in my seat. "Have you solved the case?"

"Not yet." He crossed his arms over his chest. "Is your sister around?"

"She stepped out for a bit. Why? More questions?" I straightened.

"For one, I'm still waiting for her to tell me where she was the night of the murder."

I gestured with the wave of my arm. "Why don't you sit? You look uncomfortable."

"I'm fine."

It took all of five seconds and he pulled a chair closer to me and sat.

I bit my lip to fight the urge to smile. "Any other reason you're here?"

"I noticed Megan Hunt's shop is up for sale."

"Yes, and?"

"I thought maybe Izzie knew more details. She and Megan are good friends, aren't they?"

I shifted in my seat. "I thought you had a murder case to solve?"

"I do." He drummed his fingers on his thighs.

I pointed at him. "Then how does your investigation involve Megan selling her property?"

"She's a person of interest, which means anything she does becomes part of my investigation. I find it strange she'd put her shop up for sale less than two weeks after Fiona's murder. I need to know why she's selling and leaving town."

"Who said anything about leaving town? You're making assumptions, which I know you hate. Megan has family in Whisper Cove. She's lived here her whole life. Maybe she wants a change. To take a different career path. People do that, you know." I snapped, lost my cool, and went on the defensive, which had less to do with Megan and more to do with me. After all, I had escaped New York and abandoned my dream career of becoming a successful artist. Nobody should judge. Not even Hunter Barrett.

He held up both hands. "Whoa. You're right, and I apologize. I have no idea what her plan is beyond selling the shop, but I find the timing of her actions suspicious."

I flashed on another image. Megan holding out a casserole dish while exposing the scratches on her wrists. "Well, you're forgiven because I have no idea either."

"Good. Now that we have that settled, I should go." He stood.

I rolled the sketching pencil between my fingers. "I take it you haven't heard any news about Sammy?"

"Nothing. We've expanded the search to cover a wider area. If you hear anything, you'll let me know, won't you?" The look in his eyes deepened with concern.

"Of course." I jiggled the mouse to bring up the photo of the Maine coon on the laptop screen again, debating whether to mention my conversation with Nell. The fact that Sammy had left town in a hurry and forgot to set the light timer wouldn't help him find her. On the other hand, Nell's comment that I didn't exactly look like the woman with Sammy the day she left would put me in the clear. "I should probably get back to work." I wasn't feeling up to a lecture about my behavior and how curiosity killed the cat, or something to that effect.

"Sure. Let me grab my jacket." He started for the storage room then stopped. "By the way, I made a trip to the nursing home in Sinclair this morning to check on Gwen's alibi."

"Yeah?" I lowered my gaze as I pressed down on the canvas and broke the lead. Cursing under my breath, I grabbed another pencil. Add another secret to the tall stack of them I was keeping. If I confessed the story of my call to the nursing home, everything else I'd done this morning and afternoon to interfere in his murder investigation would come tumbling out. Nerves, guilt, and the need to come clean would be my downfall.

"Funny thing. In my conversation with the head nurse, I learned someone claiming to be Gwen had called there yesterday morning to ask about Tressa Finch. What a coincidence, right?"

"Uh, huh. Strange coincidence." I added more pencil strokes to the Maine coon sketch. My stomach lurched. He clearly suspected I was the one who had called.

"Something about coincidences bothers me, which is why I stopped by to see Gwen. Turns out she and Penny had been visiting townsfolk all morning to collect last-minute donations for the upcoming sailboat race." He returned to where I sat and leaned close. "Now, I know you're too smart to do anything foolish, like pretending to be someone you're not to get private medical information."

I snapped my head around and scowled. "Well, did you find out she was lying about visiting her sister-in-law? Is that why you're bringing this up?"

"No."

"Good." I sketched the finishing touches on the Maine coon, then set the canvas aside.

"Great." He shoved his hands in his pockets.

"What did you find out?" I just couldn't help myself. The smirk on his face told me he realized how curious I was.

"Probably no more than you did. That place keeps horrible records. No sign-in register. Even worse luck, a power outage zapped their computers the day Fiona was murdered and wiped out all the entries for that week."

"Huh." I cocked my head. "What you're saying is you learned nothing to incriminate Gwen."

"That doesn't mean she's innocent."

"Yeah, but it means something." My voice lifted at the end and I grinned.

"Here's your jacket." Willow came out of the storage room.

"Thanks." He turned to leave. Reaching the door, he added, "I'll be seeing you around, Chloe."

"Bye, Hunter." I stared after him for a moment, then focused on the next sketch.

"Looks like your ex has some competition." Willow sat next to me.

My cheeks burned. "That's crazy. I don't care about either one of them."

"Yeah, but they both care about you." She laughed and bounced out of her seat. Snatching her bag from behind the counter, she headed toward the front door. "I'm stopping at Bob's for a bite. You don't mind if I take a longer break to run to the bank and do some other errands, do you?"

"No. I'm good, and Izzie should be back soon. See you later." I clicked on the next pet photo and lurched back in my seat. "Now *this* is the ugliest creature I've ever laid eyes on."

Within an hour, I finished two more sketches, which meant we were caught up. Izzie would be pleased when I told her. Of course, more photos would be coming in. We had two days left before the event, and six of the guests who'd registered hadn't responded yet. Glancing at the time, I snatched my phone off the counter. Izzie had been gone too long. More than two hours. I stabbed the button to speed dial her. After hearing a dozen rings and her voice mail message, I grabbed my jacket. Maybe it was because of Sammy's disappearance, but right now I hit panic mode. People should call when they were late. I ran outside and down the steps, and straight into Izzie. "Oh! Hey, where've you been? I imagined all sorts of horrible things and was worried you might've been swallowed up in the lake or something."

She sniffed and swiped her eyes with the back of her hand. "Well, I'm fine so you don't have to worry." A hiccup burbled out of her mouth. "Sorry."

"Izzie, what happened?" I wrapped an arm around her shoulders and guided her back inside the shop. "Sit. Let me grab a bottle of water for you."

"The one you should worry about is Megan. Willow was right. She's selling her shop. Can you believe it? I sure can't. That place was her do-over, her dream, her chance to prove she's responsible." Izzie swigged half the bottle.

"Yeah, I heard. Hunter stopped by and mentioned it."

She pointed the bottle and water sloshed out. "I know what he's thinking, but he's wrong. The sale has nothing to do with Fiona's murder. Megan's investor is pulling out because quarterly sales are too low. She has a car loan and a second loan to buy equipment for the shop, and—she can't afford to make those payments on her own." Izzie sobbed. "I feel so awful for her. I swear, if I had the money, I'd be her investor."

"But you can't. All your money is in this shop." I spoke softly and stroked her arm. "Maybe sales will pick up soon. The town fair is coming in August, which usually brings hundreds of visitors, and they spend lots of money."

Izzie shook her head. "It's too late, Chloe. Her mom and dad offered to help, but they can't do much. Deeding the building to her was their contribution. She's moving out of her condo and back into her parents' house. Can you imagine how humiliated she feels?"

My brows lifted. "We live in our parents' house."

"Yeah, but she left home and had her own place before coming back."

I kept my mouth shut about that one. "That is rough." I chewed on a fingernail for a second. "There's something I should tell you about Megan. Yesterday, when I had lunch at the Blue Whale, Megan was there. She . . . she was upset. I overheard her arguing with someone. Before I could find out what was wrong, she ran out of the place."

Izzie scowled. "Why didn't you mention this earlier? Maybe her being upset has something to do with her selling the shop. Really, Chloe?"

"Well, I'm telling you now." I lifted my chin. "The reason I didn't say anything is because I was afraid you'd go crazy and do something you'd regret later."

"Why would I do that?" She stood and anchored both fists on her hips. The creases in her forehead deepened.

I hitched my breath then let go. "Because the person she argued with was Grayson Stone."

Her face reddened. "Why that—when I find him, I—"

"I'm back! Sorry it took me so long. There was a huge line at the bank, and Bob's messed up my order, so that took a while." Willow let go of her breath. "Anyway, I'm here."

Izzie gave me a searing look, then quickly turned to smile at Willow. "Good. That means we can take care of what's left to do and go home. I'm tired and need to raid the fridge before taking a long, hot bath."

Willow chewed on her lip and gave me a quick glance. "You look tired. Why don't I finish up and you both head home?"

"No, that wouldn't be right." Izzie shook her head.

"I think Willow can handle it. I sketched all the pet photos, which means there's not much left to do." I nudged Izzie's arm. "Let's go."

"Are you sure? Okay. Lock the door after we leave and call when you get home. Until whoever set fire to Sammy's place is caught, the alley might not be safe," Izzie said.

"I'm not worried. Now, go. Have something to eat and take that bath." Willow shooed with an arm wave.

The ride home was uncomfortably silent. I didn't try to strike up a conversation. If I knew Izzie, she needed time to calm down and think rationally before asking me more about Megan and Grayson. Meanwhile, she'd talk small stuff, which was fine by me. I needed a breather, too.

Max met us at the door, hopping like a pogo stick. I had to admit, a bath sounded nice. Right after raiding the fridge with Izzie. I followed as she dragged her feet down the hall and into the kitchen.

"Looks like Mom and Dad took the boat for a sail." Izzie held up a note. "They're planning to meet up with friends for an art show and dinner."

"Such a hard life." I pulled a casserole dish from the shelf and took a sniff.

"Yes, we should be so lucky." Izzie popped open a can of soda.

I covered my chest with one hand. "We're only the poor unfortunate offspring who scrounge for food and pinch our pennies while we toil at work."

Izzie grinned. "Don't make me laugh. Please. I need to be sad." She turned down her lips. "See? This is a sad face."

"We should do something to cheer up Megan. Maybe show her the positive things in her life, friends like us." I picked a piece of chicken out of the casserole and dropped it into Max's mouth.

"I suggested a girl's night. She wants to be alone." Izzie shrugged.

"Yeah, I get that. After breaking up with Ross, I sat in front of the television for several days and binged on romantic comedies."

"Movies with a happily ever after? Isn't that counterproductive?" Izzie leaned against the counter with a tub of ice cream and a serving spoon.

"I'm into self-torture, I guess."

"Whatever you say." After a few bites, Izzie shoved the ice cream in the freezer and walked toward the doorway. "I think I need that bath more than food."

"Do you want leftover chicken piccata or takeout for dinner?"

"Chinese from Lucky Star sounds perfect."

Before Izzie disappeared down the hall, we exchanged a thumbs-up. Without saying a word about it, I got her message. All conversation about Grayson could wait. Despite the unsettling events of the day—the nursing home fiasco, Megan's curious and sad situation, and Detective Hunter's irritating visit, I was strangely satisfied. I had a good life with plenty of family and friends who loved me, and a job. I couldn't forget that. Whisper Cove would survive. Solve a murder, bring customers back to the shops, and reclaim the peaceful, happy atmosphere our town always had before all this nuttiness were all we needed to do.

With a goblet of wine, I walked out to the screened porch and plopped down in a wicker chair. The wind had calmed, and the sun peeked from behind thin, wispy, feather-like clouds. Maybe I'd take a ten-minute snooze before ordering. I closed my eyes for a moment and relaxed.

*   *   *

"Chloe. Chloe! Wake up, will you?"

A firm hand shook me so hard my teeth rattled. My eyes popped open and I straightened in the chair. "What?" I pulled my arm out of Izzie's grasp and stood. "Is there a fire? Was another event canceled? Because if it's none of those, you shouldn't startle me like that."

"None of those. It's worse. So much worse." Izzie hiccupped and moaned at the same time.

"Okay. Calm down. I'm awake and listening." I set her in the chair next to mine.

"Willow called a minute ago." Izzie snatched my glass and gulped the rest of my wine.

"Okay, so? Willow called and . . ." I rolled my hand.

"Someone broke into the shop, Chloe. *My* shop."

Chapter Fourteen

Willow sat huddled in her chair, arms snug against her stomach, while Hunter hovered with a pad and pen. Behind them, a deputy bagged evidence, dusted for prints, and snapped pictures.

I frowned. "He could at least sit down and stop the intimidation routine."

Izzie leaned my way. "I hear it's an interrogation tactic. He hopes to get more answers that way."

"Answers? Two men wearing masks trashed the place and left their calling card with a very scary and personal threat. That's pretty clear to me." I threw up my arms and swiveled side to side. "I mean, look at this place." Fortunately, nothing valuable had been destroyed or touched, including the painted canvases hung on the walls. Supplies were scattered across the room, and the front window was covered with messages scribbled in marker. I prayed they had used the washable kind. The faint odor of turpentine lingered in the air from Izzie's attempt to clean a spilled bottle of green paint off the floor.

Izzie bobbed her head and the messy bun on top fell off its perch. "I'm trying to distract my thoughts from the obvious, if you don't mind. Concentrating on Willow and Hunter's grilling is working."

"Maybe we should sit next to her. You know, for moral support?" I took a step toward them. My intentions were more out of curiosity.

"I don't think that's a wise idea. Hunter won't—Chloe!" Izzie spoke in a strained whisper.

I scooted a chair next to Willow and sat.

"I'm trying to get an incident report, Chloe." Hunter's brows inched together.

"Yes, and I'm here to give Willow moral support. You'd like that, wouldn't you, Willow?" I patted her arm.

"I, I guess?" She slumped even more in her chair.

Hunter ignored me and refocused his attention on Willow. "You said the men wore masks. Can you describe them in any other way? Tall, short, heavy, thin, maybe walked with a limp?"

"One was tall and heavy. The other maybe average height? I'm not sure. I was so scared. I only got a quick peek at them, then I hid behind the work table until they left."

He tapped his pen against his teeth before pointing it at her. "After they left, you found the note with the threat."

"Yes. That's right." She unwrapped her arms and laid them straight on her thighs. "I waited about five minutes, maybe more, to make sure they were really gone and not coming back. I was shocked at the mess and nearly missed seeing the note. It was taped to the projector screen."

Hunter flipped the page of his notepad. "'Quit snooping and asking questions, or next time we'll do more than trash the shop.' They must be smarter than the average burglar."

I shivered and my stomach lurched. So much for my moral support. "Why's that?"

"Using cutout letters from newspaper ads takes forethought." He tucked his notepad in a pocket. "I'm done here. If you think of anything else to add to your story, Willow, give me a call."

"Willow, why don't we go in the back and relax?" Izzie coaxed her out the chair.

After they disappeared, Hunter faced me. "I think we should talk."

"About?"

"I have a hunch this could've been the work of Sammy's partners." His expression darkened.

"I thought the same thing, which has me worried. The people at Infinity don't make idle threats." I recalled my employer in France. He'd let the situation go and accepted the damage to his business and reputation without causing more of a ruckus. If he'd tried to get revenge or even fight the situation, there was no telling what Infinity would've done to him. Fortunately, the Paris authorities didn't take matters further to charge my employer with involvement in the stolen items.

"You should be careful. I've told you not to interfere in police business. Now, you have another reason to stop. Let me handle the situation. It's my job, Chloe. Not yours."

I rubbed the back of my neck. "That's the puzzling part. I haven't made any attempt to find Sammy or whoever set fire to her shop."

"For some reason, they think you have." He touched my arm and drew closer. "I don't want you to get hurt. You or

Izzie or your family." In a second, he cleared his throat and backed away. "It's my job to protect people from harm, of course."

I covered my mouth for an instant to hide my smile. "Of course. I'll remember to be careful. Promise."

"What? No three-fingered salute this time?"

"Funny guy. No, really. I'll try my best." I shoved a lock of hair behind my ear. This conversation ventured into up close and personal once again. I didn't know how to take it.

"You do that. Try your best, I mean." He tipped his hand, then beckoned to the deputy before heading outside.

I lingered, watching as he walked across the lawn and to the alley road. Voices from the storage room caught my ear. I inched closer to the doorway to listen. Or maybe eavesdrop, though I wasn't sure why I would.

"I don't understand. Either you did or you didn't lock the door like I told you," Izzie said.

"I thought I did. After you left, I remember walking to the door and thinking I should watch you walk to your car because of all the scary things going on and a fire-obsessed nutzo on the loose. Maybe I got distracted and forgot." Willow's voice shook.

"Always check, double check, in fact. I mean, you could've been . . ." Izzie hiccupped. "You know."

"Yeah, I'd rather not think about it."

I stepped into the room and pointed behind me. "He's gone, so you can come out now."

Willow relaxed her shoulders. "That's a relief. He's so intimidating."

Izzie and I exchanged glances and shrugged.

"I could tell you geek stories about Hunter from our high school days that would squash that I'm-a-big-bad-cop image like a bug." Izzie winked and gave Willow's arm a squeeze.

"Thanks. That does make me feel better." Willow stood on shaky legs. "I think I should go home."

"I think we all should," I chimed in and led the way to the front door. The break-in and Hunter's warning had left me unsettled—not only because of the threatening message our intruders had left and the fact that Izzie's paint party business might take another hit. A part of me felt guilty for snooping. Like Hunter said, we should stay out of police business. The problem was, I never could stay out of anybody's business, especially when the business involved someone I cared about. This time, too much was at stake.

After seeing Willow to her car, Izzie and I rode home in silence, both confined to our own thoughts. As we passed through the intersection of Whisper Cove Boulevard and Sail Shore Drive, I spotted Gwen. She stood at the counter of Pick Your Poison with a bottle of wine. I smiled. At least somebody would go to bed happy this evening.

* * *

I took a long shower in the morning while brainstorming every excuse I could imagine to find the most believable one. After dressing in shorts and a blue sleeveless pin-striped blouse, I pulled my hair back with a matching hair tie. With a quick peek in the mirror and a nod of approval, I skipped down the stairs and into the kitchen.

Izzie, Mom, and Dad sat at the table. I flew past them to the coffee maker and poured a cup. "I think I'll swing by the hotel and see Ross."

"Oh?" Mom looked up from her plate.

"You remember he's coming this evening for dinner?" I spread cream cheese on a poppy seed bagel. "Anyway, I thought I'd stop by and give him the details."

Mom sprinkled cinnamon in her coffee and stirred. "Yes, of course I remember. Tell him we're having steaks on the grill and—"

"Please don't say anything with the word quinoa in it," I blurted out with a tormented edge to my voice.

"I was going to say twice-baked potatoes, if that's all right with you?" Mom's brows pinched together.

I munched on a bite of bagel and mumbled approval.

"Hmm." Izzie tapped the side of her mug and tilted her head.

"Hmm what?" I scowled.

"Seems you could talk about dinner over the phone rather than making a trip to the hotel."

"Your point?" As soon as the words flew out of my mouth, I winced. Talk about falling right into a classic Izzie trap.

She wiggled a finger at me and winked. "Sounds like somebody is missing her ex-boyfriend."

"Oh for—" I pressed my lips together and pictured my cream cheese bagel flying straight at her face. "I'll be at the shop after I run some errands." I swallowed the last of my coffee. "Mom, if you need anything for dinner prep, give me a call and I'll stop on the way home."

"Thanks, sweetie. Tell Ross we said hello."

"You'll see him in a few hours." I stared at the puzzled look on her face. "Sure. I'll tell him."

To keep my story credible, I made a quick visit to see Ross, then drove back across town toward Artisan Alley. That, however, was only an excuse to cover up what I really planned to do this morning. Tossing and turning last night, I had realized that I wouldn't stop sticking my nose where it didn't belong. Not until I took my last breath. I shuddered. No matter how that last breath happened.

I parked my vehicle in the usual spot and sprinted down Artisan Alley past Paint with a View. With any luck, Izzie wasn't standing anywhere near the front window to see me. She would be upset if she knew about my plan to talk with Megan. In fact, she'd be furious and swear to never speak to me again. After Izzie's meltdown yesterday, I couldn't voice my opinion to her, especially since part of me wasn't sure of Megan's innocence. I had plenty of reasons to think that way. First, her huge shouting match with Fiona and the threat about leaving before someone did her serious harm. Second, the scratches on her wrists that could've been caused by a fight, and not with a prickle bush. Third, the bizarre Nancy Drew trench coat disguise when she left the bank, waving her arms like windmills as she talked on the phone. And fourth, selling her shop without a word to anyone, not even to Izzie. The timing had to be more than coincidence. As far as the quarrel with Grayson at the restaurant went, I needed to know more. Overall, even if I hated to admit it, Hunter was right to suspect Megan's actions.

I approached Light Your Scent. The shop stood at the far end of Artisan Alley. The view of the lake was more picturesque from here, and her building was next to one of the pricier homes in Whisper Cove. Definitely a plus when it came to the value of your real estate.

Even though we weren't close friends, I'd known Megan since grade school. I had a hunch the whole detective questioning routine hadn't worked well, but maybe, given our relationship, I'd have a shot at getting more information out of her. To keep from sinking into a pool of guilt about my motives, which were a bit underhanded to be honest, I convinced myself this visit was to show concern, woman to woman, citizen to citizen, friend to friend.

I clenched my hands. "Who are you fooling, Chloe Abbington?" Izzie's business and our reputations were in jeopardy. Those issues were my main concern. "You're pathetic, and a traitor. Don't forget traitor." I took a deep breath and marched up to Megan's front door.

"Hello! Megan? It's Chloe." I lifted on my tiptoes to peer over the shelves to spot the blonde head of curls. I wove up and down aisles and around endcap displays to reach her. Getting closer, I slowed my pace. The distinct sound of sniffling in between mumbling became louder. I wanted to melt into a puddle on the floor, like the wicked witch in *The Wizard of Oz*, because that's how evil I felt right now. I pivoted on my heel, ready to bolt.

"Hey, Chloe. It's g-good to see you." Megan dabbed her eyelids with a tissue, and her lips quivered in a smile. "Are you here to buy? Everything is half p-price." She dissolved into blubbering once more.

I wrapped my arms around her, and she buried her face into my chest. "I heard the bad news and thought I'd stop by to offer my sympathies. This really sucks. Is there anything I can do to help?"

She pulled away and blotted the damp spot on my blouse with her tissue. "Sorry. I didn't mean to ruin such a pretty b-blouse." Her chest heaved. "Thank you. I appreciate the offer, but I'm good. Mom and Dad are letting me stay with them until I figure out what to do. After all, they should be used to my failures b-by now." She bit down on her fingers for several seconds. "There. All better."

I knew I should turn and walk out before saying anything else. Not ask questions, not dig for dirt or stir the pot. "So, what happened? I can't believe your investor is bailing on you like this. Such a lousy move." I might as well change my name to Judas.

"Like I told Izzie, the quarterly sales are down, and I have no capital to keep the shop from hemorrhaging." She shrugged. "I guess my investor has a more profitable use for his or her money."

"His or her? You don't know who your investor is?" I gaped. "How did that happen?"

"My dad's lawyer represents a group of investors. He offered to ask if anyone would be interested in my shop. One thing led to another, and then I had the money I needed to open. As long as I agreed to the investor remaining anonymous, that is. According to my dad, it's done that way all the time." She walked to the front of the shop and grabbed a bottle off the counter. "I guess backing out of investments is done all the time too."

"I'm sorry. Finding out from the bank that way must've been hard. Calling you to come in and dropping the news on you like that." I wasn't known for subtlety. I tiptoed like a two-ton elephant through that territory.

"I found out from my dad's lawyer, actually." She rummaged through a bag and pulled out a handful of curly fries.

I chewed on my upper lip. The visit to the bank had nothing to do with her investor. "I don't suppose your investor has a thing for Hawaii, does he?"

"What?" She stopped chewing for a moment, then averted her gaze to stare at the fast-food bag and plucked out another fry.

"Never mind. I should probably be going." I hefted my bag over my shoulder, then paused at the door. "How well do you know Grayson Stone?" At once, her face blushed bright red.

"I've run into him a couple of times. Why?" She turned to stuff the bag and the empty bottle in the trash can behind her.

"I know he was the one you argued with that day at the Blue Whale, Megan. Is he . . . is Grayson Stone giving you problems?"

A nervous titter escaped. "Don't be silly. It was all a misunderstanding. He forgot to pay for an item when he shopped at my store. Now, if you don't mind, I have to get back to work packing."

I left the shop and checked my watch. Maybe I was overreacting and her actions were innocent, but I wasn't totally convinced she was telling the truth about the argument with Grayson. Same thing with the Fizzy Orange soda bottle and fast food from Bob's Barbecue she was scarfing down, which could be pure coincidence. Lots of folks enjoyed Bob's food. Bottom line, I came away with no idea if I was right or wrong about Megan. "File those details under the Hunter's hunches-are-not-evidence column."

I kicked at stones scattered on the pavement and, instead of going straight to the shop, I steered a path to the lake. Benches skirted the shore, and I sat on the closest one. My gaze followed the sailboats skimming across the lake. I recognized the Abbington vessel with the blue and white sails and the name *No Regrets* painted in a curly scrawl of black letters. I'd listened to Mom and Dad boast for days how they would take first prize in the boat race, which really was no more than a ribbon because this event was a fundraiser, but they were excited and motivated. According to Izzie, they'd been practicing for weeks and argued about everything from tacking to backing to who tied the best clove hitch. The race was tomorrow morning, which meant Mom and Dad would go to bed early this evening. With any luck, dinner would be a quick affair. No time for Mom to poke and probe or volley hints across the table about a reconciliation between Ross and me. Thank goodness. Closing my eyes and lifting my chin, I soaked in the sunlight. My mind drifted to other problems. I wanted to help Izzie in any way I could. She was stressed because I was feeling the same way. Sister empathy in overdrive. My eyes popped open, and, on a whim, I pulled off my sandals. Taking a cue from Ross, I sprinted across the grass and stepped knee-deep into the lake. With both hands, I splashed water on my face and neck. I grinned. He was right. This was the perfect way to decompress.

From the corner of my eye, I caught sight of Megan coming out of her shop. Arms swinging side to side, she power walked across her lawn and took a turn to the left, instead of heading toward Paint with a View and Whisper Lane. I stopped splashing and let my hands drop. In a few hundred yards, she disappeared beyond the townhouse development that towered over some of the small lake cottages. I puzzled over where she could be going. Most every house along that end of the lake was a rental, and none of them belonged to Megan. I left the water for dry land and slipped into my sandals. I considered following her, but the possibility of getting caught squashed my enthusiasm. Besides, most likely what she was doing, where she was going, and who she was seeing had nothing to do with Fiona and her murder. I was grasping for any lead that took Izzie and me off Hunter's radar. I shifted my gaze toward Paint with a View and headed in that direction. All these problem-solving thoughts in my head exhausted me. I was done playing snoop for the day.

Chapter Fifteen

"Would you all move a little to the right?" I stood, lifted my chair, and waited while Izzie, Megan, Gwen, and Penny scooted over.

Ross had backed out of both dinner and this morning's invitation to watch the sailboat race. Some excuse about a web consult with a client he couldn't afford to cancel smelled of the old Ross, who put all things personal on a back burner. No shocker there. Old habits were hard to break. At least I had avoided any possibility of a mom interrogation. Maybe after this she'd back off playing Cupid. Unless there was an apocalypse or an invasion of aliens to excuse you, no one canceled on one of Kate Abbington's dinner invitations.

"Wait! Don't set your chair on my burrito." Izzie snatched a bag off the ground and heaved a sigh.

I squirmed in my seat to get comfortable, then perched binoculars on the bridge of my nose. A colorful array of sailboats sat in a wavy line, waiting for the signal.

"There!" I pointed. "Second from the far end."

Mom and Dad's vessel looked so pristine. The fresh coat of paint had certainly given its appearance a lift. With such good care, no one could tell the boat was more than three decades old. The wedding gift from Granddad Abbington had been cherished as well as used hundreds of times on trips to vineyards, to camping spots, or for a spur-of-the-moment sail around the bay.

"Pass me a donut, would you, sweetie?" Penny called out from the tail end of our queue.

"Sure thing." I handed the bag to Izzie, who passed it down the line.

We had front row seats, nestled along the lakeshore, thanks to Penny, who'd arrived at dawn to claim our space by setting out chairs. To make sure no squatters stole our spot, she had parked herself in a seat for three hours until we showed up. As far as I was concerned, she deserved the whole bag of donuts for that act of diligence.

Claire set up a portable kiosk to sell baked goods and coffee from For Sweet's Sake while Bob claimed the spot next to her, offering his signature Fizzy Orange beverage and breakfast burritos with barbecue dipping sauce on the side.

Food was my favorite part of the show, even if it wasn't the main attraction. The sailboat race was an annual event. Each year, the money raised went to a different charity or fundraiser. Businesses sponsored the participants in the race, while town residents bought raffle tickets to win door prizes. Last year, Mom won a cement swan from Bellini's Nursery and placed it in the front yard. She painted it tangerine orange to match the porch swing. Definitely a conversation starter. I smiled as Gwen and Penny argued over the last custard-filled donut.

"Don't worry. I'm sure there are plenty more. Be right back." I jogged over to the baked goods kiosk and waited in line. Even Claire and Bob gave a portion of their sales to the cause. By the looks of the crowd, the lighthouse and ferry fundraiser should make a killing.

The bellowing sound of the horn signaled the start of the race. I purchased a dozen assorted donuts and bagels, then hurried back to my seat. "Here." I shoved the bag at Izzie and snatched the binoculars from her lap.

"Hey! Not nice." She wrinkled her brow and stuffed half an éclair in her mouth.

I ignored her and peered across the lake. Mom and Dad's *No Regrets* was gaining distance, way out in front of other boats, except for one. Its bright yellow sail billowed in the wind as it skimmed at a fast pace. The name of the vessel was etched in blue. "*Hummingbird*. Who has the boat with the yellow sail?" I nudged Izzie.

"Number?" Izzie stretched the flyer across her lap.

"Hmm?" By now the *Hummingbird* was several yards ahead of Mom and Dad.

"Chloe, there's more than one boat out there with a yellow sail. What's the number? Every boat has one. You know that," Izzie said.

"Oh. Right. It's . . ." I steadied the lens on the *Hummingbird*. "Seven. Who's sailing that one?" I set the binoculars down and leaned over her shoulder to read the list of participants. "Seriously?"

"Is he even allowed in the race? I thought only residents of Whisper Cove could participate." Izzie smacked the paper with her hand. "I'm lodging a complaint."

"Complaint about what?" Gwen stretched her neck to get a look.

"Grayson Stone is number seven. Are out of towners allowed to participate?" Izzie asked.

"Who's Grayson Stone?" Penny pulled a custard donut from the bag.

"An out of towner, obviously." Gwen nodded.

"Say. Speaking of out of towners, did any of you get a letter in the mail from some company in New York City with an offer to buy your shop?" Penny turned her head side to side.

"Not me, but when I spoke to my cousin Sally—she works for the county, you know—she told me there's news about some bigwig real estate developer from upstate that's interested in building resorts and condos around Chautauqua Lake. I wonder if Whisper Cove is on their radar," Gwen said.

"Boy, I sure hope not. I'd like our cozy little town to stay just as it is." Penny nodded.

"I need something to drink. Anyone else?" Megan stood and hurried toward Bob's kiosk without waiting for an answer.

"Well, I'm saying something. It doesn't seem right." Izzie sipped her coffee.

"What's that?" I turned my attention back to her, quickly dismissing Gwen and Penny's conversation.

Izzie pointed toward the lake. "The *Hummingbird* and Grayson Stone."

The *Hummingbird* was still leading, but *No Regrets* was closing in. "Mayor Porter's in line for a burrito. Why don't you go talk to him?"

"Ha! You want to get rid of me so you can hog the binoculars." She stood and handed me the flyer. "Fine. I will because somebody needs to."

I glanced for a second as she marched over to Bob's kiosk. Fat chance she'd get anywhere with Porter. He only saw dollar signs when it came to negotiating town business. My guess was Grayson had charmed his way into the event by bribing Porter with a hefty donation to the fundraiser. Izzie's complaint would fall on the mayor's larger-than-life deaf ears.

"Would you look at that? Jake's boat is passing your mom and dad's and catching up to the out-of-towner guy." Penny sprang from her chair and waved both arms. "You go, honey! You can win this."

I couldn't help my grin. Jake Marino and Penny had been an item and top news of town gossip for several years. No one was surprised that bets were made on whether Jake or Penny would pop the question sometime in the next decade. As long as they stayed together and happy, I was glad because that meant cheaper costs for car repairs. Something about the saying "happy wife, happy life" could apply here.

I peered through the binoculars. Jake puckered his lips, then blew several kisses in a sappy but cute gesture. As quick as a wink, he returned his concentration to sailing *Penny Lane*. His love for both the Beatles and his significant other was obvious. I gripped the binoculars. Poor Jake. If his goal was to beat the *Hummingbird*, the dream was fading because the distance between the two vessels widened. My heart sank as *No Regrets* fell farther and farther behind to fourth or maybe fifth place. Our household would be quietly depressing this evening.

"What'd I miss? Oh, wow! Oh, that's not good." Izzie sank in her chair while her gaze fixed on the boat race. "Mom and Dad will be so disappointed."

"Yeah, well. So will Jake." I pointed to the *Penny Lane* as she sailed neck and neck with the vessel named *Pickles* to the finish line.

"Is that Edna Charles? I thought she sold her boat to Timothy Olebotham." Izzie leaned forward.

"She did, sweetie. Timmy's sailing *Pickles*. He promised not to change the name. In remembrance of Edna's dog, you know." Penny chewed on her éclair with ferocity. "Jake will be devastated if Timmy gets second place. I should head over to give him moral support."

"Looks like Mom and Dad are taking fourth place." I slumped in my chair. "Let's go cheer them up." I stood and tugged at Izzie's arm.

Izzie turned to Megan. "You want to tag along?"

"Nah. I'll stay and keep Gwen company." She patted Gwen's arm. "If that's all right with you?"

Gwen rubbed her thighs. "My legs are killing me. Ballroom dancing sure is a workout. And I'd love to stay for some girl talk with you."

"Okay, then. We're off." Izzie linked her arm through mine, and we headed to the far end of the lake, mixing in with the crowd that had the same destination in mind.

"What did Porter have to say?" I asked but could guess the answer.

"A thousand-dollar donation trumped my words of protest. Moving on." She shrugged.

As we drew closer, the sparks of a heated argument filled the air with a hostile tone.

"I guess we end this event with fireworks."

"Not much different than other years. Remember when Bob and Jake battled it out over who got third place? Too bad we don't have some fancy camera taking shots at the finish line to decide. You know, like in horse races or football games?" Izzie nudged a huge lumberjack of a man in front of us to move to the side and we slipped through to get a better view.

Jake and Timmy were nose to nose, their faces both the shade of ripe tomatoes, while every five seconds or so, Penny attempted to pull them apart. Meanwhile, Grayson stood farther to the side. Mayor Porter and Charlie Wales presented him with the symbolic blue ribbon, shaped like a sailboat. The polar opposites of the scene were almost comical.

"Maybe we should go. I need to open the shop so we can finish prepping for this evening." Izzie shifted her feet backward. "Besides, the outcome of who wins the fight will be buzzing through town within the hour."

She was right about the buzzing through town. More than half of Whisper Cove attended this morning's event, and it took only a handful of folks to spread the news.

"I didn't notice Willow at the lake. Did you?"

"Nope. Maybe she hates boats." Izzie unlocked the front door of the shop.

I snorted a laugh. "Then she came to the wrong town. Nothing but boats and water all around us."

The shop phone was blinking. Izzie reached over the counter to punch the message button.

Someone coughed, then Willow's voice cleared to speak. "Sorry. I can't make it in this morning, but I promise to be there for this evening's event. See you then."

Izzie anchored fists to hips. "Unbelievable."

"No explanation, and this is the third time. What are you thinking?" I studied her face.

The creases in her forehead seemed permanent nowadays. "I'm thinking if she doesn't become more dependable, I may have to fire her."

"Let's not fuss and fume over that decision. We have Paint Your Pet in a few hours. I'm excited. Aren't you excited?" I put some bubble and bounce in my tone, hoping to cheer her mood.

Izzie shuffled pages in her agenda notebook. "I'm thrilled, feeling like a giddy schoolgirl. Loads and loads of excitement in me. Yes sir." She snapped the notebook shut and smacked the counter with the flat of her hand. "How would you like to become partners? You and me. Paint with a View, owned by Izzie and Chloe Abbington. Sounds nice, right?"

I blinked. She blinked. My jaw dropped and hers set in a rigid line.

"Chloe? You're not saying anything. Please talk to me." Her voice quivered.

"Yeah, I um . . ." I wet my lips with the swipe of my tongue.

Partners. A new start. Moving forward. Something to be a part of. All of it sounded nice. So why couldn't I answer?

Izzie picked up the agenda once more, flipping pages and scribbling on one or two. "Think about it. I know it's a huge step." She swallowed and clutched the notebook to her chest. "Just know I'd really love and feel so blessed if you said yes. Okay?"

"Okay. I will. I mean, I'll think on it, long and hard and . . . long. Thank you." I pointed at the agenda notebook. "Is there anything on that list you'd like me to take care of?"

"Oh boy, is there." She ripped out a sheet of notebook paper and handed it to me. "Take this to Theo at the *Gazette*. See if she'll place an ad in tomorrow's paper. That will cover the rescheduled date for the lighthouse event and news about next week's fireworks painting."

"Sure. No problem." I turned to walk out and then stopped. I swiveled around. "Really, thanks again."

"I'd never ask if I thought you wouldn't be a great partner, Chloe." She grinned, then clapped her hands. "Now scoot. Theo will refuse to print the ad if it doesn't reach her desk by noon. She's a stickler for time."

"Yes, ma'am. I'm on it." I saluted, along with a curtsey, then flew out the doorway.

"Goofball," Izzie hollered.

"Nerd," I called over my shoulder and skipped down the sidewalk.

The *Gazette* office building sat on the corner of Main Street and Seneca Drive, near the outskirts of town and next door to the courthouse, where the usual quiet of midmorning was disrupted by the pounding of hammers and high-pitched squealing of drills. The town building was getting a well-deserved facelift.

Paper in hand, I walked into the office. "Hey, Theo. Didn't see you at the race."

Theo wore her editor's visor as she bent over the table, flipping through photos on her screen. "Hi, Squirt. Yeah, I was there. Not during but after. I heard about the scuffle between Jake and Timmy, so I raced right over to catch a few pics. You want to see?" She held up her digital camera.

"I'm good. I had front row seats to the live action." On my way to the *Gazette*, Edna had ambushed me, nearly shouting how Timmy and *Pickles* earned second place. She also commented that it was a shame some people, like Penny, were such sore losers. If history repeated itself, the town would take sides and argue about the outcome until next year's race came around.

I laid the paper Izzie had given me on the table. "Izzie wants to know if you have room to place an ad in tomorrow's edition."

"You got the money, I got the room." Without taking her gaze off the laptop in front of her, she grabbed the ad and placed it in a tray.

I puzzled over the open screen as she scrolled through articles. The name Stone appeared in many of the titles. "Is that Grayson Stone?"

"Yep. He won the race, so I'm doing a feature on him in our 'New in Town' column. Did you know he's stinking rich? Owns several businesses and is also famous for his art, *and* he plays the piano for the New York Symphony on occasion. Seems unfair for one person to have so many talents."

"Yeah, totally unfair." I leaned in to take a closer look.

The man was certainly photogenic. Add would-be fashion model to his résumé.

"Total philanthropist too. Of course, he can afford it." She tapped the screen to enlarge a photo.

Several people were included in the shot and it appeared to be a social function, with all of them dressed in suits and fancy gowns. A man standing in front and a little to the side of Grayson held out some sort of award statue. He blocked the view of whoever stood on Grayson's right so only an arm was visible. Slender like it should belong to a woman or child. I squinted at the blue marking on the shoulder, but, because of the grainy quality of the photo, I couldn't make out any details. "'The Stone family legacy lives on as Grayson Stone accepts an award for the generous donation to the Carnegie Art Institute at their annual gala.'" I read the caption, then backed away a couple of steps from the table. "He certainly is amazing." All his accomplishments suddenly made me feel small and insignificant.

"Almost too perfect, which I've never cared for in a man, especially in my husband."

My eyes widened. "I never knew you were married."

"He passed many years ago. We were living in Jamestown at the time. Stephen was killed during a break-in." Theo shook her head. "The fool thought he was some kind of hero. Took a baseball bat downstairs to confront the intruder. He never had a chance. People came from all over the country for his funeral. Afterward, I moved to Whisper Cove. I couldn't stand the memories in that house. Did you know he started this paper?" She snorted and pointed at the floor. "He nearly ran it into the ground because the man thought he was always right. Never listened to me. Thank goodness I was able to turn it around." She shrugged. "Anyway, as I was saying, imperfection makes a guy human, all humble and loveable. Puts you on level ground in a relationship, you know?" She pulled off the visor, and her mop of salt-and-pepper curls sprang out in all directions. "I never had that."

"I'm sorry, but you still have plenty of time to find that guy. Right?" I grew anxious to change topics and move on to more urgent matters. "Hey, while I'm here, have you recalled anything else about those phone call complaints you received concerning Fiona? I mean, anyone else besides Gwen that raised your suspicions?" My own personal list of suspects needed a boost.

Snooping on Megan and Gwen had led me smack into a dead end, while Sammy had simply vanished. Until I had more to go on with any of it, I needed a new target to pursue.

"Can't think of anyone." She picked up the note she'd placed in the tray and read in silence. "I can do a quarter page ad and place it next to the 'New in Town' article so everyone will notice."

"Izzie will appreciate it. Thanks, Theo. Please, if you think of someone in particular who had a grudge against Fiona, give me a call. It may sound crazy, but I can't seem to let this alone."

"I'm sure Detective Barrett has got it covered. Meantime, you have plenty to do helping your sister with the business, right? Might be wise to leave police business to the police and not take any risks. You have a great day, Squirt." Theo shoved the visor back on her head and went back to her photo sorting.

Discouraged and totally put off by Theo's attitude, I took the long way back to Artisan Alley to give myself time to think. Detective work wasn't on my list of favorite things to do because I stunk at it. A dark cloud of negativity settled over me. Izzie still refused to share where she was the night of the murder. Sammy went from being a likely suspect to a victim when someone decided to set her shop on fire. Then there was me, the unfortunate soul who had discovered Fiona's body, which made me an even more likely suspect, with time, place, and motive stamped on my forehead. To top it off, the shop had been vandalized, and we had been warned to stop playing amateur sleuths.

As I neared Sail Shore Drive, I pulled over and let the car idle. I didn't recall Mom or Dad telling me any stories about Theo's husband and his tragic death. I had to wonder why. It appeared there were a lot of mysteries and secrets kept in Whisper Cove, and I had only touched the surface.

Chapter Sixteen

"You're definitely in a good mood. Bouncing all over and whistling some tune I don't recognize." I dropped my bag on the counter and sat on a stool. "Which dwarf name should I call you? Happy? Sneezy? You are a little dopey, so maybe that one?" I grinned.

Izzie swatted me with a dust cloth. "You always tease at my expense. This time I don't care. I am in too good of a mood."

"Why's that?" I placed my elbows on the counter and tipped my head.

"Grayson Stone's bonfire party." She sang out her words.

"I thought you despised Grayson Stone."

"I don't *despise* him, or maybe I do a little. Anyway, that's not important." She anchored her rear end on the stool opposite mine.

"It isn't?"

"What's important is who will be at the party." She squealed and clapped her hands.

I groaned. "Okay, feeding me teeny tiny bits of information like this is annoying."

"Sorry. You remember the big, important clients who hired me last year to do their portraits? You're shaking your head. Okay, long story short. The Sterling brothers own several art galleries in the northeastern states. To make this story even better, I read in the news they're interested in franchising a chain of painting event shops. Isn't that fantastic?"

"I guess?" I lifted my shoulders.

"You are so dense sometimes." She threw up her arms. "They're invited to the bonfire. If we get Grayson to introduce us, maybe we can talk up Paint with a View. Who knows? They might offer to make us a part of their franchise."

I fidgeted with my hands. "Is that something you want to do? Having an investor like these Sterling guys is a huge step."

She licked her bottom lip. "I know. I'm only thinking about it. Besides, I'm sure none of what I said will happen at the party. Big dreams like that are one in a gazillion."

"Oh, Izzie." I leaned over and squeezed her arm. "I didn't mean—"

"It's fine. Like I said, big dreams and all." She sprang from her seat and twirled around. "I do have more important news. I called Hunter and gave him my alibi and the phone number of who to call to verify the story."

"That's great! Are you going to tell me too? I've been dying to know."

"An art collector from Jamestown got in touch with me a couple of months ago. His name's Martin Steele, and he's very well known for his collection."

"I've heard the name, even when I worked in Paris. Go on."

"He wanted to hire me to paint a reproduction of *The Night Watch*."

"Rembrandt. That's a challenge."

She reared back her head and scoffed. "You think I can't do Rembrandt?"

"Well, it is *The Night Watch*." I winced. "Sorry. Not here to judge."

"Anyway, he needed the reproduction to put on display so he could sneak the real one out of his house and into his bank vault."

I stood and walked behind the counter to grab a bottled water from the mini-fridge. "I don't get it. Why buy a priceless painting if you're not going to hang it on your wall and enjoy it?"

"He claims to have people in his life who have sticky fingers." Izzie wiggled her brows.

I gasped and choked on my water. "You mean art thieves?"

"Con artists and all that crowd." She nodded. "He's paying me really well, Chloe. I mean more than the total sum of what I made in the last three years. That'll buy a ton of paint supplies, for sure. Only thing was I had to promise I'd keep quiet about the whole matter until after I finished the painting and the real one was safely hidden."

"Which happens to be today. Thank goodness. I can take that one off my list."

"What list?" Izzie dusted the counter, tables, and chairs.

"Call it my dark cloud of negativity, but let's not talk about that. What's left to do before this evening?"

Izzie shoved a sticky note at me. "Three large coffees, one with cream, one with cream and sugar, and one black."

"Seriously?" I flitted my gaze from the note to Izzie's face. "I'm your errand boy, now?"

"Or girl, as the gender fits. Please, I need a caffeine fix, and you, by the looks of your antsy moves, need to exercise that energy."

"You couldn't tell me before I made the trip to the *Gazette*?" I muttered under my breath as my phone beeped with a message. "Coffee will have to wait a while. I need to stop by Brown's Grocery first. Seems Mom needs a can of chicken broth ASAP and can't leave whatever's on the stove to go buy it. Of course, Dad is out sailing with Mr. Bixby." I went outside. Reaching the alley road, I skidded to a halt. "Ross." At once my eyes narrowed. "Aren't you supposed to be chatting with a client on Skype or Zoom or something?"

"Obviously, you haven't forgiven me." Ross reached out to touch my arm, but I pulled away. "The client is one of our biggest. When he says jump, well, you know."

I sighed. "I'm kind of in a hurry. If you don't mind." I swiped an arm to gesture for him to move.

He hopped to the side. "Oh, sure. I only came by to apologize and see if we could reschedule dinner?"

"You'll have to speak to my mom about that, but I can pretty much guarantee she'll say no." I hustled along Whisper Lane while Ross hurried to keep up.

"I have a box of salt water taffy to sweeten the deal. I can be very persuasive." He grinned and gave his voice the proper dose of confidence.

"I know. You're a lawyer. Look." I brought my feet to an abrupt stop, and he nearly toppled into me. "Do what you want. I don't care." I planted one fist on my hip. "One question.

Why are you still in town? I'm sure Jake has fixed your car by now, and vacationing this long must get old and boring for such a big New York City attorney like you." The snarky attitude reared its head.

He hugged the box of taffy to his chest and smirked. "If I left, you'd miss me. Admit it."

"I would not." I stuck out my lower lip. "Now, go away. I'm busy." I marched ahead, and he didn't follow. Whether that left me satisfied or disappointed, I couldn't decide. I called out over my shoulder. "By the way, Mom hates saltwater taffy." A smile tickled the corners of my mouth.

"What does she like then?"

"Caramel-filled chocolates." I waved before crossing the street. I stepped inside the grocery store. In quick time, I purchased three cans of broth, just to be safe, then directed my steps down Sail Shore Drive.

Entering the house, I followed the sound of Mom humming an uplifting tune. The delicious aroma of chicken noodle soup cooking in the kitchen made my stomach growl. "Special delivery for Kate Abbington," I called out and laughed.

Mom wiped her brow and left a smudge of flour on her cheek. "Thank goodness. Soup should always have plenty of broth. Silly me for not taking inventory before I started cooking."

A flattened slab of dough covered the huge wooden board. "And homemade noodles?" My brow lifted. "You certainly are industrious today." I set the cans on the table, then carried one to the electric can opener. Pouring the contents into the pot, I took a sniff. "Yum."

"I was in the mood. That's all." She ladled some broth and took a sip. "Perfect."

I sat at the table. "Say, Mom, why haven't you ever mentioned Theo had a husband who died tragically?" After my visit at the *Gazette* and conversation with Theo, I was curious to know more.

"Oh boy. I haven't given that awful story a thought in years. Murder isn't exactly a conversation you want to have, is it? Plus, out of respect for Theo, I've never felt comfortable talking about it." She held a knife and cut strips of dough. She had no need for a fancy noodle maker, she'd once commented when Dad suggested buying one.

"Yes, she told me it was murder. Did the police ever catch the killer?"

"Sadly, no. I guess the Jamestown PD and the detective in charge never got any leads that helped. I heard he died recently. His name slips my mind. I'm sure Aunt Constance would know since the detective was born in Mayville. I remember my conversation with Theo, soon after the murder happened. She was angry about the case not being solved, but that didn't stop her from moving on quickly."

"How so?"

"She put all her time and energy into the *Gazette*. The business had been struggling before that." Mom wiped her hands on her apron and sat down next to me. "I don't think I could recover if your Dad passed. Especially if he went in such a horrible way." Her voice quivered.

I patted her hand. "Don't think such a thought. You and Dad will probably outlive all of us. I mean, just look at all the healthy food you eat." I managed a smile. "You know, it's strange when you think about it."

"What's that?" She returned to the stove and stirred the soup.

"You're married to someone for years, and then he or she is murdered. How do you get beyond such a tragedy that easily?"

"I don't know. I can't imagine it's easy. But I don't know that she and her husband were all that happy. I guess she wanted to invest in real estate, but he refused. While he was still alive, I remember visiting the *Gazette* on a few occasions and catching them in a heated argument. Of course, all couples squabble."

I frowned. After hearing the comments Theo had made earlier this morning, I agreed with Mom's take on the relationship.

"You know, after her husband died, as soon as she could, Theo sold their house in Jamestown and moved to Whisper Cove. Rather than purchase a new place, she lived above the *Gazette* for a couple of years and used money from the house sale to buy business property along the lake. Got the real estate she wanted, after all."

I glanced at my watch. "I better get back to the shop. Can't wait for that chicken noodle soup this evening. Love you." I planted a kiss on her cheek, then jogged to the front door. My thoughts churned and mulled over what I'd learned. Theo was a smart and determined businesswoman who, it seemed, hadn't had a great marriage.

The room glowed with festive lighting that Izzie had chosen to give this evening's event some ambiance. Several guests arrived early, anxious to see the penciled sketches of their precious pets. The hum of chatter and bursts of laughter filled the room. Proving once again to be an expert teacher, Willow had organized and distributed various palettes of colors to each station that matched their respective animal. Showing her creative side, Izzie had put on her shopping hat and found paper toweling and cups designed with an animal theme for this evening. I volunteered to find the proper music selection. I tapped my fingers to the rhythm as "How Much Is That Doggie in the Window?" played. I also added "What's New Pussycat?" even though Tom Jones wasn't singing about a feline, and "I Want a Hippopotamus for Christmas," despite the fact no one attending had a hippo for a pet and Christmas was several months away. Everything had been planned down to the tiniest detail. Izzie beamed with pride over the results. In a more subdued way, so did I.

I pointed my finger at each person and counted. "Only one hasn't arrived."

"Hmm." Izzie nodded.

"Should we start anyway? My watch reads seven." Without checking the roster, I knew which guest hadn't shown. Grayson Stone. He hadn't promised, only said he was interested. Why had he bothered emailing the photo of Major and paying for admission, then?

"You're pouting." Izzie tapped my bottom lip with her finger tip. "He's not special, you know. Money doesn't mean everything. Our parents taught us that much."

Over dinner, I'd explained the article and photo from Theo's collection to divert attention from Mom's tirade about Ross having the nerve to ask for another chance at dinner.

She'd told him she'd think about it, but gladly accepted the box of chocolates. Chances were, she'd accept his proposal, though it might involve a second box of chocolates, a bouquet of flowers, and a lot of groveling. I cherished the thought.

"I'm not pouting. I'm thinking."

"Thinking about Grayson, of course." She nodded.

"No, I'm thinking that it's a waste of a canvas and the time it took to sketch his dog. That's all." I rolled my eyes. "Whatever. Can we start? Because it's now five after seven. Every minute counts. Isn't that what you said?"

Izzie stared at me and opened her mouth, but then quickly shut it. Stepping onto the platform, she clicked on the projection screen. "Welcome, everyone. I have to say, you all have some adorable pets. We enjoyed sketching them, and we hope you'll enjoy painting them too." She gestured to me, then Willow, who stood near the front counter. "My sister, Chloe, and assistant Willow will be joining me to float around the room and help guide you through the steps to complete your paintings. You'll notice each of you has an individual printout with some tips. Willow came up with the brilliant idea to help you. You can thank her for that. Of course, whenever you have a question, please shout out to us. Good luck, everyone."

We each took a row of five patrons to monitor. My row was missing one. The sketch of Major looked lonely propped up at its station without his master. On a whim, I decided I'd deliver the sketch tomorrow evening at the bonfire. Somehow, having another reason, a more practical one, to attend Grayson's event put me at ease.

A couple of the locals were supportive and had signed up to paint their pets. Megan and Edna Charles, who owned three poodles. Somehow, I'd managed to fit all three headshots on the canvas. Moving up and down my row, I pointed out what each person needed to do and answered questions, but my gaze never left Megan for more than a minute. I'd given up snooping on her for the most part, or maybe I was merely taking a break. Giving up entirely seemed extreme. Guilt slowed me down. Her being best friends with Izzie dampened my enthusiasm. Still, something about her behavior didn't add up.

"How's it going?" Izzie whispered over my shoulder.

I gasped and dropped the brush I'd been holding. "Good grief. Why do you sneak up on me like that?"

"Sorry. I didn't want to interrupt the artistic flow." She waved her arm up and down.

"Weird." I stepped away from Edna Charles and cupped my hand around my mouth. "You know as well as I do, she can't paint a straight line. Thank goodness poodles are all curls."

"Just do your best." Izzie whispered in my ear. "We don't expect them all to be Michelangelo, you know."

"Picasso with misplaced body parts is more like it," I muttered and walked over to the fridge for a beverage. Leaning against the wall, I swigged my water and perused the room for hands to go up.

A warm breeze flowed into the room as the door opened wide. Hunter walked in and shifted his gaze until it fell on me. He nodded and crossed the room. "Evening, Chloe."

"Hunter. What brings you here?" I kept my words short and civil and my mood tempered, even though every time he showed up, he wanted to talk about police business. I doubted he ever clocked out and took time to relax. "Any news?"

"About?" His brow inched up.

"Oh, let's see." I tapped my lip, then pointed. "You're a detective, so how about police matters? Isn't that why you're here? Seems you always are. What's the saying? All work and no play makes—"

"I get it. Well, I did hear from one of the department's men searching for Sammy."

I gasped. "You weren't going to say anything?"

"I planned to call you, but then I got sidetracked. Besides, it's not my habit to share police business with civilians." He popped a stick of chewing gum in his mouth.

"Even when this civilian is a close friend and when our business is at risk? Or how about the fact that while a killer—and I'm not saying she is one—runs free, my sister and I remain suspects? Does none of that count?" I gritted my teeth.

We couldn't get through one tiny encounter without him making my blood reach the boiling point.

"Like I said, I was going to call." He chewed slowly. "The news is someone spotted her in Altoona. At least we know she's alive."

My jaw dropped. I didn't know whether to be angry or relieved, though angry pushed its way to the forefront. How dare Sammy not let us know she was okay? She had to realize we'd be worried.

"Too bad she managed to get away before our man could catch up to her. Anyway, that's not why I'm here. I'm looking for Megan. Ah, there she is." Without asking for permission, he stepped toward her.

"What's that about? He does realize he's interrupting our event, right?" Izzie sniffed as she stood next to me.

"I'm sure he doesn't care. What the . . ." My eyes widened.

Hunter bent over to whisper to Megan, who frantically shook her head. Finally, she bolted out of her chair, grabbed her bag, and ran out of the shop, with Hunter close behind her.

Izzie started for the door, but I pulled her arm. "Don't. She can take care of herself. Besides, we have a painting event to finish, right?"

Her chest rose as she took a deep breath. "I'll deal with him later."

"Who needs help?" I walked back to my row and mingled with my group.

We finished up with fifteen minutes to spare. I suggested the guests stand together with their artwork in front of the stage for a photo, which would be added to our website. Nothing like free advertising. After handing out flyers for future events and bidding the last guest goodbye, I closed the door.

Izzie grabbed her phone and stepped to the front. "Would you two take care of the clean-up? I need to make a call."

Before I could comment, she disappeared outside.

I turned to face Willow. "How about I start washing down the tables and stations while you carry supplies to the storage room?"

"Got it." She tossed paints and brushes in a plastic bin.

Halfway through washing, I ran out of cleaner. Twenty minutes passed, and Izzie hadn't returned. I worried she might have gone to find Megan and what would happen if she found Hunter instead. I shuddered at the picture in my head. In defending her friend, Izzie would give her former classmate a tongue-lashing he'd never forget. Or worse. I stabbed her number on my speed dial and stared at the phone while rushing to the storage room.

Willow stood at the utility sink scrubbing a paint stain on her shirt. "Oh well, this is hopeless. I'll toss it in my rag pile at home." She shrugged.

"Here." I opened the locker we used to store coats and aprons. "You can borrow this so you don't have to wear a wet shirt home."

"Thanks." She pulled the top over her head. Wearing only a bra, she reached for the clean shirt I held.

I quickly turned away to give her privacy. "You were a big help this evening." I waited a few more seconds, then turned around to smile at her.

"I do love this work. Art has been my dream since I scribbled in my first coloring book." She laughed. "You too, I bet."

"Oh, trust me. I didn't have a choice. In my family, it's art of some kind or you'll be disowned." I laughed along with her. "Why don't you get going? Try a bit of turpentine on that stain before you wash it . . . which I'm sure you already know."

"You sure? Okay. See you tomorrow."

"You'll come with Izzie and me to the bonfire on Friday, won't you?"

"I don't think so. I've got other plans. Have a good evening, Chloe." She hurried to the front.

The door slammed shut.

"Guess bonfires aren't her thing after all." I checked my phone but didn't find any messages. My call had gone straight to Izzie's voice mail. I told myself not to worry. I'd give her ten more minutes then try again. As if my thoughts had telepathic powers, the phone buzzed to life. "Where have you been? I'm waiting here at the shop and ready to go home."

"Sorry. Everything has gone crazy and I forgot to call," Izzie said, out of breath.

"Crazy. Crazy how? Izzie, are you okay?" My heart pounded.

"I'm fine. I decided to go to Megan's place and see if I could comfort her. She was so upset." She hiccupped.

"Did you find her? Is *she* okay?" With a tight hold on my phone, I sat in a chair.

"She's fine too."

"I'm confused. She's fine. You're fine. When does crazy come into the story?"

"Oh, right. On my way to Megan's—she's still living in the condo but has to be out by the end of the month. That greedy landlord won't give an inch and—"

"Izzie!"

"Oops. Sorry again. On my way to Megan's, I passed by Quaint Décor, of course. Such a mess with all that fire damage. Yes, well, I saw a light inside. A flashlight, I'm thinking, because the beam moved around. Why would someone be in a badly burned and unsafe building at night? Anyway, I was too scared to check it out, so I hurried past."

"That's it? That's the crazy part of your evening?" I scoffed. Maybe living in New York had toughened me.

"I'm not finished." She drew out her words. "After I made sure Megan was okay, which she really isn't, but she won't say why, I had to pass Quaint Décor again. This time, someone came out of the shop, walking as if they didn't want to be seen. Slouching down, looking side to side."

"Yeah, I get it. Go on. Did you see who it was?"

"A man. Or maybe a woman dressed like a man?"

I slid down farther in my chair and dropped the phone to my side for a moment.

"Do you think it was Sammy? Or maybe her goony partner from Infinity?" Izzie said.

I pressed the phone to my ear. "I don't know, but I'm tired and want to go home. Are you almost at the shop?" I didn't have the energy to tell her Hunter's news about Sammy being spotted in Altoona. That could wait until morning.

"No, I'm home. I thought you'd be here. That's why I called. You shouldn't stay there so late. Besides, Max is moping. I think he misses you."

I clenched my jaw. "I'll be home in a bit, but give Max his evening doggie treat. That's what he's missing." I ended the call, then rummaged through the fridge, looking for the bottle of wine we'd started and I hoped not finished. "Yes."

The bottle was a third full. Enough to calm my nerves before going home. I poured a glass and sat on a stool, mulling over what Izzie had told me. Whatever someone was looking for in Sammy's shop, it must be important enough to take the risk of getting caught. The question was, what could it be?

Chapter Seventeen

"I'm tired of waiting for answers and getting bits and pieces of information Hunter dishes out. I say we start our own detective team." Izzie slipped into a denim skirt, then pulled a peasant top over her head. She brushed strands of hair away from her face. "Are you with me?"

After spending Thursday with family to celebrate Mom and Dad's participation and finishing in fourth place in Wednesday's race by sailing to a nearby winery, it was time to get back to work.

I tipped my head to the side. "I think that's what one or both of us have been doing since this murder investigation started. Didn't we visit Sammy's shop to pump her for information? Though you might have pushed too far since she practically threw us out. How about stopping by the *Gazette*? We got a great story from Theo. I know you don't like to think Megan could be a suspect, but you came up with the Bob's Barbecue connection to the evidence found in the dumpster." I paced back and forth across her bedroom. "Of course, I did some snooping on my own. Like calling the nursing home, though I didn't really learn anything. Oh, and I should confess that I visited Megan the other day to see if she'd talk more about selling her shop. She was munching on Bob's food and acting kind of strange. Then there was the day we dressed in costumes to hand out flyers. She came out of the bank dressed like Inspector Gadget, with a trench coat and hat pulled over her forehead, talking to some guy in a Hawaiian shirt. I mean, who does those things? Looks pretty suspicious to me." I heaved my chest to take a breath.

Izzie's eyes bugged out and her mouth flapped. "What about Sammy? She's off doing who knows what in Altoona. Maybe she's the killer *and* the one I saw prowling around her shop the other night. She might've come back to town to finish off some more victims. Did you consider that?"

"Yeah, sure I have. I've considered her, Megan, Gwen, even Penny, who's a bit weird if you ask me. I've given them all equal time, and my brain is fried from thinking too much. I'm only saying we've done a lot already and learned quite a bit, even if it's not all useful, but we're not detectives, Izzie." My voice was tinged with a pleading tone.

Izzie fiddled with her shirt buttons and then glanced at me. "Megan isn't a killer."

I barely heard her muffled words. This wasn't going well. As usual, I didn't have the first clue how to be subtle. I just charged in like a rhino and said whatever was on my mind. "Look. I'm sorry, and I don't want to argue. We have a bonfire to attend this evening. Let's have fun, okay? We deserve it."

"I guess, but I plan to stop by Megan's this morning and get her to talk. Something Hunter said has her so upset, and I want to help."

"You want me to come with you?"

"No. She'll think we're ganging up on her. It's better if I go alone." She shoved her phone and keys in her bag then turned. "Maybe we're not detectives, but that doesn't mean we shouldn't do what we can. Like you said, we've learned a lot. No reason we can't find out more. In our bungling, amateur way, of course." She smiled and held up her hand.

"Agreed." I gave her a high five. She was the cheerleader this time. I was happy to let her take a turn. "I'll see you later at the shop. Mom's expecting us back here for dinner before we go to the bonfire."

"She and Dad still won't say yes, huh?"

"They're too old to have that sort of fun. That's what she told me. I laughed until I cried, then handed her the brochure that came in the mail from Greenbrier Assisted Living facility. She didn't see the humor, only grumbled something about me being a wise guy." I chose a shell necklace out of her jewelry box and held it to my neck. "I think Ross is going."

"I'm not surprised. Didn't you say he was staying in Whisper Cove to relax and enjoy himself?"

"Yes, but I would prefer he take his fun somewhere that's not around me." I dropped the necklace back in the box.

"You're so mean to him. I think Mom is going to cave and invite him to dinner again."

"After three boxes of chocolates, two dozen roses, and a million compliments thrown her way, no wonder." I scoffed with a wave of my arm. "He managed all that in twenty-four hours. Trust me. If she invites him to dinner, it's because she wants the gifts to stop. I don't think Dad cares for it either. Did you see how he moped around the kitchen this morning? Practically sobbed while munching on his quinoa muffin."

"You can stop with the melodrama." She giggled. "I've gotta go. When you get to the shop, will you answer all the emails we received in the past two days? I haven't had a chance to take care of them."

"Sure thing." I hugged her tight, then waved goodbye. Grabbing the necklace, I placed it around my neck. "I wonder if she has earrings to match." I picked through the jewelry and, after a minute, gave up and left her room. I had time for one more cup of coffee before going to the shop.

At least several dozen emails sat in the inbox, waiting to be answered. People from as far away as Buffalo had heard about our shop. Even though the painting event business was beginning to explode, ours was rather unique with its picturesque location and view. Izzie had talked about scheduling some daytime events and taking the classes outside to sit by the lake. We still had a couple of months before the cold weather arrived, which gave us time to include one or two.

Thinking of fall reminded me of Izzie's proposal. I had to make a decision soon, even though she hadn't pressured me to hurry. If I became a partner in the store, that meant staying in Whisper Cove. Permanently. Maybe giving up on my dream to become a successful artist forever. On the other hand, I could start small from here. New York City wasn't that far away. If I painted in my spare time and submitted the work to my contacts in the Big Apple, maybe at some point I'd snag that gallery showing I'd always dreamed of. Despite my impulsive nature, I used an Izzie move by making a list of pros and cons. So far, the pros were winning. "Paint with a View, owned by Izzie and Chloe Abbington. That does have a nice sound to it." I grinned as I skipped down the stairs and into the kitchen.

*　*　*

"Would you stop squirming? I'll stick you with this needle for sure." Izzie held the strap of my sundress between her finger and thumb while she sewed. "If you weren't so short, none of this altering would be needed."

"Quit griping. Are you almost finished? It's nearly eight. I want to get to the bonfire before dark."

If Ross showed up, I didn't want to be ambushed or cornered by him. I needed more time to think about my feelings. I thought I had figured out everything about our relationship when I left New York. Our priorities were too different. Now, since he'd arrived in town, I wasn't sure.

"There." She snipped the thread with scissors and stood back. "You look great in yellow with your black hair. I'm jealous."

I snorted. "Yeah, right. You and your model figure and gorgeous long hair couldn't possibly think so."

"You sell yourself short, Chloe. You're smart and witty. You have the most beautiful green eyes and bright smile. A cute figure. Haven't you heard the saying? Good things come in small packages." She grinned and squeezed my hand. "Now, let's get out of here. We've got a party to go to."

Grabbing my sweater off the bed, I ran to catch up with Izzie, who flew down the stairs. Just as we reached the foyer, Mom was in the open doorway greeting someone.

"Well, this is a surprise." I chuckled. "I thought you had other plans?"

Willow wrinkled her nose and lifted upturned palms. "Plans change."

"A case of guy slime?" I asked.

"Yep." She gestured with a thumbs-down. "No great loss. Besides, like I said, a bonfire sounds fun."

Izzie tapped her watch. "We should go. I'm driving."

After a quick goodbye, the three of us walked to Izzie's jeep. We parked along Whisper Lane, then made the rest of the journey on foot, following the trail to the other end of the lake. The bonfire, with its orange and yellow flames, brightened the dim evening light of dusk like a beacon, while the shadowy images of guests moved around it.

I walked in step with Izzie while Willow trailed behind. "If she's at the bonfire, are you going to speak with Megan?"

This morning's effort had come up empty since Izzie had found no one at Megan's condo or her shop. Even a phone call to her parents' home had gone straight to voice mail.

"I think she's avoiding me, but she can't hide forever. This is Whisper Cove. There aren't that many places to go without being seen." Izzie sniffed. "I want to help her. I wish she understood that."

I wrapped an arm around her waist. "She'll come around. Give her some time, if that's what she needs." I wished I had Izzie's confidence that Megan was innocent. Call it my New York, big city, skeptical attitude. I needed more time in Whisper Cove to soften my edges.

Within yards of Grayson's condo, conversation and laughter echoed across the lawn. Splashes of color brightened the scene with red, green, and blue paper lanterns hung from wire that stretched from the condo to the lakeshore. For the seafood lovers, a table was filled with serving trays of baked clams, oysters, crab legs, and lobster, while another displayed barbecued ribs from Bob's and grilled steaks, along with plenty of sides and beverages. Music piped into speakers played a tune by the Beach Boys.

I sniffed the aromas and groaned. "Good thing I brought my appetite. Look at all that food."

"What's the matter? Didn't Mom's beef stew appeal to you?" Izzie jabbed me in the side and snickered.

I wrinkled my nose. "I don't think that was beef, but we'll save that debate for another time."

"Hey," Willow shouted, then mumbled a quick goodbye as she ran off toward a couple of girls who jumped up and down. They hugged her, then the three of them linked arms and walked off toward the bonfire.

"Guess she rebounded without a problem. The healing power of female bonds never fails." I laughed.

"Oooh. I see Megan by the seafood table. You want to tag along and be my wing woman?" Izzie gave me her signature pouty lips.

"Won't work this time, sister dear. I'm heading for the barbecue ribs and potato salad. This empty tummy cannot be ignored." I rubbed my middle, then jogged off toward the table where Bob and Millie stood at opposite ends.

Observing their expressions and lack of conversation, I figured the boat race feud was in full swing. Bob was good friends with Timmy, while Millie was a second cousin of Jake's. I pressed my lips to hide the grin. I so missed small-town drama. I scooted toward Bob's end first and cautiously piled my plate with ribs while keeping a sideways glance on Millie. She daggered me with a scowl. I quickly shifted toward the middle of the table and neutral ground. Plopping a heaping spoonful of potato salad next to my ribs, I then hurried away without dessert or a bottle of Fizzy Orange soda. No way would I get in the middle or take sides.

Spotting an open seat next to Gwen, I skirted around a group of teenagers playing hacky sack and sat down in a lawn chair. "I hope you're not saving this seat."

Gwen held up her plastic goblet of wine and took a sip. "Only for my date, but he won't arrive until much later."

"Great. I mean because I don't need to move, not the part about your date coming much later." I chewed on a bite of rib and recalled Mom's comment. "You never mentioned who you're dating. Is he someone from Whisper Cove?"

She emptied her goblet and refilled it. "Would you like a glass? I have an extra cup. And another bottle of wine, if needed."

I blinked. "That's okay. I'm going back to the table for a Fizzy Orange, whenever it's safe."

She wrinkled her brow in a puzzling way. "Why wouldn't it be safe?"

"Never mind. You were saying something about your date?" I wondered if she had something to hide. Maybe her guy was an ex-con or something.

"You wouldn't know him. He lives in Rochester. Anyway, enjoy your meal. I need to mingle and see if I can drum up some kite business. Nothing like a party to find potential customers, you know." She walked across the lawn, or more like staggered.

I stared at the empty bottle lying next to her chair. It wasn't uncommon for people to drink too much when they were troubled or sad or lonely. I wondered if that was the case with Gwen now. I eyed her duffle bag with the other bottle and a few personal items. An envelope stuck out of the bag. It had been torn open. Biting my lip, I lifted my gaze and searched the crowd until I spotted Gwen. She was engaged in conversation with a couple standing by the lakeshore, several hundred feet away.

I lowered my arm and pinched the edge of the envelope. Slipping it out of the bag, I read the return address. "Sinclair Point Nursing Home." I gasped and quickly lifted it from the bag. With one more glance at Gwen, who worked her way across the lawn and stopped to talk with another guest, I slid the contents out of the envelope and read. My eyes widened and jaw dropped.

"I see you went for the land lover's choice."

I squealed and jumped in my seat. Shoving the letter back in Gwen's bag, I looked up to find Hunter hovering above. "I can never resist Bob's barbecue ribs." In an effort to slow my racing heartbeat, I took a deep breath and another for good measure. "I'm surprised you came."

"Why wouldn't I?" He chewed on the end of a toothpick.

I studied him from head to toe. Dressed in a cotton shirt, unbuttoned at the top, a pair of khaki cargo shorts, and canvas deck shoes, he appeared ready and relaxed for the occasion. "I'm too used to seeing you in your professional gear. Like I said before, you always seem to be on the job." I waved my arm. "This never happens."

A smile teased his lips. "Stick around long enough and you'll find there's more than one side to me. Besides, who says I'm not working the case right at this moment?" He winked.

A bite of potato salad caught in my throat. I swallowed and wished I'd accepted Gwen's offer of wine.

"Here." He handed me one of the bottles of Fizzy Orange he was carrying. "Seems like you need a drink."

"I'm fine." I strained the words but took the bottle he offered and swigged half the contents.

Hunter sat in Gwen's chair and popped open his own Fizzy Orange. He took a sip and nodded. "I can see what the fuss is all about. Does Bob make this?"

"Yep. Well, his dad came up with the recipe. Bob is keeping the family tradition going, I guess." I set my plate on the ground. "Supposing you are on the job, here and now. Is there any news you can share?"

"Well, I could." He leaned back, lifting his chair's front legs off the ground.

I rolled my eyes. "Is this a game you enjoy playing with me?"

The chair landed on all fours. "Not sure what you mean. You asked if I could, which I took to mean if I had the ability to share."

"Oh for—just tell me what you know." I spoke through gritted teeth.

"Now, that's clear enough. A bit rude, maybe, but clear." He took a few more swigs of his drink.

I drummed my fingers on the chair arm and held my temper. If I wasn't curious to learn what he had to say, I'd get up and walk away.

"We caught the arsonist. His name is Milo Lewis. He was in the middle of another arson job up in Rochester. Once the RPD threw him in jail, he begged to make a deal with the information he had on Infinity. I have to admit we sure caught a break. In no time, he spilled all he had on the guy who hired him for the job. Lewis knew how Infinity played dirty. So, as added insurance, he had recorded the conversation with the contact from Infinity. Everything we need is on there—time, place, and what Infinity would pay. Enough proof to charge both of them for arson. Of course, I imagine Infinity has a strong team of lawyers on retainer, and their guy won't serve much jail time, if any." Hunter chewed on the toothpick again.

Fireworks popped and whistled as they reached the sky, then the spirals of color spread and fell into the water.

"Did they say anything about Sammy?" My heartbeat held for several seconds. Despite the foolish and rather hasty decisions she'd made and my wavering suspicion she could be Fiona's killer, I didn't wish her any harm. Especially harm from Infinity goons. Nobody deserved their kind of vengeance.

"Only that she owed them money for breaking her contract. Since she wasn't around to pay, they made sure she'd never do business with anyone again. As far as they're concerned, the score is even."

I shuddered. "I warned her, but it was too late. She was in pretty deep by the time I learned about her partnership."

Of course she wouldn't want anyone to know. That was why I had to wonder if Fiona had somehow found out and threatened to write about it, or maybe even blackmailed Sammy. I rubbed the goose bumps on my arms and stared in silence at Hunter, with his deeply furrowed brow and tense jaw. Was he drawing the same conclusions? One thing for sure, exposure and blackmail were strong enough motives to commit murder.

"The team will keep searching until they find her. After they spotted her in Altoona, she gave them the slip. Turns out her cousin lives there. I looked up her driving record and got a close look at her photo and description. Short, black hair, five feet three inches, one hundred forty pounds." He smiled. "Sammy's neighbor was spot on. You can see why I assumed the woman was you."

I glared and exercised my jaw back and forth. Seriously? How could men be so dense? I wasn't an ounce over one thirty. "Well, you know what they say when someone assumes."

He widened his eyes. "You're right. I shouldn't make assumptions. I go by facts and evidence. In this case, the facts prove the woman Sammy's neighbor saw was almost an exact match to you, but I—"

"You are so exasperating. And that's not me assuming." I picked up my plate and bottle, then sprang out of my seat. "For your information, I already knew. Nell Sampson told me herself when I spoke with her. She said I was too skinny to fit the description. So there. See you around, Detective." I marched away without looking back. Fuming over something as trivial as assumptions about my appearance reeked of insecurity. I had zero respect for women who were shallow and worried about each wrinkle and every pound. Something more was at work here, but I didn't have time to dwell on why I was feeling this way. Spotting Izzie and Megan sitting near the lake, I tossed my plate and bottle in a trash bin and, without breaking stride, headed toward them.

Izzie snuggled close to Megan and wrapped her arm around her shoulders.

I plopped down in the sand and nudged Izzie. "Is this one of those private moments between you two, or can I join?"

Izzie patted my leg. "You're welcome to stay. In fact, you should hear Megan's story to give you some perspective."

Her gaze pierced through me and sent a message.

"Sure. I'm listening."

Megan's breath hitched. "The police received an anonymous tip in the mail. It's a time-stamped photo of me picking up an order from Bob's Barbecue close to nine the evening of Fiona's murder, but that's a coincidence, right? I mean, plenty of people were there at the same time."

"How could you be there at that time? You were . . ." I stopped as the notion hit me. The empty seat at the event before we'd finished. "You left the paint event early. Why?"

"I got a call from the jewelry store in town that my dad's birthday gift was ready to pick up. Mr. Finnigan agreed to stay open late for me if I promised to stop by Bob's to grab his order since he'd missed dinner. Dad's birthday was the next day, you see. My aunt Susan arranged a family gathering at her home in Buffalo to celebrate. My parents decided we should leave first thing in the morning. I had to pick up his gift the evening of your event, and that's why I left early." She sniffed and wiped her eyes with the back of her hand.

"Seems reasonable. What did Hunter say when you told him?" I asked.

Izzie sighed. "He wanted proof. Her word wasn't good enough. Such a tool."

"Izzie, stop. He's a detective. He goes by evidence, not assumptions." I made a mental eye roll. At least most of the time he did.

"I had proof." Megan straightened her shoulders, but her lips trembled. "I gave him the receipt from Finnigan's, which had the date and time."

"Thank goodness, Hunter was satisfied. Megan heard he followed up by talking with Finnigan and Bob," Izzie added.

"That's great. Isn't it?" I frowned. "Of course, I'm so dense. You're worried about your shop."

"Thanks. Truth is, I'm not in the mood for a party." She stood on wobbly legs, then turned to stare into the crowd that circled the bonfire.

I followed her gaze and spotted a group of four people off to the left of the circle. Grayson Stone was among them. Our gazes connected, but then his head turned a fraction. He didn't smile, which was a surprise. He'd always been so friendly, so charming.

A tiny gasp escaped Megan.

"Are you okay, Megs?" Izzie touched her shoulder.

Megan gave her head a hard shake. "My leg cramped for a second. Going up and down stairs a million times to move my stuff will do that, right?" She managed a tiny smile. "I think I'll head home. I have lots left to pack before I move out of my condo."

"Did you get her to tell you what the argument with Grayson was about?" I asked as Megan wove her way around guests to reach Artisan Alley.

"Just some disagreement about him not paying for some merchandise."

"At least she's consistent," I mumbled under my breath.

"What?" Izzie turned to stare at me.

"Nothing." I pulled her toward the nearest boat dock. "I have something to tell you."

I kept my voice lowered. No telling where Gwen might show up as she worked her way through the crowd, promoting her kites to anyone who had a pulse.

We sat on the edge with our legs dangling and feet touching the water.

"What's so urgent and private that you had to bring us out here?" Izzie asked.

"I found a letter in Gwen's duffle bag."

Izzie gawked. "You went through her things?"

"Never mind that. You want to know what it said, or not?" This wasn't the time for lectures on respecting people's property.

"Fine." She pointed her finger. "But only if it has something to do with the murder case, which I remember you said to leave alone."

"Old news. Anyway, the letter was from that nursing home where Gwen's sister-in-law is staying. Or I should say, *was* staying."

Izzie's eyes popped open as she slapped a hand over her mouth. "She died? How awful."

"No, she didn't die." I scowled. "She was moved to a state facility in Buffalo this week. Anyway, the letter was addressed to Gwen. It stated that her ex-husband, William Finch, was the one who signed the order of transfer. Also, it mentions insufficient funds as the reason for her moving out of Sinclair Point." I clutched her wrist. "Izzie, here's where it gets even more important. The letter stated that if Gwen had questions or concerns, the director was free to meet with her any time after six on Thursday, two weeks ago. You know what day that was? The day Fiona was murdered."

Izzie frowned. "I don't know. Seems far-fetched. Why would someone from the nursing home send Gwen a letter about moving Tressa?"

I scooted closer. "My guess is someone felt Gwen should know, maybe since she visited Tressa often. Remember I told you about the phone conversation I overheard Gwen having? She argued with someone, saying how cruel the person was and warning that he or she would pay. What if she was talking to William and the conversation was about Tressa?" I shook my head. "Now everything makes perfect sense. The excessive drinking, her strange behavior, and talking about some man she's dating."

She braced both arms behind her on the dock and leaned back. "And this connects to the murder how?"

"Gwen's story about where she was that night has to be true. The letter is postmarked two days before the murder. She probably went to Sinclair on Thursday evening, like the director invited her to, to see if there was any way to stop them from transferring Tressa. So sad, that phone call could have been her hail Mary, hoping she could change William's mind."

"I'm glad if this puts her in the clear, but it really narrows down the suspect list. Maybe we'll never find out who killed Fiona. Does Hunter know about all this?"

It hit me. Of course, he had to know. After talking to the director at Sinclair Point, he would've learned about Gwen's visits, including if she'd been there the evening of the murder.

The director wouldn't need a computer log to jog her memory. Residents didn't get booted out all that often. "He does! He has to know. Instead of sharing the whole truth, he talked about the nursing home's computer snafu and power outage. Such a tool."

"Hey! I'm the one who gets to call Hunter a tool." Izzie winked. "Don't fume about it too much. He's the detective, and we're the bumbling amateur snoops. Isn't that what you said? Nothing says he has to share his information."

"You're right. Teaches me to stay out of his business, I guess." I kicked my feet in the water.

She jabbed my side with her elbow. "Which you won't do. You never could stop poking your nose into what you shouldn't. How many times did Mom or Dad ground you?"

"I lost count." I grinned. "But it was a heck of a lot." I bounced onto my feet. "I'm glad I snooped this time, though.

"Me too." Izzie stood and brushed off her bottom.

I pointed over my shoulder. "I'm heading over to our host's deck. I think there's a wine bar set up. You want to tag along?"

"Nah. I'm visiting the seafood table. I haven't had lobster in weeks, thanks to Mom and her 'save the sea creatures' campaign."

I laughed. "Don't worry. Her next crusade will come along soon. What about the Sterling brothers?"

She smiled. "Oh, they must like seafood too because they're standing next to the crab legs."

"My sister the multitasker. Good luck." I waved and walked back toward the bonfire, searching for any sign of Ross. Maybe he'd changed his mind. Or another web conference with a client was keeping him busy.

I snorted. "Why should I care how he spends his vacation?" A heavy feeling settled in my stomach, along with the huge rack of ribs I'd eaten. I wormed my way through the crowd when I spotted Grayson. "Maybe that's who I should focus my attention on." I was speaking into my chest, while stepping onto the deck.

"What can I pour for you? We have red, white, sweet, dry, any number of both domestic and imported wines." The bartender smiled at me.

"I'll take a glass of Merlot, please." I tapped my foot while twisting to look behind me.

Grayson remained in his spot.

"Here you go, miss."

I clutched the stem of the plastic goblet and stepped off the deck. Making my way toward Grayson, I scrambled to think of something clever to say, anything that would impress a rich, famous, and talented man. I moaned and took a healthy sip of wine. Who was I kidding? I was totally out of his league. Within a few yards, I pulled up short and frowned.

Through the crowd, someone with a bob of pink and purple hair approached Grayson. As she reached him, I gasped. Willow grabbed his arm with one hand and waved the other around. Their mouths moved as if in a heated exchange. Within seconds, Grayson led the way toward the side entrance to the condo and Willow followed. They disappeared inside, but I could still hear the sound of raised voices.

I looked side to side. No one else seemed to notice what was going on. In a snap decision, I set my wine glass on a bench and made my way to the sliding door entrance. I was worried about Willow. After the quarrel between Megan and

Grayson, I was beginning to question my judgment. Grayson might not be such a nice guy after all. He was certainly showing a side of himself I didn't care for. Quietly, I opened the slider and tiptoed inside. Staying close to the door, I listened to their voices coming from down the hall. On tiptoe, I inched my way closer until I could peek around the corner of the room in which they stood.

"I asked you to do one thing. Just one," Grayson said. The muscles in his face knotted in anger.

Willow shrank away. "I couldn't. I'm sorry, Grayson. I tried but it was just too hard."

"You're a silly little girl. Never will amount to anything." He waved an arm. "Get out of my sight. I don't ever want to see you again."

Willow sobbed and reached for his hand, but he stepped back. "Please don't say that. I love you. I'd do anything for you."

He shook his head and laughed. "Silly *and* pathetic. Now leave. Before I have someone throw you out."

I cringed at the anger and the coldness in his voice. My heart skipped as Willow cried and ran out of the condo. It took no more than a second. I flew down the hall and outside, hoping to catch her. Instead, I collided with one of the servers carrying a tray. Shrimp and puff pastries scattered across the patio.

"Oh! I'm so sorry." I threw up my arms, then sidestepped to move around him. "Sorry!" I called over my shoulder as I hurried across the lawn, nearly colliding with other guests. I strained to catch sight of Willow, but by now she had been swallowed up by the crowd.

"Hey! Leaving so soon?"

A hand gripped my arm. My head snapped around. Grayson smiled in his charming way that no longer appealed to me. A sour taste filled my mouth. "I'm not feeling so great. Thinking of heading home and turning in early."

Several thoughts collided in my head. Willow and Grayson knew each other, but how? She hadn't mentioned this when I had brought up the invitation to his bonfire, which puzzled me. My stomach clenched with concern. The decision to go after Willow and see if she needed help jarred me. I feared she was in some kind of trouble, and the cause of that trouble was standing right in front of me.

"You look stunning, by the way. Maybe you could stay for a bit longer?" He stroked my arm.

"I really should go. Maybe we'll get together some other time." I spoke while slowly stepping away from him. The casual, smooth talk sounded fake now. Like all of it was an act to cover up some underlying anger or something I couldn't understand. What I did know was the impression I'd had of him had vanished.

"I've been meaning to visit you at the shop. Business keeps getting in the way." He chuckled and kept moving forward as I backed away. "How is the shop doing? With all the trouble going on, making a go of it is a struggle, I'm sure."

My gaze scanned the area, searching for a familiar face, like Izzie or Ross. "We're doing great. Izzie has scheduled several events and slots are filling up faster than ever." I lifted my arms with palms face out. "Look, I really have to go. Nice party," I hollered as I turned to weave my way through the crowd. I couldn't escape quickly enough.

"Chloe. What's wrong?" Izzie came from behind me.

"I'm not sure." I wrapped my arm around her waist and snuggled closer to warm myself. "But I think Willow might be in trouble."

Chapter Eighteen

"We've tried the shop and her apartment and called her phone a dozen times. What more can we do?" Izzie dropped into the living room chair.

I checked my watch. An hour had passed since we had left the bonfire, and everything was shadowed in darkness. Searching more now would be pointless. Frustration put my nerves on edge. "How far did you go in checking her background?" I had an idea that wouldn't involve stumbling around blindly.

"I didn't call the FBI or hire a detective to see if she's been on a crime spree, if that's what you mean." Izzie narrowed her eyes and grew rigid.

"I'm not judging. After seeing her on the job and all she can do, I'd hire her on the spot." I sipped my water and leaned forward. "There's a good chance she left town and has gone to stay with a relative or friend. That's why I asked. Did she give you an emergency contact name and number?"

Izzie frowned. "No. In fact, she mentioned not having any family and how she came to Whisper Cove for a do-over since she lost her last job due to the business closing."

"Hmm. What business was that?" I pulled out my phone and opened a window.

"Paint and Play? She described it as a small shop offering activity workshops for kids, but I already checked and found a dead end."

I typed in the name. "The link to the website shows the domain is for sale. You're right. Nothing more is listed." I scratched behind one ear. "We could call the police, but they won't search for her yet."

"Maybe we're being premature. I wouldn't be surprised if we walk into the shop tomorrow morning and find her there." Izzie hiccupped.

"Ah, your words say everything's fine, but your hiccups say you're still worried. Be glad you weren't there to see them. Grayson was so angry, and Willow looked really frightened. I can't stop until we find her and I know she's okay." I sighed. "I'm heading upstairs to use my laptop and search online for more info. If you have Willow's résumé and application in your files here at the house, text me her SSN and any other personal info that might help me, would you?"

"I do and will. In the meantime, I'll make a few more calls and check with her landlord and places I know she likes to go." Izzie stood. "What about Grayson? Maybe we should go back to the condo and speak with him."

"Are you kidding? I wouldn't trust him being anywhere near us. Not now." I shuddered. "If someone needs to question him, let it be Hunter."

I went up to my room. Max trotted after me. We snuggled together on the bed, and I booted up my laptop. North was a common name. If I was going to get results, some extensive searching would be necessary and would involve database programs I didn't have at my fingertips. "We'll work with what we've got, right, Max?" I scratched the top of his head, and he immediately rolled over on his back. I laughed. "Always looking for a belly rub."

My phone dinged. I read the text from Izzie with the information I needed. "Okay, let's do this."

A half hour later, my search ended with a list of several addresses where Willow had lived, all of them in and around New York City. Other than the fact she had never stayed in one place for long, I had nothing. I tapped the sides of the laptop while contemplating the pros and cons of my next move. I hated the idea of owing him anything. "Oh, what the heck." I picked up my phone and dialed the familiar number. Chances were he wouldn't answer. I pictured him doing something fun like dancing with some hottie, taking full advantage of his summer vacation. I still didn't fully buy into this new and improved Ross who played in the lake water and wore clothes fit only for a tourist. "Hi! You answered." I sat up straight and cleared my throat.

"Ah, yeah. That's what happens when my phone rings. I answer and have a conversation. Are you at the bonfire? I looked for you," Ross said.

"Something happened and we had to leave early." I picked at the fringes of my blanket. "Are you enjoying the party?"

"It was a total bore without you. I left and came back to the hotel. So, what's the something that happened? Are you and Izzie okay?" His voice shifted to a somber tone.

"We're fine but worried about Willow. After having an argument with Grayson Stone, she was upset and ran away from the bonfire. We tried to find her, but it's like she vanished."

"From all you've told me, that guy sure seems to have a problem with women. Anyway, what can I do to help?"

I smiled. I didn't even have to ask. Maybe I was being too harsh. He hadn't been such an awful boyfriend, just unavailable most of the time. "You have access to databases, don't you?"

"Me and the NYPD are tight. You want me to search her name. Willow North, right?"

"Her last address was in Manhattan, and she worked for a small business called Paint and Play. I'm texting you her social security number." I pressed send, then added, "I can't get over the two of them knowing each other. She never once mentioned Grayson by name. When I told her about meeting him by the lake and his invitation to the bonfire, she asked who he was. So strange."

I heard the tapping of keys. I set my phone and laptop aside, then leaned against the bed frame to wait. One thing was for sure, Ross excelled at research. On almost every case he worked, he needed very little time to prepare his brief.

"It seems she's got a criminal record."

"Oh? I didn't see that coming." I gripped the phone. How Izzie could've missed that important detail was beyond me.

"Wait. Only a couple of misdemeanors for shoplifting. One incident involved a Quicky Mart, where she stole a package of ground chuck and a box of rice mix."

"Oh lord. Poor, starving, living on the street, selling sketches for any money people would give her. It's horrible." I squeezed my eyes shut.

"I see you haven't lost your wild imagination. But before you play the sympathy card, these addresses she's lived at are in some upscale neighborhoods. Hardly poor and starving."

"Yeah, well, we're all one paycheck away from living on the streets, you know."

"Hold on. I found something interesting."

I thought aloud while his key tapping resumed. "If she lived in comfort, why come to Whisper Cove? I mean, she could be running away from something or someone." My mind jumped to the argument between Willow and Grayson. "My gut tells me she and Grayson Stone have a history, but I can't imagine what that could be."

"I'm switching to video chat. You won't believe this until you see it with your own eyes."

I clicked to accept the video call, and Ross's face filled the screen. "You're right. I thought I was talking to someone who sounded exactly like you. How relieved I am now." A smirk crossed my face.

"Funny lady. No, look." He turned his phone to view his computer screen.

"What am I looking at?" I squinted and leaned closer. "Would you hold the phone still? No, move in closer so I can read. It's too blurry."

"Oh, for—" He groaned and switched the camera back to him. "There's more than one of her. Willow North, Willow Noel, and Willow Singer. Her photo ID is the same, only the name changes."

"I don't understand. She has fake IDs?"

"It would take a while to explain how these databases work. Trust me. Willow has these aliases, and I'll probably find more if I keep searching. Why, I don't know. I could wager a couple of guesses. Running from the authorities or maybe escaping an abusive home come to mind."

I'd already done a search for Grayson Stone, but I didn't have the advantage of using Ross's toolbox of tech goodies. "One more favor? Can you search Grayson Stone in your database?"

His face blushed and he glanced away. "Already did."

"And why's that?" I stabbed my finger at the phone screen. "Let me guess. You checked him out because Izzie asked you to, or maybe she told you I was interested in him, which I'm not. Ross Thompson, when will you give up? We're not getting back together." I slammed my back against the headboard.

He rubbed his jaw with one hand. "Your sister cares about you and your safety. I do too. No matter whether we're together or not, Chloe, I'll always look out for you."

"Totally not necessary, but thanks." I slouched in my seat. "What did you find?"

"No criminal record. His accomplishments run a mile long. The guy's a saint." His eyes brightened. "But you're not interested in him, so none of it matters."

"That's not why I asked, you goof." I squirmed in my seat while Max curled in a ball with his rear end pushed against me. "What about the connection to Willow? Did you check the social pages? Any details about his personal life, family, girlfriend?"

"A few articles mention his parents, who, by the way, are wealthy enough to be in the top one percent. As for siblings, he has a brother who lives in San Francisco and works for some software company. There's also a sister who's much younger.

She attended prep school, then started her freshman year at a private college, but that's when the information on her stops. For some reason, she fell off the radar."

"None of this helps, does it?" I sighed. All the information we'd found created more questions than answers.

"There was one credential about Stone that raised my curiosity." Ross grabbed a paper off the table in front of him. "Besides his sculptures, his philanthropic efforts, and appearances with the New York Symphony, he also runs a real estate development company, which has completed several projects across the country."

"Of course, he has the money to start a dozen companies. Doesn't sound fishy to me."

"I'm not finished. What surprises me is how his company makes some of these deals. I searched the court records. On one occasion, Stone was able to persuade a zoning committee to change a residential area to a business zone by cutting through the red tape. There's even a case I found where someone accused the company of using pressure tactics to convince property owners to sell. No charges have ever stuck, but still, the pillar of society might have a crack in his reputation."

My stomach soured. To be honest, I wasn't totally surprised, after what I'd experienced this evening. All the charm and good looks meant nothing. "Thanks for your help and digging up a ton of info, even if none of it leads to finding Willow."

"Always glad to help you, Chloe. Hey, I'm free tomorrow. Would you like me to help in the search? If Willow doesn't turn up by then, that is."

"Thanks, but let's wait and see. To use Izzie's optimism, I'm picturing Willow at the shop in the morning, eagerly ready to work."

"In any case, I think I'll do some more digging and see what else I can find out about her."

"Don't stay up too late. You know how grouchy you are in the morning when you don't get a good night's sleep." I caught myself before adding more and quickly ended the call. I didn't need distractions by stirring up old memories. I had to focus on Willow. A glance at the clock showed me it was late, but I could research a little while longer before retiring for the night. I pulled the laptop closer and booted it up before the house phone rang. I answered quickly, hoping not to wake Mom and Dad, who were probably sound asleep.

"Hello?"

"Izzie? Chloe? Kate? Whoever this is, I've been trying to get a hold of one of you."

"This is Chloe. I—"

"Thank goodness you answered. I called Izzie's cell phone but can't seem to get through. Keeps going to voice mail. At least your folks are sensible and keep a landline. Anyway, I would've left Izzie a message, but this is urgent. Or at least I think it is."

I laid the receiver in my lap and sighed, then pressed it to my ear again. "Who is this?"

"Oh, guess I should've led with that. This is Penny."

"Hi, Penny. Is everything all right?" I shut the lid on the laptop. "You said something is urgent." My breath held. After all that had happened along Artisan Alley in the past two weeks—the murder, the break-in, the fire, Sammy's disappearance, and now Willow's, I expected the worst.

"After leaving the bonfire, I checked on my shop and then made my way over to Whisper Lane, where I'd parked. Passing by, I noticed there were lights on in your sister's place. With all the scary things happening around here, I got suspicious. I mean, you and Izzie don't stay that late, from what I've noticed. Anyway, I knocked on the door, figuring somebody might be hurt and need help. Not totally far-fetched, considering. But nobody answered. Now, I'm pretty brave but sure not foolish. I took the matter that far, and that's when I started calling your sister. See what I mean?"

"Yes, thanks, Penny. You did the right thing. We'll take it from here."

"Don't be a fool and go there alone. You should call that detective for help."

"I will, if necessary. Good night and thanks again." I set the receiver back in the cradle and scrambled out of bed. Penny was right. If I was smart, I'd call Hunter. However, the thought pressing me was that the person in the shop had to be Willow. At least, I was ninety percent sure. Maybe more like eighty. I pulled on my shoes and grabbed my bag and keys. If Izzie hadn't gone to bed yet, she would come along. Safety in numbers gave me confidence.

I tiptoed down the stairs and into the living room, where I'd left Izzie. Finding no sign of her, I searched the rest of the first-floor rooms, even peeked out the front window, but her jeep was parked in the drive. I retraced my steps and tiptoed to the second floor and Izzie's bedroom. If she wasn't in there,

I'd give up the search. "Izzie?" I whispered and gave the door a soft tap.

Dad was a light sleeper. If I made too much noise, he'd wake up and grab his baseball bat, ready to charge down the hall.

I inched the door open and heard the rumble of snoring. The lump under the covers and the tousled brown curls spread out on the pillow told me I wasn't getting my backup. I stepped lightly down the stairs and pulled out my phone. Staring at the screen, I debated whether Penny was right. I scanned my most recent calls but couldn't find the one I needed. "Darn." I clutched my bag and at once I gasped. "His card!" On the horrible, tragic day we met, Hunter had given me his card. I rummaged through my bag and found it. While dialing the number, I walked outside and to my car. After three or four rings, the call went to voice mail. "Good grief." I waited for the beep. "This is Chloe. You said to call if I needed you. I think someone, or rather Penny Swanson thinks someone might've broken into our shop. She claims there are lights on." I took a big gulp of air and steadied my hand. "Willow is upset and ran away because Grayson yelled at her, and Izzie and I have looked everywhere but can't find her. Maybe we should've reported it, but we're not sure if she is in trouble, and you won't start searching until—" I gripped the phone and took several deep breaths. "Sorry. I'm rambling. I ramble when I'm nervous. Okay. I'm going to the shop and wanted to let you know. Bye."

I stabbed the end call button and tossed the phone back in my bag. Sliding into the driver's seat, I fired up the engine and sped toward Artisan Alley. Fool or not, I had to do this in case Willow was the intruder and needed help.

I slowed to a crawl down Whisper Lane, then pulled into the usual spot when my phone rang. I snatched it out of my bag and answered. "Thank goodness you called."

"I didn't expect that sort of response. I figured you'd be angry with me."

I gripped the phone. "Sammy? Oh my gosh. It's you."

"Yep. Runaway me." Her voice sang out. "I'm coming home for good and wanted you to know. Things were left hanging a bit." Her nervous laugh echoed over the line.

"A bit?" I shook my head. Getting out of my car, I noticed no other vehicle in the parking area. My confidence wavered a little, but if Willow was in the shop, she could have come on foot.

"Okay, a lot, but I had good reason. After we talked that morning, I got a call from my contact at Infinity. Seems he has a conscience after all. He wanted to warn me that some people from the company were coming to meet me in an hour to convince me one way or another that I shouldn't break my contract with them. I needed to get out of town right away."

"You should let the authorities know about this. I have Detective Barrett's number." The strong breeze drifting off the lake made me shiver. I rubbed my arms, then marched around the corner and up the walkway. Sure enough, lights brightened the rear of the shop, while the front remained dark.

"I already did, this evening. Chloe, I wanted to call sooner, but I was afraid. My shop is destroyed, so I'm not sure what I'll do next, but I had to let you know I'm sorry. I should've listened to you."

My brows peaked. "Were you the one sneaking through your shop the other night?"

"Yeah, I had to see for myself. Everything's destroyed." She sighed. "I didn't stay long. Until the men from Infinity were put behind bars, I couldn't stay in Whisper Cove and feel safe."

A shadow passed by the back window. "Look, Sammy, I'm sort of in the middle of something. We'll talk more when you get home. Okay?"

"Oh! Yeah, of course, but I wanted to make sure Detective Barrett contacted you. I told him who I suspect killed Fiona. He said he would call you as soon as he could. I know it sounds crazy, but to think she . . ." The crackling sound of static came over the phone.

"Sammy?" I scowled and pressed to end the call. "Everything happens all at once," I muttered as I dug in my bag to retrieve the shop key. On a hunch, I jiggled the handle first and the door swung open. A shuddering breath moved through me as I stepped inside. I checked the phone once more before tucking it inside my bag. Still no answer from Hunter. "Guess I'm going in solo." Tilting my head, I listened for noise coming from the lighted storage room. Steps softly shuffled and a shadow darkened the doorway for a second as if someone was moving around.

If Willow was back there, at least she was alive. I swallowed to clear my throat. Before losing courage, I clenched both fists, then put my feet in motion and marched across the floor to the storage room. I stopped at the doorway. Willow was pulling clothing out of the locker and tossing the items on the floor. "Willow?"

She startled at the sound of my voice and whipped around to face me. Her eyes grew wide. "Chloe. What are you doing here?"

"I should be asking you the same thing." I inched closer, then paused when she backed away.

"I forgot my shirt the other day and came to find it." She shifted her weight from one leg to the other.

"No, you didn't. Remember? I told you to use turpentine to remove the stain, then you put the shirt in your bag."

"You think you know everything." She turned to pace the floor, pausing for a second to stab her finger at me. "But you don't. There's plenty about me you don't know."

As she passed near me, I caught a closer look at the mark on her shoulder. I'd noticed it before, the day she borrowed my shirt. The image had slipped my mind, but now I paid attention. A blue butterfly. I'd seen something similar. I snapped my fingers. "The newspaper article! Slender arm, blue marking on the shoulder. You were the one in that group photo taken at the Carnegie art gala. You were standing next to Grayson, but someone blocked the view of your face. I'm right, aren't I?" For a moment, I forgot about what had made me frightened in coming here.

Instead, my brain worked and shifted through the tiny details, hints I should've known something was wrong. Willow's aliases, her arrival in Whisper Cove after responding to a job ad Izzie had placed in the *Gazette*, her claim she had no family, the argument with Grayson, those times she hadn't shown for work or left early because her stomach was upset or she had to visit the doctor. And what about the date who dumped her?

I asked you to do one thing.

My eyes brightened as I gasped. "Are you pregnant? Is that why you came to Whisper Cove? You were following Grayson to tell him he's going to be a dad? Kind of old for you, but I'm not judging."

Her jaw dropped. "What? God, no! I'm not . . . He's not . . . I think I'm going to be sick again." She plopped down in a chair and covered her face with both hands.

I hesitated but then stepped closer. "I overheard your argument with Grayson. You said you loved him when he called you silly and pathetic. What is the one thing he asked you to do that you couldn't?"

Glaring at me, she clamped her mouth shut and crossed both arms.

"Why didn't you say anything to Izzie about the shoplifting charges? She would've understood and given you the job anyway. She's forgiving like that. Just a bit on edge most of the time."

Willow widened her eyes. "How did you find out? I wasn't—"

"You weren't Willow North when you shoplifted." I spoke softly.

"I had to keep changing my name because I didn't want anyone following me."

"Willow North, Willow Noel, Willow Singer. Are there any others?"

She sniffed and wiped her cheeks with the back of her hand. "He asked me to come to Whisper Cove and help him with a deal he was putting together. I didn't know the details but came anyway. He's my brother. I'd do anything for him." Her gaze darkened and pierced through me. "Anything, you understand. When Fiona spouted off that she knew what my brother was up to and how I should be ashamed for doing some of his dirty work, I—" She sobbed, then lifted her chin. "I couldn't let her ruin him. I owe him so much."

My phone buzzed. "It's about time, Hunter." I pulled the device out of my bag and stared at the text from Ross.

> Willow has another alias. Willow Stone, and my guess is that's her real name. Call me.

"Just a little too late, Ross." I glanced back at Willow while shoving my phone in my pocket. Her gaze darted side to side while her hands and jaw clenched. The back of my neck tingled. Taking a step nearer the supply counter, I did a quick scan of brushes, knives, and cleaners. If she attacked me, I'd spray her face with cleaner and run as fast as I could. I was too squeamish to stab her with a knife or even the pointy end of a brush. "You killed Fiona. That's why you wanted to leave early that evening. You had a date all right. One to commit murder!"

"No! I didn't. I mean, I wanted to and planned to." She raked fingers through her hair. "Oh, God, it sounds crazy saying the words out loud. I tried to catch up to her after she left the event, but I couldn't find her. She said she would go to the authorities and let them know she had proof Grayson planned to tear down every shop along Artisan Alley, no matter what it took, so his company could build the condos and resort." She shook her head. "Somehow Fiona discovered he'd pressured Megan and threatened to destroy everything she had unless she sold him her business. I couldn't let that despicable woman hurt Grayson."

"Willow." I smiled sadly, suddenly not afraid any longer. "There's no point in lying. The truth has to come out. Whether you confess or not, Hunter will figure out you killed her."

Her shoulders shook. "I'm telling you the truth. Don't you see? Someone else got to her first. I don't know who, but—" Her eyes widened as she gasped. "Chloe! Watch out!"

Chapter Nineteen

I stirred awake and winced at the effort. Sharp clinking and clanking sounds pierced my ears, followed by a loud tirade of expletives. I touched the top of my head with my fingertips and moaned. Any effort to recall what had happened and why I was sitting here, wherever here was, came up empty. I pushed to stand but cried out in pain. My ankle was swollen and bruised.

"Eh, eh. Stay where you are. I expected you'd be out for hours. Not that it matters. Just because you have a bum leg, I won't think twice to bop you over the head again."

I blinked to clear the blurry image in front of me. The words bop and head triggered my memory. When I fell, I must've twisted my ankle. Willow's warning hadn't come quickly enough. "Willow!" I tensed at the thought of her, then searched the room. Sharp pain stabbed at me like daggers, and the bump on my head throbbed.

"She's fine. Threw a few punches at me, so I tied her up. Let that be a warning. I'll do the same to you if you don't sit still."

I rubbed my eyes. Willow was huddled in the back corner of the storage room. Her mouth was taped and both arms and legs were tied. I leaned against the box behind me, relieved she was alive. Still, the wild look of panic in her eyes hinted we were in deep trouble. Scooting my rear end to face the other way, I squinted to see who was talking. The voice sounded familiar, but my ears were ringing and her words echoed in my head. Pain threatened to make me pass out again, but I strained to make out the image of a woman. "Theo! What— why are you here? I don't understand."

She sat, straddling the chair and pointed above her toward one corner of the ceiling. "Cameras. I have one installed here, another in the front room, and one outside the shop. I told your sister they're for safety, in case someone breaks in. It's a convenient excuse. I use them to see who comes and goes. The building belongs to me, so . . ." She shrugged. "I watched Willow come inside the shop, and then you followed." Her eyes narrowed. "Didn't I tell you to stop snooping? But I knew you wouldn't. You're the same little girl who was always too curious for her own good. Ever since you stopped by the other day and asked more questions about Fiona, I've kept an eye on you." She stood and looked up at the camera. "Such a nuisance. Now, I'll have to delete this mess and won't have the chance to watch and enjoy it."

The wild eyes sparked with anger and showed something in her I'd never witnessed before. The painting knife made sense now. She could've easily entered the shop and stolen it. Most likely, she hoped to focus the investigation on someone who worked here or attended the event. I started as the distant ring and buzz of my phone sounded. My gaze darted around the room. I hadn't remembered placing the phone anywhere except in my pocket. Ross or maybe Hunter and especially Izzie would be frantic if I didn't answer. I stopped and stared at Theo's smug expression.

"Don't worry. I have it tucked safely away." She patted her shirt pocket. "You won't be needing it any longer."

I gulped. I'd read how victims should keep their captors occupied with questions, maybe stroke their egos and get them to talk about themselves. Anxious, I scratched the palms of my hands. I had to do something to delay whatever Theo had planned, until someone came to the rescue. *If* someone came. I squeezed my eyes shut for a brief moment and forced my mind to work. *Keep her talking.* That was the only card I had to play. If Izzie's optimism had a chance of working, now was the time. Otherwise, the ending to this story would find Willow and me dead.

"Please. I think, under the circumstances, I deserve to know why you're doing this."

"Isn't it obvious? Use that pretty head of yours and think." She reached out as if to touch my forehead, and I flinched. A throaty chuckle escaped. "I killed Fiona. There, I said it. Whew! That's a relief to admit it out loud." She pointed. "I know what you're thinking. Why? Why would someone like me kill her? There has to be a reason, right? I mean, look around you." She waved her arms. "So many people in this town had better motives and opportunity. Sammy, Megan, Gwen, even your little thief over there." She lifted her chin. "But me? Not a thing. Detective Barrett and his team of idiots, even you and Izzie, worked so hard to figure out who committed the crime, and never once did you think of me.

Until the other day, that is, when you stopped by the *Gazette*. You were getting too close to the truth. That's when I decided something had to be done. Put this story to bed, as we say in the newspaper business."

I licked my bottom lip while Willow mumbled and groaned in a muffled tone. Theo was insane. I couldn't argue with her. Mainly because I didn't have a clue what she was talking about. Something told me no amount of reasoning would change her mind.

"What possible reason could you have to kill your employee? Didn't you say she helped sell newspapers? Sure, she was difficult to work with, and plenty of folks called to complain about her column, but that didn't matter. That's what you told us." I glanced at my watch. It was past ten thirty, more than a half hour since I'd called Hunter and almost as long since Ross had texted. By now, one or both of them had to be worried and panicked. I gave myself a mental thrashing on the safety rule I'd overlooked. Since I hadn't left a note, Izzie and our parents had no clue where I was. Neither did Ross. Only Penny, but she had warned me not to go alone. Even worse, Hunter might not check his voice mail until it was too late. I dug fingernails into my palms as anxiety threatened to pull me apart.

"You're right. She wrote those articles, and, despite the horrible things she said about shop owners, people loved to read her column." Theo pulled out a phone and began punching at the keyboard.

I recognized the pink cover and heard Willow's voice pitch higher as she mumbled louder.

"Now, what will the message be? How about 'I'm sorry but I couldn't stop myself. She threatened to make sure my brother went to jail. I got so angry, and, before I could stop and think, I stabbed her with a knife, just like I murdered Fiona.' Does that sound believable?" She looked up, and her lips lifted into a smile that didn't reach her eyes. "I think it will do."

My heart raced as I understood what she meant. "You haven't answered me. Why would you kill Fiona?" My voice grew raspy.

She waved an arm. "That's the surprising twist to this story. Turns out Fiona was an excellent reporter. Seems I wasted her talents on that silly column. Totally underestimated her. Small town, older widow with no employment history, who knew?" She stood and walked to the supply counter, then picked through the utensils, lifting and examining each one. "She claimed she was researching a cold case for a book on unsolved murders she planned to write." With a knife clutched in her gloved hand, she turned to me. "I told you my husband was a fool when it came to business. Always had to have the last word and make the final decision. The paper was spiraling toward bankruptcy. I couldn't let him get away with running it into the ground. Why, I gave up having children to help make the *Gazette* what it is today. I sacrificed everything. Can you believe it?" She smacked the knife on the palm of her hand.

I jerked and swallowed hard. "What did Fiona find out?" My voice trembled and the words were barely audible. Theo had murdered Fiona, and, from the look in her eyes, she was crazy enough to kill me. I had to wonder who else had become her victim. She seemed well-practiced at this sort of thing.

"When she first came to me with what she discovered, I didn't react, other than to wonder how she could have possibly figured it out. I was clever and careful. I had left no tracks. Heck, even the insurance company never suspected." Her brow furrowed as she glared. "Not Fiona. She was sharp . . . like this knife." She stabbed at the air and laughed.

From the corner of my eye, I saw Willow struggling to loosen her ties. Theo was too busy with her story to notice. I had to keep it that way.

"Yes, but what possible evidence could she have on you?" I scooted a few inches to my right and away from Willow.

Theo's gaze followed. "Stay put." She pointed the knife in my direction. "Flimsy at best, but I feared the information was enough to make the authorities and the insurance company take another look. I was so careful. Looking back, I admit I was in too much of a hurry that night my husband died. One tiny slip-up. That's all it takes." She stood in the storage room doorway and snapped her head around to glare at Willow. "If you don't stop trying to loosen those ties, you'll be the one who ends up dead."

Willow dropped her shoulders and leaned back.

"You know, despite everything I hated about him, I loved my husband. Maybe that was my weakness." She fingered her necklace. "Authorities never found the murder weapon. I buried the knife in our backyard, beneath the rose bushes. Nothing led them to believe I had anything to do with the murder." She sighed. "He grabbed hold of my necklace, the one he bought me for our first wedding anniversary, and the chain broke. After I . . . afterward, I picked up all of the broken pieces and stuffed them in my pocket. The next day, I went to the jewelers to have the necklace fixed. This one." She lifted the gold herringbone chain with the diamond pendant. "Beautiful, isn't it?"

"Yes, but what made Fiona suspect anything?" I took another glimpse at my watch. Only ten minutes had passed, but it seemed like hours.

"Oh, she was clever, the way she got me to talk about things, including my life with Stephen. Of course, I enjoyed venting and unloading stories about all those frustrating moments I'd had with him. I probably said some pretty nasty things that got her curious. Who knows? Fiona had a suspicious attitude and never thought well of anyone. It was the necklace that tipped her off, though. I guess she saw an opportunity and thought I'd be an easy target." Her eyes darkened. "Fool that she was."

I thought of Willow and her account of Fiona's threatening comments. "What about the necklace?"

"I had to read the investigative report. Otherwise, how would it make me look? Grieving widow, who only wanted justice for her husband, had to be concerned when no one was arrested for his murder. Anyway, I read the report, or skimmed through it, then never gave the matter another thought. I underestimated how thorough the authorities were. The team collected everything to test for prints." She clutched the necklace again. "Including the link from this chain I'd evidently missed finding." She walked to stand beside the shelf, then turned to face me. "Never leave anything to chance. That's the lesson I've learned." She looked away to set the knife on the shelf. "Like I said, I underestimated Fiona. I don't know how she persuaded the authorities to let her take a look at the evidence, but she did. She boasted how she'd questioned every jeweler in town until she found the one who'd fixed my necklace. He had records, she said. And my repair job was dated the week my husband was killed. I should've waited. It was foolish to be so sentimental over a silly anniversary gift." She heaved a sigh. "I fell right into her trap. As soon as she mentioned the necklace and what she had learned from the jeweler, I snapped. I said things that must've hinted to her I was guilty of Stephen's murder. I don't even remember what I ranted on about. I should've denied it, made up a story of how the necklace broke, but I panicked and then lost my temper. There's only so much a person can take, you know?"

"Before I realized what had happened, she threatened to go to the authorities and claimed I'd be in handcuffs before nightfall."

In that instant, I shifted my gaze. Willow spread her arms apart. She'd freed them from the ties. Just as quickly, she put her wrists back together.

I gave my head a slight nod then faced Theo. "Why would she think the necklace had anything to do with your husband's murder in the first place?"

"I have no clue. She was like Woodward and Bernstein. I don't know how she managed to figure it out, and, at the time, I didn't care. My only thought was how to get rid of her and end this mess."

My phone rang for the second time. "Whoever that is will worry if I don't answer." I nodded, not sure if my suggestion would work. I could say something to make Izzie or Ross think something was wrong, but not Hunter. We didn't know each other well enough. Two out of three were odds I was willing to take.

Theo lifted the phone from her pocket and stared at the screen. A smile spread her lips as she handed me the phone. "Might as well have a last word with your sister. Say something nice for her to remember you by." She grabbed the knife. "Be careful. I won't hesitate to end this now."

With a trembling hand, I tapped the button and brought the phone to my ear. "Hi, Izzie. I'm surprised you're up." Under the weight of Theo's stern scowl and the knife in her hand, I struggled to keep my voice cheery. "I tried shaking you awake to let you know I was going out, but you know how you sleep like the dead. Anyway, I decided to go searching for Willow one more time."

"Put the call on speaker." Theo whispered under her breath.

"Oh! Well, I guess that's okay. You had me worried, though. Ross has called here a couple of times. One went to the house phone, and Dad answered. He was not a happy man. You know how he likes his sleep." She chuckled.

"I sure do. Tell him I'm sorry. I should've left a note or something. I tried calling Hunter, but that went straight to voice mail." I shot a nervous glance at Theo. "I'll be home soon, right after I make a quick stop at the shop to get that list you forgot. Go back to sleep. Love you." I stumbled over the last words and rushed to push the end call button before Izzie could respond.

Theo grabbed the phone away from my hand and turned it off. "That better not have been a hint, telling her you'd be stopping here." She tossed the phone on the counter.

"We talked about the list earlier. She won't think anything of it." I steadied my voice to hide the fact I was close to losing all hope. I'd given Izzie plenty of hints, but if she came, it would probably be too late. Even worse, if Theo was still here, Izzie might walk straight into a trap that I had caused. I prayed she would call Hunter or Ross for help, even Dad, before she'd come here alone.

"I think we've talked enough. I don't want to be late and miss the eleven o'clock news." Theo walked to the back door and opened it. "How about same crime scene, different victim? If I leave the right clues, along with the text message from Willow's phone, our dear detective will be convinced she's the killer."

I closed my eyes and held my breath to stop the pounding against my chest. My head hurt and my mind was exhausted. I couldn't even think of any other questions. The situation was hopeless, and I was out of time. As if I had already accepted what was about to happen, my thoughts drifted. I pictured Ross's face and that crooked smile when he motioned for me to join him for a dip in the lake. Izzie with her long brown curls, waving to me from the front porch. Mom handing me a bag with her latest quinoa concoction. Dad smothering me with one of his bear hugs as he called me Shortcake. So much good in my life, and I had no more time.

A groan and loud thud sounded from across the room. I snapped my eyes open and gasped at the sight.

Willow stood over Theo's still body. The heavy canvas held in her hands had a huge hole in the middle, the size of someone's head. Theo's, to be exact. "Well, looks like that large-order discount on canvases paid off in more ways than one."

Despite the tears streaming down my face, I laughed. "Yeah, I guess it did. I promise never to question any order you make." I nodded at Theo. "She isn't . . . ?"

"No. She'll be fine, but maybe you should make a call to Detective Hunter before she wakes up. I wouldn't want to ruin another canvas." Willow set the damaged one aside and rubbed her wrists.

"Are you okay? Those wounds look bad." I struggled to stand and hobbled on one leg. My eyes blurred for a second while my head remained woozy.

"I'm okay. How about your head and ankle?" She pulled a chair next to Theo and sat.

"I'll live. Nothing some rest and pain reliever won't cure." I took a seat near the doorway and picked up my phone to redial Hunter. Before the call went through, the front door burst open. Pounding footsteps traveled from the front.

"Oh, my God! You're okay." Izzie bent down to grab my arms and smother me with hugs and kisses. "I didn't know what to think." She hiccupped. "The call and your words made no sense. You know I'm a light sleeper, and I never forget my lists. They go where I go. You know that too." She stood straight with her fists anchored to her hips.

"Those were hints, Izzie. My S.O.S., which you figured out." I pulled a hand away from her hip and held tight. "Thank you."

Hunter and Ross stopped in the doorway, shoulder to shoulder, as if they were fighting over who would enter the room first.

I rolled my eyes. "What a pair."

"Who?" Izzie turned to face the doorway. "Ah, yes. Men are so immature."

Hunter pushed through and crossed the room to where Theo lay unconscious, while Willow distanced herself by retreating to the corner. I could guess what she was thinking. Even though she had saved my life, she had plenty to answer, starting with her involvement in Grayson's deal, whatever that was about. If his actions were as underhanded as Fiona had claimed, when the news came out, the people of Whisper Cove, especially the shop owners, would be furious. Then again, I had a strong hunch Theo and her crime spree would be the story to make the front page. No matter the outcome, in my heart, I believed Willow would do the right thing and tell the shop owners about Grayson's plan to tear down their businesses so he could build his resort.

"I guess you're going to tell me what went on here this evening?" Hunter glanced my way as he squatted to take Theo's pulse, then called for the EMTs.

I brushed my hands along my thighs. "How about Theo is your not-so-prime suspect who committed Fiona's murder and planned to take victim number three? That person would be me. At least I was until Willow stopped her."

Hunter gave Willow a second's glance before turning back. "Wait. Who was the other victim?"

"Actually, victim number one was Theo's husband. Fiona figured it out and confronted Theo, so she became victim number two." I shrugged. "You already know those murder details." I pointed at the camera. "In case you need a recap, check the camera."

"She confessed to all this?" His brows lifted.

"She bragged about her horrible deeds and how she planned to murder me while making Willow look like the killer. I guess you never can tell about some people. Theo Lawrence, owner of the *Whisper Cove Gazette*, a well-respected citizen of our town. None of that matters now."

"How did you end up here this evening?" His eyes narrowed while he tensed.

"That's partly my fault." Ross stepped in.

"Ross." I laid a hand on his arm.

"I've got this, Chloe." He smiled. "I did some research and shared the information with Chloe."

"I don't understand." Hunter stood. "Research about what? How does that bring her to the shop?" He turned to face Willow. "And why are you here?"

Ross opened his mouth to speak.

"It's because of me." Willow interrupted and stepped forward. "I'm the research. Chloe came here to find me."

"Because I thought she was in trouble." For what good my attempt would do, I wanted Hunter to know the whole story. "Willow was upset after arguing with Grayson Stone. Izzie and I—but you know all that from my rambling voice mail, right? After Penny's call, I came to the shop and found Willow. If it wasn't for her, I'd be lying on the floor, probably dead. She knocked out Theo. She saved me." I pulled back my shoulders and stared at Hunter without blinking.

"No, Chloe. He needs to know the whole truth. I have to tell him. My brother can't get away with what he's been doing for years. Not any longer." She lifted her chin. "I'm not afraid to come clean."

"Brother? Who's your brother? I don't understand. Chloe?" Izzie tilted her head and a blank expression surfaced.

"Willow?" Hunter crossed his arms.

"Grayson Stone. My real name is Willow Stone. I came to Whisper Cove to help my brother with his plan to build a resort along Artisan Alley." Her chest heaved. "It was my job to snoop on everyone and find any personal information Grayson could use against shop owners to make them sell. He'd even resort to blackmail if it helped him close the deal . . ." Her bottom lip quivered. "But I couldn't. Everyone here is so nice." She gave her head a hard shake and swiped away tears. "He's so angry with me."

"Maybe we should wait and give her some time to pull herself together before asking more questions. We both went through a traumatic experience this evening." I touched the knot on my head. "I'm hurt. I'm tired. And I imagine Willow feels the same."

Hunter raked a hand through his hair and glanced at Theo, who moaned as she started to wake. "I suppose—"

"No. Let me finish. You should know I wanted to kill Fiona. After she threatened to go to the authorities with information that could put my brother in jail, I was furious. In my mind, I saw myself killing her, but Theo beat me to it." She held out her arms. "Fiona was a despicable person, and I'm not sorry she's dead. I guess you can arrest me too because I would've killed her if I had the chance."

"Thinking about murder won't get you arrested, but if there's anything else—" Hunter raised his chin.

"No! I promised to do what he asked, but . . . like I said, I couldn't, not to such good people." She looked my way and a half-formed smile surfaced.

At that moment, the EMTs rushed into the room, interrupting the awkward silence that followed Willow's confession.

I leaned my head on Izzie's shoulder and squeezed Ross's hand.

Hunter stepped to the side and got on his phone while the EMTs checked on Theo.

"Send two deputies to Artisan Alley in Whisper Cove . . . yes, same place as last time." He glanced at Theo and the EMTs with a questioning gaze.

"Her vitals are fine, but we'll take her in for observation, in case of a concussion." After fitting her with a cervical collar, both men helped Theo into a wheelchair.

Hunter held his phone against his side. "She's under arrest, so I'll send a deputy to the hospital to keep watch until you release her. His gaze shifted to Willow before he lifted the phone. "Send someone to the condo where Grayson Stone is staying . . . Yes, it's where the bonfire was held. Tell him he needs to come to the station for questioning. If he resists, cuff him."

Chapter Twenty

Sitting next to Izzie on the porch swing, I reached down to scratch my ankle underneath the bandage. The morning had brought sunshine, and a pleasant breeze drifted off the lake. I closed my eyes and took a deep breath. Hard to believe only three days ago I had faced a crazed killer who had threatened to take my life. Yet here I was, listening to my sister chatter on about this evening's paint event. Other than a nod or two, I kept quiet. Nothing could ruin this moment.

"Well, well. If I ever witnessed two more beautiful ladies, let lightning strike me down."

My one eye popped open then closed. "That can be arranged."

"Stop. He's only being polite. Thank you, Ross. That's kind of you," Izzie said.

I pushed off with my uninjured foot to set us in motion, then eyed Ross. His dejected look with those pouty lips made me laugh. "Okay. I'm sorry. Come sit." I dug my heel in to stop swinging and patted the open space next to me.

Without a second's hesitation, he squeezed into the narrow opening and sat. "I figured I should stop by and see how you're doing." He raised his arm and placed it along the back of the swing.

"Ross, please. You've called me at least a dozen times in the past three days. I think that qualifies for checking up on me." I smiled. "Besides, I needed time alone with my family." I nudged Izzie.

"Your wounds are healing, I hope."

"My head's fine. My ankle is just a sprain, and I get to take off the bandage this evening."

"Beautiful day." He lifted his head and took a deep breath.

"The best Whisper Cove and Chautauqua Lake have to offer." I kept my gaze on the lake view. Fishermen sat in boats while ducks bobbed their heads in the water to catch fish for their breakfast.

"I'm heading back to the city tomorrow," he said.

"Oh?" I shifted to face him and grinned. "Going through work withdrawal, are you?"

"No. If I could stay, I would. I have a trial at the end of the week. Obviously, a Zoom conference won't work." He studied me in silence. "Why? Are you going to miss me?"

I snapped my head around to view the lake again. "You wish."

Izzie reached across me and patted Ross's leg. "Of course she'll miss you. I will too. You plan on coming back here soon, I hope."

I jabbed her in the side.

"Hey!" She scowled. "Not so rough."

"I hear Grayson Stone has left town." Ross's tone was somber.

I had to admire how smooth he was to change the subject. "After Willow told merchants what he had planned to do, he couldn't leave fast enough. I've never seen so many angry faces." I chuckled.

"Must be a hard thing to do. I feel sorry for her." He took up where I left off and pushed the swing in motion.

"I always knew he was trouble. When I think of how he used his dirty tricks to convince poor Megan she had no choice but to sell her business to him, I see red," Izzie added.

"I don't understand. What could he have possibly found? Megan isn't a criminal and hasn't done anything to warrant blackmail."

Izzie chewed on her fingernail and winced.

"Izzie, what are you keeping from me?"

"I can't tell you. I promised." She wrapped her fingers around my hand. "But it's nothing that serious, only a little indiscretion from her college days. Grayson found out and threatened to tell the bank, unless she sold her business to him. You see, she hadn't disclosed the information on her loan application, and you know how bank people don't tolerate lying or covering up your past. Still, the incident was so minor and happened several years ago. The issue most likely wouldn't have mattered in getting the loan, but you know Megan. She panicked and imagined the worst."

"Oh wow. That's awful. What a slimeball." I cringed to think I had found him attractive when we'd first met.

"Yeah. I have to give her credit for resisting. Poor thing was so desperate to find another way out of her mess. Can you imagine? She even went to that weasel extortionist, Oscar Sealy, to pawn her jewelry."

Seeing that Hawaiian shirt and panama hat disguise, I hadn't recognized him at the time. His attire usually consisted of sweats in the winter and cut-off jeans in the summer. At the dinner table yesterday, I'd brought up the subject of Megan and her strange behavior outside the bank. After I described the man she'd spoken to, Mom laughed and Dad explained that Oscar had spent the last several months living in Maui. Despite his less-than-respectable role as the town pawn dealer for the past twenty years, he kept his business legal. "At least Megan got her jewelry back, and, with her parents as cosigners, the bank agreed to extend the loan on her business."

"Adding even more to this happy ending, Willow told me this morning that she's decided to accept her parents' invitation and go home for a few weeks. Nothing like mending family fences after a falling out. Did you know she hasn't seen them in over two years? I can't imagine being apart from Mom and Dad for more than a couple of weeks, especially if the last time we were together we'd argued. I told her if she still wants to keep it, the job at Paint with a View will be waiting for her when she gets back." Izzie smiled. "I can't afford to lose such a talent."

"It's a shame how her pathetic excuse for a brother abused her with his manipulation." I fumed, thinking about him. He deserved a life sentence for those actions alone.

"Well, let Megan know that if she changes her mind and wants to press charges against Grayson for extortion and harassment, I'd love to represent her and maybe at the same time get a conviction. That guy needs to suffer for once," Ross said with an edge to his voice.

"Meanwhile, he can take his company's plans to build that resort elsewhere." Izzie slapped her thigh.

Ross pushed off from the swing and stepped away. "I should go. I have lots of packing and other errands to run before I leave tomorrow."

I leaned on the arm of the swing to stand and braced myself for the hug and kiss goodbye. I refused to choke up with some pathetic emotional meltdown, but my heart did skip a beat or two. "Have a safe trip home, Ross."

"Aw, see? You will miss me. I can tell." He smiled and tweaked my nose. "Don't worry. I plan to come back in August for the town fair."

"That's only a month from now." I scowled. "I won't have time to miss you."

"Only takes a couple of hours to pine away for me." He winked, then jogged across the lawn. "Bye, Izzie. Take good care of my girlfriend."

"I'm not your girlfriend," I hollered back, but a grin worked its way to the surface.

"Did you see?" Izzie placed the paper in her lap. "Front page news."

Since Theo's arrest, her cousin-in-law had taken over the *Gazette*. We'd heard they never got along. Probably their squabble had to do with Stephen's murder. "I love the part about Fiona's story. She was pretty darn clever the way she hid her reasons for coming to Whisper Cove."

"Yep. Listen to this. 'Fiona Gimble's husband, Terrance Ford, was the chief investigator in the case of Stephen Lawrence's murder. When asked, men he worked with stated Ford never gave up on his theory that Theo had committed the crime, but he could never prove it. A call to Fiona's sister informed our sources that, after the death of her husband, the grieving widow was determined to solve the case, which brought her to Whisper Cove.'" Izzie folded the paper and set it aside. "Such a tragedy she died."

"Here we thought she was such a horrible person." Despite the spiteful things she wrote about our town and her abrasive behavior, she'd come to Whisper Cove to find justice.

"That's all in the past now." Izzie checked her watch. "We should get inside. Mom will be furious if we're late for breakfast."

I limped alongside her. "Quinoa muffins, quinoa oatmeal, quinoa shakes. What shall it be today?"

"Quinoa keeps the digestive system regular." Izzie held up one finger.

"Gives you energy to last the morning." I held up another finger until I broke down laughing. We smacked palms and entered the house. Life was good, and I was grateful.

* * *

"Open it." Izzie clapped her hands and wiggled. The grin widened while her eyes sparkled.

I held the tiny box in my palm and puzzled over what could possibly make her so excited.

"Oh, come on. I'm dying over here." With an exasperated sigh, she snatched the box out of my hand and opened the lid. "See?" She held up a card.

I took the card and studied the engraving. "'Izzie and Chloe Abbington. Co-owners of Paint with a View. The paint party experience you'll enjoy.'" I glanced up. "Looks nice, but I haven't—"

"I know, but I thought if you saw this and . . ." She swallowed, then chewed on her fingernail. "I shouldn't have, right?

307

I'm not trying to pressure you. Honestly, I'm not." She closed the box and set it aside.

I held the card up and tipped it side to side. "Not bad. Although, when you reorder, I think the lettering should be in neon pink. A color that will make the message pop." I pressed my lips together in an attempt to keep a serious face.

"You mean . . . you decided? I—oh my gosh. Chloe, this is fantastic." She grabbed my shoulders and shoved my head against her chest in a tight hug. "You are the best sister ever."

"I can't breathe, Izzie." My words came out muffled as I tried pushing away.

"Oooh, sorry." She let go and smoothed my mussed hair. "Thank you. This will be great, you know? I'll have the lawyer draw up the paperwork, and we'll make it official. Did I say thank you?" Her chest heaved and a quivering breath escaped.

"Don't thank me yet. I could be a pain in the rear and you'll regret your offer before the week is over." I gave her shoulder a gentle nudge and winked.

"Not a chance. Okay, we should scoot. Without Willow's help, we need the extra time to set up for the event. Beach Fireworks will be a hit. I can feel it." She laughed and linked her arm through mine.

We took her jeep and sped down Sail Shore Drive toward Artisan Alley. I stuck my arm through the open window. The cool evening breeze tickled my fingers. This was real, and, for the first time in a while, I felt I had a purpose. Maybe I wasn't meant to be a world-famous artist showcasing my work in some posh New York or Paris gallery, but the shop was something even more special, and, because of Izzie, part of it would belong to me.

I turned to smile at her. "You're a wonderful sister too."

Izzie laughed and turned up the stereo volume. "Now, this is what I'm talking about."

As we passed through the intersection, I spotted Gwen walking arm in arm with a man. When she had come into the shop with him yesterday, nobody was more surprised than I. Turned out the boyfriend she'd been bragging about wasn't make-believe. "It's nice to see she found Winston. Seems like he makes her happy." I pointed.

"After so many years of being alone, she deserves to have some fun." Izzie steered into a parking spot.

"I'm just relieved she didn't have anything to do with Fiona's murder." I exited the car and walked alongside Izzie to the shop. Blue and red balloons attached to the porch roof waved to and fro. A banner sign with the words "Congratulations, Partner" painted with glitter hung above the door. I clutched my throat and eyed the scene with surprise. "What the . . . ?"

"I'm the optimist, remember?" Izzie leaned against me. "Sorry the balloons aren't purple. I know that's your favorite color, but the local gift shop only had red and blue. They overstocked and had a great sale, though."

I kept myself from crying or falling apart with some other sappy display of emotion. "They're perfect, but please don't tell me there's a crowd of people on the other side of that door ready to pop out and yell surprise."

"Nope. Just a few friends. Come on." She dragged me up the walk and inside before I could escape.

I gawked at the dozen or so people wearing party hats and grins who were spread across the room decorated with even more balloons and signs. "You guys are unbelievable. Thank you." I managed to get the words out but looked away for a second to hide my teary eyes. "Well, heck." I sniffed, then lifted my chin. "Is there wine to go along with this party?"

"You bet!" Megan raised a bottle then popped the cork. "Champagne is even better."

"Okay, people." Izzie clapped her hands. "We have thirty minutes to celebrate before I boot you all out. Unless you paid to paint this evening."

"Always the bossy one." I bounced my hip off of hers.

"You will be too, now that we're partners." She held up her glass. "Cheers."

I sipped my champagne and circulated through the room to talk with everyone. My steps froze as I came face to face with Hunter. "You're here."

"Invited guest." He smiled and raised his plastic cup. "Though I've got to say, I feel like this is me back in high school when I crashed the A-listers' party. Weird, right?"

I chuckled and shook my head. "You are way beyond high school, and I see no signs of the dork Izzie described."

"That's good, I guess." He shuffled his feet while glancing at the floor.

Heat rose in my cheeks and I hurried to take the conversation elsewhere. "I bet you're happy the case is solved."

"Absolutely. Especially for her." He pointed at Megan. "I admit there were moments I thought she was the one. Theo confessed she staged the clues—wrapper and soda bottle behind the shop and the photo of her being at Bob's right before the murder."

"Well, Megan's fight with Fiona didn't help matters. I don't suppose Theo had anything to do with the fire or the break-in at our shop?"

"Nope. Infinity is solely to blame. Oh, and Sammy is coming home. She contacted the sheriff's office and asked if we would please call off the bloodhounds tailing her. I had to laugh. She's got a sharp eye." He rubbed his finger along the cup, then took the last sip.

"I know. She called me too. She's relieved the owner of Infinity will be facing jail time."

"I'm glad."

"Did she tell you who she believed killed Fiona?"

"She was ashamed to admit she'd snooped on Megan and found a receipt in the trash bin behind her shop. It was for the purchase of a knife and dated the day before Fiona's murder. Adding that to Megan's financial problems and the argument she had with Fiona, Sammy was sure Megan was the killer. Turns out she'd bought a wax knife, which I've since learned is used for making candles. Hardly capable of stabbing someone in the neck."

"When Izzie and I had spoken to her, Sammy insisted Megan had a bigger motive than anyone to want Fiona dead." I sighed. "I'm glad she was wrong."

"Well, I should be going." He tossed the cup in the trash can.

"So soon? There's plenty of champagne and good conversation to last. Until Izzie shoves you out the door, that is." I could blame the champagne for the warm glow inside me, but that would be wrong.

"Duty calls." He tapped his watch. "I have a lead on another case to check out. Congrats, Chloe. I'm sure you and Izzie will do great."

"Thanks." I tilted my head. "Same goes to you. You solved the case and did so without rubbing too many suspects the wrong way."

"Including you?" His eyes brightened and a slow smile stretched across his face.

"Detective Hunter, it takes more than being accused of murder to rattle me." I winked.

"I'll remember that." With the tip of his hand, he saluted and turned to walk away. "In case there's a next time."

I rolled my eyes and listened to his deep, throaty laugh as he walked through the doorway.

"I think somebody likes you." Izzie nudged my arm.

"I think somebody's got a crazy imagination." I poked her back.

"Well, either way, we don't have time to discuss men. We have a paint event in an hour." She hopped up on the stage and whistled. "Party's over, folks. Toss your cups in the trash and shuffle on out the door." Facing me once again, she added, "Let's get this show started. Partner."

Acknowledgments

F irst, I'd like to thank my agent Dawn Dowdle for guiding
me, encouraging me, and being my advocate in this pub-
lishing venture. I am blessed to have you in my corner. To my
editor, Faith Black Ross, and all the other staff at Crooked
Lane Books, thank you for taking a chance on my Paint by
Murder series and for helping to make *A Brush with Murder* a
better story. It's been such a great experience, and I look forward to the next.

It takes a lot of building blocks to nurture an idea that
turns into a plot and develops into a story. Two of those blocks
were especially important. First, my visits to Bemus Point,
New York, a quiet little town set along Chautauqua Lake,
inspired the setting for this series. Such a beautiful place made
writing my description of Whisper Cove so easy. Second,
choosing a business—all cozies have them—like paint parties,
seemed a perfect choice. Why, who knew even ten years ago
how this type of recreational fun would explode and become
such a popular scene? I have my daughter Jenn to thank for
introducing me to this experience. Pushing me to take a chance
(I am a horrible artist!) and tag along to our local Painting

with a Twist shop to create trees in fall colors, snow globes, snowscapes, and so many more subjects on canvas inspired me to make this a part of my story. Besides, a paint party shop is definitely not an overdone theme in cozy mysteries. I figured it was a win.

I want to include a shout-out to our author brainstorm group—Julie, Cari, Jane, Wendy, and Shellie. They are the cheering squad ready to help when you need one! And finally, to all the wonderful readers who gobble up cozy mysteries faster than we can write them. You're the reason books make their way to the printed page. Thank you so much!